All I Want for Christmas

Also by Jenny Hale:

Christmas Wishes and Mistletoe Kisses
Coming Home for Christmas
A Christmas to Remember
Love Me for Me
Summer by the Sea
Summer at Oyster Bay

All I Want for Christmas

JENNY HALE

bookouture

Published by Bookouture

An imprint of StoryFire Ltd.
23 Sussex Road, Ickenham, UB10 8PN
United Kingdom

www.bookouture.com

ISBN: 978-1-78681-079-3

Chapter One

Leah used the scissors from her Christmas wreath-making project to open the package from Nan, her hands trembling. She missed her grandmother so much that she held her breath from the moment her fingers touched the envelope. She set the scissors next to the pile of spruce needles that were still on the kitchen table and ran her fingers through her thick, blonde hair. She'd straightened it that morning, but after all day in the rain and sleet, it had started to curl back up.

Tipping the package upside down, Leah caught a lone key in the palm of her hand, recognizing it immediately. She pulled out a stack of documents with a note in Nan's scratchy handwriting clipped to the top. The notepaper was pink and lacy, the edges rounded delicately with little holes punched out. She laid the documents on top of a few Christmas cards that had come in the mail and focused on the letter, aching to hear Nan's soft, reassuring voice again.

"Mama," Leah's daughter, Sadie said, pulling her out of her thoughts. She was still wearing the red-and-blue leotard Leah had gotten her as a surprise for her birthday. Sadie had seen it in her gymnastics magazine and she'd kept the page open to it all the time. When Leah had asked her about it, she'd said that one day she'd like to have one of her own. Together, they'd made the matching bow clip in her white blonde hair. Every day after school she put it all on to practice her gymnastics. And she was quite the natural.

"The Girls are here," Sadie said. She bent down, placing her hands on the tile floor, between the table and the kitchen counter, keeping her feet in place until she lifted a leg into the air. Slowly, from a perfect standing split, she put her other leg up, straightening out into a handstand. Sadie had learned to do this move slowly, as swift movements used to send Leah leaping across the kitchen, throwing her arms around Sadie's legs while simultaneously grabbing dishes and knick-knacks to keep them safe. But when Sadie did it slowly, Leah was able to see the precision in her movements, her skill evident, and she didn't worry at all. Leah grinned.

Sadie righted herself and opened the side door that led to the driveway, sending a wave of wintery air in past the new wreath Leah had made from evergreens she'd found in the woods. She'd just hung it today. Leah slid the contents and the letter back into the envelope and put the key in her pocket. Another gust sent a chill through her as The Girls came in chattering together, Roz short and Louise tall, both swaddled in their winter gear.

"The Girls" was the name Leah had given to herself and her two best friends when they'd first met. They'd started out as a single mothers' group of around seven women, which Leah had joined after meeting Roz, her coworker at the florist's. But over the years, The Girls had dwindled to three—Leah, Roz and Louise—and they'd become more than a support group. They'd become *best* friends. Tonight, Leah was having them over for a late dinner.

"You're early," Leah said with a grin as Roz, all bundled up in a dark burgundy, double-breasted peacoat and striped fingerless gloves, set a bottle of wine on the counter dramatically. It was some sort of cutesy specialty wine with a gold, swirling Christmas tree on the label.

"Louise was insistent that the snow was going to fall all at once and if we waited any longer we wouldn't be able to drive here," Roz said, pulling off her gloves and dumping them on the counter. She ran her hand around Sadie's ponytail affectionately and gave her a wink. Then she shrugged off her coat. Roz walked over to the cupboards and started rummaging around for wine glasses. Leah smiled—she liked how Roz felt as comfortable as if she were in her own house. She was like family.

"At least I can say we're safe," Louise said, giving Leah a side hug as she was holding a bowl of salad and a tin of cookies in her other arm. She was covered from head to toe, with a hunter-green, wooly scarf wrapped tightly around her neck, covering her long, red hair. "And you're sure we can camp out here if the snow does start to fall?"

"We hardly ever have that kind of snow this early in the season," Roz said, busying herself at the sink. "But I brought my toothbrush just in case!"

Leah's house was small—a brick rancher tucked away behind a thick strip of woods that separated it from the main street, a four-lane expanse of pavement which was teeming at this time of year with holiday shoppers as they crawled along in traffic to get from one shop to another. But the woods allowed some privacy, and at night, in the dark, it seemed almost secluded. She had rented the house for its proximity to work and the cozy feel of the living room. Although quite crowded when everyone got together, it had offered a comfortable space to make memories with Sadie.

Louise looked at Leah thoughtfully for a second, as if just noticing her. "How are you?" she asked, studying her face until the pop of the wine cork behind them pulled her attention away.

Her friend could always read her. Leah was dying to see what Nan's letter said, but she didn't want to bring everyone down tonight by bursting into tears. It was supposed to be a fun night with The Girls. "I'm fine, thanks." Leah smiled. "I was just going through the mail..."

"Well, ignore it!" Roz said, swinging a glass full of red wine her way. The purple color of it nearly matched Roz's dark hair. It was bottle-black, her latest beauty experiment, and in the light, it had almost a reddish-purple tint to it. "We're going to have an amazing night of..." As she pressed her bright red lips together in thought, she handed the other glass to Louise. "What are we doing tonight besides drinking wine and having dinner? Did anyone get a movie or anything?"

"I thought we could play cards," Louise piped up, taking a dainty sip from her glass and looking back and forth between Roz and Leah. "I brought some. They're Toy Story though."

Roz snorted as Louise pulled her five-year-old's cards from her handbag.

"I couldn't find mine so I took some from Ethan's room," she said.

Sadie climbed up into a kitchen chair and reached for one of the silver, foil-wrapped chocolates that Leah had put out for tonight. The two of them had started their Christmas decorating today, and they'd been nibbling on those chocolates since early afternoon. Leah gave her daughter her best not-too-many face.

Roz poured one more glass of wine for herself and then filled a glass full of fruit punch for Sadie. Both Roz and Louise had the weekend free since their children were with their fathers, but Leah didn't have anyone to help with Sadie, so Sadie always joined them. She was like an honorary member of The Girls.

Sadie, who'd taken a seat next to Louise, sipped her juice and said, "May I stay up to play?"

Leah raised her eyebrows at Sadie. They'd agreed she'd go up to bed when The Girls arrived. Sadie flashed the playful smile she always used because she knew it made Leah laugh, and Leah chuckled. "One game," she said, "but then it's teeth and pajamas time."

"It's the weekend. She needs to let loose." Roz offered Sadie a conspiratorial smile.

"She's seven!" Leah said with another laugh, standing next to Sadie and tousling her hair. "She's still developing that perfect little brain of hers, and I don't want her to look back on her childhood and realize that her mother hadn't raised her right." She wrinkled her nose and smiled at her daughter. Sadie looked away lightheartedly, as if she were trying not to roll her eyes.

Leah felt so lucky with Sadie. They just *got* each other. While Leah's parents had always done their best, it was clear how different she was from them, how she was so much more like Nan. While Leah relished quiet time in the familiar surroundings of Nan's Virginia plantation house at Evergreen Hill, her parents craved the fast pace of city life, traveling the globe, spending years in Paris, her father taking jobs just to allow their travel. Leah had never spent long enough in one place to settle, and she'd only ever called Evergreen Hill home. With both her parents working long hours, Leah had made a lot of her own decisions about bedtimes, school, and studying. She wished she'd had someone to guide her like she could now guide Sadie.

She'd gravitated to a simpler life most of her childhood, opting to stay with Nan every holiday, and because of that she was fiercely independent, but she found comfort in the support of those who understood that about her. As a young girl, she had gotten that support from Nan, and now she got it from Louise and Roz, but there had been times with her parents when she'd felt very alone. She didn't ever want Sadie to feel like she didn't have anyone to turn to, but being a single parent sometimes made it tough. She'd had to take a second job to make ends meet, and spent many hours studying for her evening class in business management and corporate event planning, Sadie was often left with other people, and the guilt was difficult to bear.

Letting Sadie stay up felt more like indulging herself than giving into Sadie.

Sadie turned and pressed herself up against Leah affectionately. "We're supposed to get a snowstorm anyway. It was on the news! We probably won't even have school on Monday because of the snow. I can get my sleep then."

"All right," Leah said. She didn't want Sadie to miss out on a fun night.

"Awesome!" Roz said, leaning back on the two legs of her chair to grab Louise's tin of cookies off the island. Leah and Sadie had re-covered the vinyl kitchen chairs themselves to match the cream-colored Formica tabletop. They'd found the set for an amazing price at the second-hand shop in town, and it looked so nice with the greenery they'd placed in the center today alongside the dishes of chocolates.

Roz popped the tin lid open and handed one to Sadie—a sugar cookie the size of her palm with red-and-white icing swirled in a pattern resembling a peppermint candy. Sadie took a bite, a delighted grin on her face that showed two front teeth that hadn't completely come in yet, her big brown eyes bright and excited.

"Well, I suppose we should eat before we do games or anything," Leah said. "Sadie, do you want something else to eat?" Sadie had eaten earlier, but now with her bedtime routine out the window, Leah figured she might as well ask.

"I'm okay with the cookie," she said, brushing crumbs from her lips. "I want to paint with you. When are you going to do that?" She pointed through the large open doorway separating the small kitchen and living room, where a small pile of canvases lay on the floor by the blue recliner they'd gotten as part of the rental, left by the previous tenants.

"The arts-and-crafts store had a clearance," she explained to The Girls, "so I bought us canvases and a few paints. I got Christmas colors. I figured we could paint something tonight. But it can wait if you want to play cards."

"Oh! I love that idea! We can do both!" Louise clapped her hands. Then, she sobered, as if something had just occurred to her, and turned to Leah. "You didn't have to buy anything," she said, a grateful smile on her face.

It was hard for Leah to open up about some things, and she'd never told anyone how difficult she was finding supporting her little family, but after Nan passed she'd just felt overwhelmed and had confided in Louise one night about her financial situation. She wasn't struggling completely, now that she had the other income from part-time waitressing, but things were tight, and she didn't know how she'd be able to pay for gymnastics lessons for Sadie. Sadie had never asked, but after the sports day at school, Leah and all the other parents had been blown away by Sadie's floor routine, and the gym teacher had taken Leah aside and said that, with the right coaching, there was no limit to where gymnastics would take her.

Leah had signed her up at a shabby little gym—all she could afford—and Sadie got to go once a week, but the coaching wasn't great, and Sadie often showed more skill than what the gym could offer lessons for. There was barely enough room to have floor routines. The tumbling mats were short, so she couldn't get a big sequence down, and their uneven bars were supposedly being repaired, although they hadn't seemed to change at all since they'd enrolled. Once Leah had finished her degree, she hoped to start a career that could earn her real money to provide for her and Sadie. And then there was Leah's ultimate dream. She wished she'd had a chance to read Nan's letter.

"I know I didn't have to buy anything, but I wanted to. It's December; we can make some new decorations. Maybe we could do something that represents the three of us."

"I've already got ideas for mine," Louise said to Sadie, her perfectly lined eyebrows bouncing in excitement.

"Mama and I went all through the woods today, looking for greenery to decorate. She held me up over her head just to get the perfect sprig of holly," Sadie said, her eyes round with excitement as she giggled. She turned to Leah. "I'm going to paint that holly, Mama."

"Oh, Sadie, that's a great idea," Leah said, smiling as she thought of their time in the woods together. It was something they had done for the last few years. Leah would continue to look for that perfect piece even after she'd gotten what she needed—just so that they wouldn't have to end their walk in the woods. Sadie talked the whole time, telling her about her friends at school and things she was doing in class. She'd spilled the beans about a clay dish she was making in art as a Christmas present for her. "What a great memory to save, Sadie," said Leah. "I can't wait to see what you paint."

"You want me to be sentimental?" Roz teased with a crooked grin from behind her trendy new black-framed glasses. She took a big drink of her wine.

"Yes," Leah said.

Louise giggled.

Roz pursed her lips playfully. "I don't do warm and fuzzy."

"Make yours modern art," Louise said. "Christmassy modern art."

"If you're going to make me do Christmas, I'd better have more of this." She pulled the bottle from the island and topped off her glass.

Leah understood Roz's feelings on Christmas.

It was that one time of year when Leah's life choices really stood out to her, and she knew Roz was the same. Leah had always wanted a big family, rows of fuzzy-socked feet in front of the fireplace, an enormous tree with too many presents to fit underneath it, rooms of bunk beds for the kids and their friends, the golden glow of lamplight, and walls of shelves full of books and board games.

She'd had a taste of that life growing up whenever she went to Nan's. Nan lived in an old brick Georgian-style manor house with double chimneys and view of the river. When Leah was very young, before Nan bought the house outright, a little boy, his mother, and his grandmother had all lived there with Nan. Nan would have tea parties for the ladies in town, and they were always encouraged to bring their children. Nan made every small affair feel as though it were the most important event. She'd spend the day baking a pie, cookies, finger sandwiches, and all sorts of side dishes, and she'd display them on the center island in the kitchen. While the ladies had tea, all the kids would line up along the hearth of the fireplace to keep warm, an endless supply of homemade treats on hand-painted china in their laps. Leah had enjoyed that memory so much that she'd recreated it with Sadie, asking Nan for her recipes.

Making memories was so important to Leah. That was why, when Sadie asked to stay up, almost all of the time she'd let her. With a grin, she looked at her daughter now. She was in the living room, showing Louise her handstand. Her fingers spread on the old carpet, her ponytail dragging the ground, she had her toes perfectly pointed, her feet in the air. Louise was clapping and Roz had brought in their glasses of wine, all topped off. Leah got up and joined The Girls.

Chapter Two

Leah sat in the small living room of her home, cuddled under a quilt with a cup of coffee. The three painted canvases from last night leaned against her bookshelf, the tall oak case overflowing. She'd separated the shelves by her favorites, the ones she'd yet to read, and all the textbooks from her coursework. She shifted on the warm tweed sofa and looked over at the colored lights shining on the small tree in the corner, Nan's package in her lap.

She peered down at Nan's familiar handwriting, thinking of all the plans they'd had. Her whole life, Leah had visited the plantation, Evergreen Hill, where Nan had made her living, hosting weddings and other events. As soon as she was old enough, Leah had joined Nan, working there on holidays and summers. Nan had retired when she hit sixty-five, but had immediately started missing it.

Leah was the first one up, and the sun had barely begun to peek over the horizon, casting a pink glow on the edge of the sky through the window, despite the forecast of snow. She slid the key off the side table and held it in her hand.

The Girls had stayed the night last night, having had a little more wine than they should. Not to mention, the roads were getting icy. Sadie had slept with Leah, and Roz and Louise had stayed in Sadie's double bed. Whenever they stayed over, it was always a tight squeeze, but they'd all agreed that it brought them closer together.

Leah quietly fiddled with the torn edge of the package to retrieve the documents, so as not to wake The Girls or Sadie, and slid Nan's letter out with the other papers. She held it in front of her for a moment, knowing she was about to hear from Nan. She missed her so much.

Tears welled up in Leah's eyes as she read "Dear Leah" in Nan's writing. It was like her grandmother was talking to her from Heaven.

As a child, it had been Nan who had had those long, giggly conversations into the wee hours of the night with Leah; it had been Nan who would listen as she talked about boys or her school problems. And, when she'd gotten pregnant, and the child's father refused to be a part of their life, she'd gone to Nan to find out what to do. Nan had raised Leah's mother, Marie, and her uncle, William, by herself, and she was the strongest person Leah knew.

Leah could hear her grandmother's voice perfectly as she read— soft like a whisper, the way she'd been when she'd tucked her in during her visits when Leah was a girl. As the words "Evergreen Hill" slid in front of Leah's eyes, she could feel the warmth in her cheeks, and she knew what it was: hope welling up that she'd be allowed one last way to be near Nan. Leah had just one class left before she'd have her degree, and while she'd entertained finding a job as a corporate events planner to broaden her experience, the plan had always been for Nan to teach her the business—but only after she'd finished the classes. Nan wanted her to be prepared and also to have enough background to build her own vision for Evergreen Hill.

She had planned to finish her degree, wrap up Sadie's school year, then drive the two hours to Evergreen Hill with all their worldly possessions and start a new life. Nan had always said she hoped Leah would be throwing big white weddings on the lawn, opening up the library for local historians, and showing school kids round the vast halls and servants' quarters long after she'd gone. She had even promised that Leah would inherit the house.

That hope was burning Leah from the inside, telling her she might be able to give Sadie the life she'd always wanted her to have—the life Nan and Leah had planned. She blinked over and over as she read her inheritance: the plantation was hers. Evergreen Hill, with its winding paths and acres of open land, would now belong to her and Sadie. It was bittersweet, but she could hear Nan telling her to relax and focus on the positives.

Leah looked up at the paintings but she wasn't focused on them. She hadn't wanted to admit it to herself, but she realized that part of her had been dreading Christmas. It just wouldn't be the same without Nan. But now it might feel different—still sad, but as if Nan were watching over them, spending Christmas with them, taking care of her and Sadie even after she was gone. And now, more than ever, she needed Nan. Leah imagined driving up the long drive, lined with oak trees. Snowy woods wrapped around three sides of the house like a familiar hug, the rest of the property sprawling out behind it—the old tobacco fields now enormous green pastures. The dark of the deciduous tree limbs a stark contrast to the white snow as they towered over the smaller evergreens; the cold juxtaposed with the yellow champagne-colored warmth radiating from every window of the house.

The plantation, Evergreen Hill, got its name from the wild evergreens that grew in the woods out back. It looked like the forest was full of Christmas trees, and during the holidays, Nan would string them all with white lights, making the snowy woods look like some sort of fairytale.

Sadie had grown up visiting Nan at Evergreen Hill just like Leah had. Leah delighted in the fact that Sadie had memories of family Christmases there, long summer breaks, climbing the old trees, picking vegetables and fruit from the garden out back, and hiking along the river. But in the last six months or so, Leah had just been too busy with work, and hadn't been able to visit. Of course there was no way they'd miss the family Christmas, and that had become Sadie and Nan's sign-off on the phone: "See you at Christmas!" But Nan passed away in November.

With the inheritance, Leah could retreat to the place she and Sadie loved most in the world. They'd go on long, winter walks with hot chocolate. She'd make them big fires in the colossal fireplaces and they could roast marshmallows to relax, away from the hustle and bustle of the Christmas season. Hosting special events and opening the house up as a museum would give her a chance to use what she'd learned and to make much better money in fewer hours, allowing her to bond with her daughter—just the two of them. She'd have to work fast so she could open the doors as soon as her classes finished or she'd never be able to afford the upkeep. It'd be tough, but Leah was sure she could do it.

She looked down at the old key in her hand, the memories of that house washing over her. Once, Nan had given Sadie that key to hold while they planted tomatoes together in a garden at the far edge of the plantation. It was hot, and Leah had worn her thinnest pair of shorts to keep as cool as possible in the sun. Sadie had alternated twirling and watching her sundress balloon around her with planting, and Leah had called out for her to "keep track of that key."

When they were finally finished, their hands swollen in their gardening gloves from the heat, Sadie reached into her pocket, only to realize the key was gone. They had dug through the tomato plants, combed the soil together, searching, the heat nearly unbearable. Sadie's face had fallen, worried, after about an hour of looking, that Nan would be upset with her for losing the key. Instead, Nan made up stories of how they'd have to camp out under the weeping willow tree and live on tomatoes.

"Like castaways," she'd said with a laugh. Leah could still picture her face as she smiled, the lines around her eyes and along her cheeks, the bright white of her teeth, the way the wisps of hair had escaped from her bun and wrapped around her ear. It had been Sadie who'd finally found the key in a nearby patch of grass where she'd been twirling. While Leah was relieved, Nan had snapped her fingers, pursed her lips, and said, "Well, my dears, I suppose our castaway days are over."

Life was perfect there. While Leah really enjoyed the history of the house, Sadie had found her niche as well. Every Christmas, Nan and Leah would take Sadie to the local high school's national-level gymnastic show, and talked about how maybe one day Sadie would be a part of their gymnastics team. The team was the top in the state, its coach a local celebrity, having been mentioned on several news programs for her coaching talents.

The schools in that county were as highly rated as the gymnastics program—a far cry from Sadie's small elementary school where the teachers' time was consumed by students with larger problems than simply schoolwork. While Sadie grappled with math, Leah knew that her daughter's overworked teacher was struggling just to make sure her class had pencils and hot meals. In a different classroom, would Sadie have as much trouble understanding?

"Good morning," Louise whispered. She shuffled in, her thin body hidden by Leah's pajama bottoms and a T-shirt that she'd borrowed, her long fingers wrapped around a mug of coffee. She sat down beside Leah and her face shifted from groggy to more attentive as she looked at her friend. "What's that?"

"I didn't hear you get up," Leah said, blinking to push the tears back. "Did you find the cream and sugar okay?"

"Yes. You always keep the sugar to the left of the coffee maker and the cream's in the fridge. Now, tell me what you're reading. You looked deep in thought just now." Louise folded her feet underneath her and pulled a corner of the quilt across her lap, concern on her face.

"I was just reading a letter from my grandmother."

"Oh." Louise had been the first person Leah had called when she'd finally wanted to talk about it. "What does it say?"

"She's giving me Evergreen Hill."

"Wow. That's huge…"

Leah took in a deep breath and looked at the little Christmas tree in the corner of the room. It was adorned with ornaments Sadie had made in school and when they'd had craft nights together.

"Are you going to open the plantation again?"

Leah nodded.

Louise took a sip of her coffee and wriggled into a different position. "You're really going to move." She frowned. Roz and Louise had always known Leah's plans, but since Nan's death everything had been up in the air. Now those plans were suddenly starting to feel real.

Leah thought about leaving her friends, and admitted to herself it would definitely be hard, but if she could give Sadie that kind of lifestyle, it would be a sacrifice worth making. "You and Ethan are coming every single holiday, remember?"

"I'm still going to miss you. Who will I make cookies for?"

Leah smiled. "That guy, Bret, at your office."

"Stop," she said with a giggle. "I'll bet you'll be glad to quit your job at the restaurant," she said more seriously, a delighted look in her eyes. Louise hadn't liked the idea of Leah taking on another job—Leah could tell when she'd told her for the first time.

Leah nodded, trying not to let that idea get her too excited, and looked back down at the letter, flipping to the next page. She still needed to see what was involved before she let herself get carried away. "I haven't finished reading the letter. Do you mind if I read the rest?" Leah pulled the quilt up higher. The house was drafty in the winter.

"Not at all." Louise scooted closer and took another sip of her coffee, the steam showing itself in the cool morning air.

I struggled my whole life with regrets... the letter said. *I know we've made plans together, and plans are good. But you can't plan for everything. I certainly know that. I've learned that sometimes you've got to put your heart before your head and do what makes you happy right in that moment, or you'll always regret it.* She read on about how Nan had things she'd never said, large parts of her life she'd never lived... This didn't make any sense to Leah. What was she talking about? *Never have regrets, Leah...* Then, as she continued to read, Leah's eyes nearly popped out of their sockets.

"What?" Louise said, turning her body toward her, apprehension on her face. Not within arm's distance to an end table, she set her mug on the floor and leaned closer to Leah.

Leah had to close her gaping mouth. She re-read the line over and over, trying to make sense of what she was seeing. She pulled the packet from behind the letter and flipped through it. "Holographic will?" she whispered as she tried to figure out what was going on.

"*What?*" Louise said again. "What is that? Tell me. The suspense is killing me!" she said in a loud whisper.

She read Nan's words. "'I've written a holographic will, Leah. I wanted to get it down on paper as quickly as possible to override what I had originally planned…'" She looked up. "I only own half of the plantation. Something about a change in her will," she said, hearing the shock in her own voice. "Nan gave the other half to someone named David Forester…"

The coffee pot beeped in the kitchen, alerting them that it was shutting off. The sound rang in Leah's ears as she tried to visualize the person from the letter. Like snapshots in her brain, she saw him: sharing her ice cream, gathering leaves to do leaf drawings, playing kickball in the back yard.

"I know who that is," Leah said.

"Who is it?"

Leah looked up from the letter, still making the connection as she focused on Louise. "He used to live there—his grandmother sold the house to mine. But he moved away when we were young. I haven't seen him since I was probably five or six years old, he was ten or eleven—something like that… Davey Forester." She hadn't said that name in such a long time.

"That's weird. Why would she do that?"

"I have no clue. When his grandmother sold it, they all moved away. Why in the world would she give it to some kid who had barely lived there?" Leah turned the page over, looking for more explanation, but that was all Nan had said. She thumbed through the packet that accompanied the letter—a bunch of paperwork, granting her the inheritance. She scanned the legal jargon, stopping at times to try to take in what would be expected: *estate considerations… each owner is free to sell or allow interest to pass by will… Contribution toward maintenance, repair, payment of property taxes, assessments, liens on the property…* She set the papers down onto her lap, feeling overwhelmed all of a sudden.

"I'm going to have to call Nan's lawyer to see what's going on."

"Definitely."

As Leah slid the letter and packet back into the envelope, she stopped, noticing the P.S. that was written on the back of the envelope. She'd seen it earlier, but there were so many thoughts going through her mind that it hadn't registered the first time. It said, *Leah, if I could drive home one piece of advice, it would be to never have regrets like I did. Don't do it. I told David the same thing. He's a good man, but he needs a little nudge every now and again. So do you. Act on your impulses, go with your gut, and follow your heart. Every time. I love you.*

"Good morning!" Roz said, plopping down beside Louise, on top of the quilt, wearing only a T-shirt and big, wooly socks at the end of her long, bare legs. She had her glasses on, no make-up, her dark hair spiking up in haphazard points.

"Morning, Roz," Leah said with a friendly smirk.

"How are we?" With a sneaky grin, Roz took Louise's coffee from her hands and had a sip.

"I was drinking that," Louise said, shaking her head.

"You can have it back."

Leah knew that Louise wasn't really upset because being a nuisance was how Roz showed affection. She would have their backs in a second if they were in trouble.

"That's okay. We can make more," Leah said, standing up and stretching. She dropped the key into the envelope and took the package to the kitchen to make some more coffee. Louise hopped up and followed, grabbing Roz by the arm and pulling her off the sofa.

"What's up?" Roz asked, entering the kitchen, taking the coffee can from the cabinet under the coffee maker, and setting it next to the coffee pot. "The two of you looked intense." She clicked the light on above the stove; the small counter was dark in the mornings before the sun came in through the double window in the breakfast nook.

Louise took the carafe from its base and rinsed it in the sink then filled it with fresh water as she eyed Leah for the go-ahead to tell Roz the news. Leah nodded. "Leah inherited her grandmother's plantation." Then, Louise turned to Leah, as if waiting for her to offer further explanation.

"Dang, girl! You just hit the lottery! I guess it's full steam ahead then on the big plans, huh?" Roz said, scooping coffee grounds and filling the coffee maker as she looked back over her shoulder at Leah. After she finished, she turned around, giving her friend her total attention.

Leah sat down at the kitchen table, toying with the chocolates in the bowl, the foil papers making a crinkling sound. She was too preoccupied to make coffee. "I don't know. I don't own the whole thing, so I don't know if I can. Someone else owns it with me—a man."

Roz made a dramatically excited face, her lips pushed together suggestively. "What kind of man? A gorgeous, wonderful man?"

Leah rolled her eyes. Roz was obsessed with finding Leah a future husband, telling her she just knew that Leah would be the perfect wife. She called all the time, trying to set Leah up with people she knew. The first few times, Leah had actually gone on the dates, but they were disasters, so she stopped listening to Roz's suggestions. She picked up the thin package of documents and waved it in the air. "David E. Forester III."

"Maybe he'll let you run the business. I'm struggling to imagine a man with a name like David E. Forester III—" Roz said the name in a deep, dramatic, manly voice "—fluffing wedding dresses and arranging flowers. That name sounds more like some sort of big executive to me. But who am I to stereotype?"

Leah laughed. "You don't know anything about him!" But neither did she when it came down to it. She hadn't seen him in years. "But I hope you're right. Sadie has her heart set on that school with the gymnastics team. She hasn't said it, but without Nan, I think she's been terrified that dream won't ever come true." Leah sighed. "She just adores Evergreen Hill. I can't believe I haven't taken Sadie in so long."

"You haven't taken me where?" Sadie said, coming in and setting her stuffed bunny on the island. She turned to look up at her mother, and her tiny ankles barely showed under her pink terry-cloth robe and fluffy slippers. Her hair was like a bees' nest in the back.

"To Nan's house."

Sadie's face dropped in sadness. "I miss her." She rubbed her eyes and yawned.

"I miss her too." There was a moment between them—they'd had many of those in the last few weeks since Nan's death. She could see the same sadness in Sadie's eyes that she felt.

"Nan said, when we moved there, I could have the yellow room," Sadie said. She pushed a wild strand off her face with her little fingers, her sparkly nails that Roz had painted last night bright against her milky skin. "She let me leave some of my books there, and my jump-rope. Do you know if we're moving there yet?"

"I'm not sure," Leah said, trying to keep her face as neutral as possible to keep Sadie from worrying. "I really hope so."

Roz shot a look at Leah and then poured a cup of coffee. "If you move, I'll have to work the showroom alone. Who will protect me from Stan?"

Leah laughed. Stan was the florist's delivery driver. He often pulled around back, let himself into the floral arrangement staging area, and basically threw himself at Roz on a regular basis. He was shorter than her, and he talked with his hands and laughed a lot, making a snorting sound they thought could fall into the wild boar category but they weren't sure. He would follow them into the showroom and walk around after Roz like a little puppy, calling her "Sweetcakes."

Stan didn't mean any harm, and he was funny most of the time, but Roz would run the moment she saw him coming.

Roz sat down at the table across from Leah and slid a mug toward her, Sadie joining them. "You really want to move there, Sadie?" Roz asked.

Sadie nodded slowly. "I couldn't see my friends or you, but I've met some of the kids around there and they're cool. And it's so beautiful. And there's this school with the most amazing gymnastics team I've ever seen." She tipped her head toward Roz. "I'd miss you though."

Leah knew that Sadie was very grown-up for only seven years old, but she still felt a twinge of anxiety at her response. Sadie and Roz were very close, and taking her a two-hour drive away would definitely be hard on her young daughter. So much so that the thought of it worried Leah enough to give her pause. But Sadie would have the best of everything instead of this shabby little rental house in Richmond with barely enough to make ends meet. Leah was going to give it all she had to get them to Evergreen Hill.

Chapter Three

Leah had the phone in her hand, dialing David Forester's number. She'd originally lain on her bed and covered up with her purple-and-yellow plaid comforter to keep warm, but her nerves got the better of her and she'd sat up, her back against the white wicker headboard she'd found at a thrift store for an absolute steal. She'd always wished she could change the colors out for winter, but she'd had to prioritize her spending, and new bedding when she already had a perfectly functional set seemed extravagant. She grabbed her pillow and stuffed it behind her back, but before she'd dialed the last number, she found herself pacing out of the room and into the kitchen.

The kitchen just felt a little more like the place where she should be talking to David. She wasn't sure if she should be more formal or friendly, a quiet listener or chatty. She didn't even really want to be the one making the call.

She had spoken to Nan's lawyers, and they'd confirmed the holographic will was legitimate, so she needed to talk to David. Maybe she *should* call him Mr. Forester. She let out a huff. She used to call him Davey, for goodness' sake. She leaned on the small kitchen window by the table. The sun was out enough to melt the icy roads—the snow had never materialized.

All that morning, and throughout her shift at the restaurant last night, thoughts had run through her mind as to how David had ended up part owner of the plantation. How had he been able to get Nan to leave such an inheritance to him when he hadn't been present in their lives since he was a kid? Leah had spent nearly every moment she could at Evergreen Hill, and Nan had never once mentioned him. So what had changed?

In her early years at Evergreen Hill, David had always been present. Back then, he was as much Evergreen Hill as she was, and they were inseparable. Even though he was older than her by about five years, they found ways to connect with one another, being the only two children for miles. He drew her hopscotch lines on the sidewalk out back, his chalk boxes bumpy on the uneven, original brickwork. He'd taught her how to climb a tree…

She had many fond memories of David, but the truth of the matter was that he moved away at the age of ten, and she couldn't fathom why his brief time there would entitle him to half of the plantation. Nan was of such sound mind and a great judge of character—what had happened between Leah's last visit and Nan's death to make her completely rewrite her will to include David?

She hit the last number and put the phone to her ear.

Sadie was over at Roz's house, playing with her daughter, Jo, who'd been with her father until today. Roz had offered to take care of her today so that Leah could get things straight with the inheritance. It had been a kind gesture, and really, it would've been fine to make the calls with Sadie there, but Sadie had been so excited that Leah had agreed to let her go. Roz had also asked if Sadie could spend the night, but, with another threat of snow on the horizon, Leah hadn't given her a definitive answer.

There was a click, causing Leah to stand up straight. She walked over and sat down in the kitchen chair, facing the oven, her eyes on the Christmas towel hanging from the handle.

"David Forester." His voice was deep but still gentle like she remembered. She fiddled with Sadie's breakfast spoon, left on the table from this morning.

"Hello," she said softly. "This is Leah Evans…"

"Ah, hello," he said. "I'm glad you called. I was going to call you. How are you?"

"Fine, thank you," she lied, for the sake of her manners. She didn't quite know what to say. It had been so many years, and he was a stranger now, yet they had this small slip of time where they'd known each other very well.

A short silence fell between them, and she wondered if he felt the same way.

Then, he finally said, "I'm sure you've heard that we both own Evergreen Hill."

"Yes. I was hoping we could talk about that." She stood up, gathered Sadie's dishes, and began to tidy the table to expel her nervous energy. She was dying to know how or if he'd been back in touch with Nan.

"Absolutely. I'd like to go over a few options with you."

Options?

"Would there be a place we could meet? I could come to you. You're in Richmond, right? I could be there in just a couple of hours."

She knew this wasn't going to be a quick conversation. Leah wanted answers. "I can't meet today." She had work tonight, and she wanted to get Sadie. "We could meet another time at Evergreen Hill."

The line was silent for a moment—just long enough for her to worry. Had she said something wrong? She knew she hadn't. She'd only said she could meet one day, and there was nothing wrong, sure-ly, with staying at Nan's. But he wasn't talking.

"Is there a problem with me going to Evergreen Hill?" She walked into the living room and sat down, but then stood up, the call mak-ing her uneasy.

"It's quite a drive. The roads get icy in the evenings," he said care-fully. "I'd assumed we'd meet somewhere closer to you."

"Well, I don't mind. I'd like to see the house."

David cleared his throat. "It's just… I wouldn't want to put you in an awkward position if the weather got treacherous, having to stay the night with a near stranger."

She stopped, standing still in the middle of the living room. Her gaze fell on the paintings—three cartoonlike Christmas trees and Sa-die's holly, their bright colors drawing her eye every time she passed them. She was trying to make sense of his statement. Had he already planned to stay there? "What do you mean?"

"I'm currently residing at Evergreen Hill."

"What?" The question sounded as baffled as she felt.

"Would you feel comfortable staying in the guest suite?"

She sat down again, this time so that her legs wouldn't give out on her. What was he doing living in Nan's house with all her things still in it? Muriel, Nan's friend who'd promised to look in once a week after the funeral, hadn't mentioned anyone living at Evergreen Hill. When had he moved in? She wasn't staying in the guest suite! She would stay in the room next to Nan's, like she always had. Leah scrambled for something to say. Finally, when words started to filter back into her brain, she said, "I think we should speak to our lawyers before we go any further."

* * *

After her evening shift, when she'd picked up Sadie from Roz's, Leah hadn't mentioned anything more about Nan or the inheritance. Once Sadie had gone to bed, she spoke to her mother on the phone. Her mother and father both thought the will would surely be thrown out, but Leah had re-read Nan's letter and she wasn't so sure. She struggled to think of any talk of David in her phone conversations with Nan over her last months. She just couldn't remember a thing. But then it occurred to her that once, when she'd apologized again for not being able to come till Christmas and said she hoped Nan wasn't lonely, Nan had mentioned having a renter. "It's all impromptu, won't be for long, but I really enjoy his company." Leah tried to remember what happened after that but couldn't. She had probably been interrupted by something and forgotten all about it.

Even though it was getting late, she called David again, her knee bouncing uncontrollably as she sat at the kitchen table.

She coughed to relieve the tension in her throat. "I've changed my mind," she said when he answered. "Nan wouldn't have done this if she expected us to sort it out through lawyers." She could stay late, and take Roz up on her offer to have Sadie spend the night if need be. She didn't want Sadie to witness any possible arguments over the house.

She closed her eyes and prayed she could handle the situation like Nan would. Nan was the calmest, most poised person Leah had ever known. She approached every situation with a smile on her face and wisdom in her eyes. She was a quiet listener, and she took in every side carefully; she surrendered completely while someone was speaking, hearing every word and mulling over her thoughts until she had just the right thing to say.

"I can be there tomorrow," Leah said to David, trying to channel Nan's control.

"Okay," he said. "I'll see you tomorrow."

The next morning, Leah dropped off a bag of overnight things for Sadie so that she could stay at Roz's if Leah got home too late, packed herself a bag in case of emergencies, and then headed straight for Evergreen Hill. She knew the route by heart. The last time she'd been there was the funeral. She'd organized it with her mother, barely able to hang on to the details due to her grief. On the day, she'd only gone as far as the parlor, where they'd put out food for the guests—she just couldn't manage seeing anything else. The place had been completely packed, standing room only, so she'd made sure to greet her family and the close friends of Nan's that she knew, but the house was full of strangers—all there to pay their respects to the most amazing woman. Now Leah wondered if David had been there.

All the way to the plantation, she prepared herself for seeing Nan's things without the distraction of friends and family. And without Nan. She also prepared herself for seeing David Forester answering the door of Nan's house as if it were his. When they'd known each other, David had been very sweet to her. He'd seemed so big, but it must've just been the age difference. She could see him wearing a baseball hat, the curls of his dark hair coming out around the edges. He loved baseball. She still remembered his favorite player was Pete Rose.

One day, David had been sitting on the front stairs, tossing a baseball into the air, as she walked over. She had tripped on a step and she felt herself start to fall, but he reached out and caught her. His baseball tumbled down the stairs and rolled away, and when she'd thought he was going to run after it, he went the other direction, into the house, and got her a bandage for her bleeding elbow.

On the ride to Evergreen Hill, Leah called her mother, Marie, again to discuss the situation.

"You're going to have to demand that David give you the whole plantation," her mother said. "He can't expect to keep it, given his short time there. That would be crazy."

"Nan wouldn't just give it away unless she had good reason. I have to talk to him first," Leah said.

"As soon as you want me to come, I'll be there. I'll call your Uncle Will and we'll be on a plane in a second. Don't feel like you have to do all of this yourself. We'll help you go through Nan's things."

"Okay. I'll call you if I need reinforcements."

As Evergreen Hill came into view, Leah slowed down to take a look at the place she'd always called home, her vision blurring, causing her to blink. Even though snow had been mentioned in the forecast this week, it was still a little early in the season for it, but not too early to be spitting frozen rain. The rolling hills where she'd played as a child and the trees beneath which she'd sat and read to Sadie as a young mother were dusted slightly with an icy white glaze, the dark brick of the house contrasting dramatically with the gray skies. Even the original slate roof had a glassy surface. Leah felt her breath catch in her chest as she blinked to get a clearer view of the house.

The windows of the manor, which were usually aglow, were all dark except one, and the furniture under the big oak tree was empty, like her heart. Normally, on cold but dry days, Nan would hang brightly colored lanterns, lit by flickering candles, in the trees, and she'd set out cushions and large quilts. Leah used to curl up on the bench, facing the river, and Nan would bring her hot cocoa or homemade apple cider. Now it just looked cold, and as she looked at it, she could feel her heart breaking again for Nan. With a deep breath, she hit the gas and headed up to the house.

Her car came to a stop beside a black Mercedes. She got out and bent down to look at herself quickly in her side-view mirror, suddenly aware of her appearance. Tears were streaming down her face, her nose all red and sniffly. There wasn't much she could do about the way she looked now. Leah wasn't sure if her shiver was because of the cold or her nerves—either way, getting into the house would help, so she bounded up the front steps, dragging her fingers under her eyes.

Her first inclination was to slide the key in the lock and go in, but she hesitated this time. She looked at the large, thickly lacquered black door. She'd never really stopped to notice it before, always too excited to be on the other side of it. All the wood in the house had been collected from trade ships that had carried supplies to the original colonies from Europe. With irritation gnawing at her, she hit the bell.

Footsteps pounded down the hardwoods inside, and her heartbeat sped up in anticipation as the sound neared the door. She was composed and ready to tackle whatever David had to say. Her shoulders were squared, her face set in concentration. She pushed the emotion that was welling up as far down as she could.

The door opened.

There was a brief pause as they both assessed each other. She sucked in a tiny breath, her cheeks warm, despite the temperature outside. David was tall, but then again, he'd always seemed tall to her. His hair was still dark brown; she remembered those charcoal gray eyes; he had a slight stubble on his jaw—that was new. She could still see that little boy she'd known in his face, but he had definitely grown up. Into a very handsome man. She willed the red from her cheeks. She needed to focus.

"Hello," he said, opening the door wider so she could enter. He had on jeans and a casual sweater. She looked down at his feet and he was wearing shoes. Nan never allowed them to wear shoes in the house—only guests. "It's nice to see you."

She took her shoes off and set them by the door, curling her toes to hide her rainbow polka-dot socks. She needed to be professional, intimidating, businesslike, if she wanted to get him to listen to her; she should've thought through her outfit better, but all she'd wanted to do was get there, so she'd jumped in the car as fast as she could.

He shut the door behind them, the smell of Nan assaulting her senses. Nan used to always burn sage; it relaxed her, she'd said. The earthy perfume of it had soaked into the wood over the years, giving the house a scent all its own. If Leah closed her eyes, she could almost smell the citrus of the lemons that Nan would boil at the same time to freshen the house, taking her back to those barefoot summers when they'd spend all day refinishing antiques out on the cool grass in the shade and then find new places for them in the house. The smell reminded her of all those little things that seemed so much bigger now.

The grand staircase fanned out in front of them from the second floor, its dark-stained treads like piano keys against the glossy white finish of the risers and spindles. She stepped onto the colonial-blue, floral runner and let her eyes rest on the empty, antique entry table against the wall, where Nan had always placed a crystal bowl of gumdrops every Christmas. There were no gumdrops. There was no bowl. That small difference welled up in the form of tears. She tried to blink them away, but then she saw there were no decorations anywhere, a stack of platters from the wake still sitting on the bench by the coat rack, and Nan wasn't hurrying down the hallway toward her to say hello.

Her chest heaved as she leaned on her knees to keep from losing her balance, the pain in her heart overwhelming. Every time she took a breath, her lungs filled with the unique perfume of her memories with Nan, and she felt like she was suffocating. Frantically trying not to completely lose it, she tried to focus on things in the room, but everything told her a story of the woman she couldn't bear to live without.

"Are you okay?" David said, placing a hand on her shoulder.

She stood up, the motion making her dizzy. She leaned toward him in an attempt to get her balance but found herself against him, her legs failing her. The grief was too much, and the mental energy it was taking to deal with the issue at hand was beyond her. Unable to keep herself together, she buried her head in David's chest and sobbed.

Pain shot through her chest and into her back as his strong arms wrapped around her, seemingly holding her together. Without them there, she felt like she might just fall apart right in the entryway. She squeezed her eyes shut, breathing in deep breaths of the clean scent of his shirt to clear her head. He held her for what seemed like forever until she finally calmed down.

"I'm so sorry," she said, pulling back, the guilt and mortification of what she'd just done setting in.

David offered a consoling smile, as if her breakdown had been totally normal behavior. "For what?" he said. "You're allowed to miss her."

For fear that she might not recover, she didn't respond to his comment.

As if he knew not to press any further, he said tenderly, "I took the liberty of making coffee. Do you like coffee?"

She nodded, still trying to get herself together. She straightened her spine and produced the most believable smile she could make under the circumstances.

As they walked down the wide hallway to the kitchen, she couldn't help but notice the confidence in his stride, the way he turned his head to smile at her as he walked, how completely calm he was, even after everything that had just happened. And she realized that it was probably because he had nothing to lose. This inheritance had most likely been a lucky surprise for him. He hadn't spent long nights with Nan, talking until his eyes almost closed by themselves, had he? He hadn't sat next to her while she made her legendary banana nut muffins, explaining each step so the next generation of the family would know it. He hadn't wrapped himself in one of her handmade quilts and sipped champagne by the fire just for fun.

He pulled out the chair at the period table where Nan usually sat and motioned for Leah to have a seat. "Cream and sugar?"

She didn't sit, channelling all her energy. She would turn her sadness into drive and focus on the issue at hand. "I'll get it," she said, suddenly not wanting to make eye contact. She looked down at the unfamiliar mug on the counter. Her emotions were getting the better of her again. Nan's porcelain creamer slid into her view and then a spoon. David moved the sugar toward her.

Leah filled her cup and added what she needed. As David made his, she went over and finally sat down at the table. She didn't want to. She wanted to get up, move around, rifle through Nan's things until she had answers. But instead, she kept her eyes on the table. It looked almost exactly the same as when Nan had been there. Nan was extremely neat and quite up on the trends for her age. She could always mix the old with the new in the most perfect ways. The table was dark wood, white placemats with a light-blue zigzag pattern giving it life. But in the center was a smooth, white vase that would normally have had sprigs of holly, berries, and evergreens, offering a pop of color. It was empty, like the gumdrop bowl.

She was trying to be strong but she suddenly felt tired, like she had no fight left. She had been working so hard, but having Evergreen Hill in her sights, as soon as college was done, had kept her going. Since Nan's death, living in limbo, she'd just about managed to hold it together. But now, knowing she had to fight made her exhaustion worse, and she felt the tears come back.

David handed her a napkin and sat down beside her. "It's okay to be sad, you know. Give yourself a break. We don't have to talk about anything right now."

She dabbed her eyes with the napkin, now slightly damp from where she'd balled it up in her clammy fist. She twisted it nervously. She was struggling to talk. How would she ever demand anything from David in this state? It was all so draining. She tried to remind herself: Nan could have given the house to charity, or to the local museum, or split it between everyone in the family who'd have then voted to sell it.

"Do you know one of my favorite things I remember about her from my childhood?" David said, his head tilted to the side, his face so composed and caring that she forgot for a moment what she was there to do.

She shook her head.

"If we got scared during a movie or at bedtime, she'd hum this little tune. Do you remember that?"

Leah nodded, the tears returning. She could hear the tune right now in her head. They'd both slipped into their memories, and Leah tried to silence them all. It was too much. She honed in on the ticking clock on the wall, trying to get the thoughts out of her head. She looked through the kitchen window next to the table, its glass original and flawed in a magnificent way. If one didn't know that rather than having the glass shipped from England, the original owner had local glassmakers make custom-sized windows using the sand from the James River outside the property, it would seem like it was just the ice outside giving them their cloudy appearance. She could still imagine Nan wiping that big window down. In the bright sunlight Nan was just a silhouette when she stood in front of it to clean it. Leah could just make out the woods out back, the sight of them calming her. She noticed David had turned toward that window as well.

"Remember how she wouldn't let us go as far as the garden because it was past the woods, and she couldn't see us?" he said. "She'd tell us that if we went out to the blueberry patch without her bear spray, the bears would come. It took me years to realize that there weren't any bears on the property!" He chuckled.

She wanted to smile, to feel the ease in her heart, the explosion of happiness that she used to have when she reminisced about her childhood with Nan, but right now it just felt like a dagger in her chest. She sat silently, trying to steel herself so she could talk to David, but she couldn't. She rubbed the pinch in her shoulder as she worked unsuccessfully to get herself together.

When she was with Nan, she felt like the sky was the limit, like she could move mountains if she just planned for it—and Nan had helped her plan. The ease with which they communicated, the elation she felt whenever she was in Nan's presence, when she could experience Nan's complete excitement for life—her body felt heavy without it. Just knowing Nan was there to cheer her on made her feel invincible. Now, she just felt alone, as if someone had removed that piece of her that made her feel like anything was possible. She spent her days pushing back tears, trying not to think about how great she had had it with Nan. Her quiet support was gone, and in the silence that remained, it was up to Leah to figure out how to survive without it. She put on a brave face for

Sadie, hoping to make her believe that her mother would have all the answers just like Nan had, but inside she felt empty without her.

She longed for those moments when Nan danced around the kitchen, when she squinted her eyes just before laughing at something funny, when she ushered Leah outside to see a wild flower that had bloomed in the woods. Just one more time. Leah and David sat silently together as the memories flooded her mind.

"She told me what was in her secret bear spray once my daughter Sadie was roaming around," she said, finally able to speak. Leah watched the interest in David's eyes, the way his expression lifted as he waited for the rest of her story. She took a sip of her coffee. "It was water and lavender." She smiled, the memory washing over her like a warm bath, soft and gentle. That was Nan. "She had monster spray too. Did she ever use that with you?"

David nodded.

"That one was water and lemon. Sadie thought it worked so well that she made Nan send some home with us. We used to refill it whenever we came back, so we'd have to conserve it between visits. Sadie would only let me use it when she was too scared to sleep. Otherwise, she'd try to be brave so as not to waste it."

"That's a good story," David said. His shoulders were relaxed, his arm propped on the back of the chair beside him. Leah noticed a small spot of her mascara on his shirt and she felt another icy stab in her chest as the feeling she'd had when she'd first arrived came spiraling back toward her.

"I miss her."

"Of course you do. She was the most wonderful woman."

They drifted into silence again. As she sipped her coffee, she watched David out of the corner of her eye, thinking about how, under any other circumstances, she'd have thought it was simply amazing to see him again. There they were, strangers who could've passed each other on the street, yet they shared these rich memories. She noticed the strength of his hand as it hung off the back of the chair—the vascular look of it, how completely unrecognizable it was from that little boy's hand who'd helped her across puddles as a girl.

As Leah thought about little Davey, she realized how great he'd been. She hadn't fully appreciated what a great kid he was, but now, looking back, with her own child… He had been an old soul, so empathetic and caring, and she couldn't help but think how he seemed that way right now. She didn't want to discuss the house—it was just too much—so she focused on him. "What happened after you moved away? What was your life like?"

"It was definitely different from growing up here, that's for sure." He smiled at her and she felt herself smiling back. He had nice eyes.

She relaxed a bit and wrapped her hands around her coffee mug for warmth.

"We moved to Chicago, into a small rental house just outside the city. It was fine. I had a lot of friends, played baseball through high school. I tried to play in college but found my studies more of a priority."

"And what do you do now?"

"I.T. and real estate. But I want to shift my focus to entirely I.T." He took a sip of his coffee. "People always glaze over when I start talking about that, but I really enjoy it. I get to understand companies inside and out, and figure out what systems will make them more efficient." He waved a hand as if to dismiss it. "How about you?"

"I manage a florist." She decided to keep it simple.

"I could see that. As a kid, you were always helping Nina—your nan—with flower arrangements." She noticed his glance at the empty vase on the table. Quickly, he looked back up at her. She knew that he was probably thinking about Nan and the house just like she was, but he wasn't mentioning it either.

"I enjoy my job," she said, although she refrained from telling him what her dream job would be. "It's where I met my best friend, Roz. I couldn't make it without her."

He smiled again, the gesture reaching his eyes. "And you have one little girl?"

"Yes. Sadie. She's seven going on forty-five."

He chuckled, the laugh coming out like little huffs of breath.

"She keeps a better calendar than I do and makes her bed without any reminders every morning. She's amazing. Once, I was running late for work and I had to leave as soon as she'd gotten the bus. I had my keys in my hand and was standing outside ready to leave the moment she did. On the way to work, I realized I hadn't had breakfast. When I got there, I looked in my handbag for a dollar to get something from the vending machine. I didn't have a dollar, but Sadie had slipped one of her Pop-Tarts in my bag."

His smile widened, and it was clear by his eyes that the story had warmed him.

"And you? Any kids?"

"No. It's just me," he said.

Leah went to take a sip of her coffee and realized it had gone cold while they'd been talking. She stood up and walked over to the sink to rinse it out. David rose and followed her lead.

"Why don't we go into the sitting room?" he suggested. "We'd be more comfortable in there." He looked at his watch. "It's after lunch. Forgive me for not asking. Are you hungry?"

"I had something on the way here, but thank you. Feel free to eat if you're hungry," she said, the air between them unclear. She didn't know how to act all of a sudden. He'd had his arms around her, comforted her, and they'd shared wonderful memories. But they hadn't broached the subject of house.

"I had a late breakfast," he said. "But I'm kind of hungry. I might just have a sandwich and a glass of wine. Want some?"

"Yes. Thank you." She needed it to take the edge off, and a sandwich would be good.

"Red or white?" he called as she left him in the kitchen.

"White, please," she said walking into the sitting room. Her eyes went straight to the basket beside the settee and the sight pulled her right over to it. Gently, she took one of Nan's quilts from the basket and ran her hand along the threads that held the tiny squares together. Nan had made all the quilts in that basket, and she'd used every single one of them at one time or another.

She sat down and covered her legs with it. It was red and white with little berries at the corners. She'd helped Nan cut the red fabric for the berries. While Nan respected the period décor of the house, built in the eighteenth century, she loved to add personal touches to warm the large spaces. She had baskets of quilts and pillows everywhere.

"I don't have the fresh foliage that Nina always had in this room." David handed her a glass of wine, two sandwiches on a plate that rested on his arm. He set his glass and the plate down on the coffee table and sat beside her on the settee. "You could probably whip something up, I'll bet." He smiled. "So, you like working at a florist's shop?"

"It allows me to be creative."

"Your grandmother was creative. She used to bake like crazy. She made me these delicious banana nut muffins once. She had quite a talent for cooking. She tried to teach me the recipe a while back." He shook his head, amusement on his face. "I'm a lost cause when it comes to cooking."

A guarded curiosity swam around inside Leah when she heard that Nan had tried to teach David how to make her muffins.

"Do you remember that year we all decorated cookies? You might not. You were probably four or so. You had colored icing all over your mouth and she kept asking you if you'd had a taste. You'd shake your head and tell her you hadn't. Then you flashed that big smile of yours," he said, laughing.

"I vaguely remember," she said, smiling more at his laughter than the story.

His whole face lit up when he laughed, his eyes lingering on her for a moment, that smile of his resting on his lips.

Their laughter dissipated and they fell silent again. Leah took a bite of her sandwich and let her eyes roam the room. She looked over at the rocking chair in the corner that Nan had always moved at Christmas to make room for the tree. There was no tree this year. There were no stockings hanging from the mantle, no wreaths with the big red bows on every front window. She couldn't help thinking how, whatever Nan's reasoning had been for giving it to both her and David, this place needed Leah, and Leah needed to be there.

Chapter Four

The alcohol had given Leah just enough of a buzz to feel comfortable. As the sun had gone down, one glass led to two, and then another, Leah losing count as the hours passed. David had disappeared to find another bottle. She didn't know how it had happened, but Leah had found herself talking about those first few months after Sadie was born. She'd never told anyone how hard she'd found it, or tried to explain why she couldn't ask for help. But David had nodded and even opened up to her, talking about the loans he'd taken out to go to college, the long nights waiting tables followed by longer nights pouring over his course texts. And now, they were so sleepy neither of them could hardly keep their eyes open, but they found themselves cracking up over a scene they both remembered from *Groundhog Day*.

She leaned over and looked at David's watch.

"It's midnight," she said with a grin. "Do you remember what we used to do if we were up at midnight?"

The corner of his mouth twitched in amusement. "We used to sneak downstairs and make snacks. You even woke me up one time to do it! I can't believe you remember that."

"Neither of us had a real dinner, and I'm hungry," she said, getting off the settee.

David stood up, collected their empty wine glasses, and they headed into the kitchen.

"What can we find in here?" Leah asked, digging around in the pantry. She grabbed a bag and held it up.

"Marshmallows?" He was looking at her, warmth in his eyes. "You want to eat marshmallows? Hang on," he said walking around her. "I have an idea." He grabbed a pack of bacon, cream cheese, and jalapeño peppers from the fridge. "I can't make a midnight snack for you and feed you marshmallows."

"What are we making?" she asked as he sliced the jalapeños longways, scooping out the seeds.

"A little appetizer that gives the appearance that I can cook," he said with a grin. "I use it to impress people. Would you preheat the oven to four hundred, please?"

"So you're trying to impress me?" she said, feeling the flush in her cheeks.

He let out a little huff of laughter, but he didn't deny it. He scooped the cream cheese into a bowl and began to grate a block of cheddar over it. "We're going to just scoop this into the peppers and wrap them with the bacon," he said.

Leah yawned as she opened a drawer and pulled out two spoons, handing him one.

"Aw, don't make me—" He covered a big yawn.

She reached over, mid-yawn, and grabbed the air right in front of his mouth, making a fist. He immediately stopped yawning and looked at her. "Nan used to always do that. She called it 'stealing my yawns.' It made you stop yawning, didn't it?"

"Yes," he said, yawning again.

They both laughed.

When they'd filled the peppers and they were laid out in nice, neat, bacon-wrapped lines, she slid them into the oven. Then they went into the sitting room.

David sat down next to Leah on the settee. "Now, we can't fall asleep, waiting for them to finish cooking," he said.

Famous. Last. Words.

They chatted for a moment about how melted cheese was probably the best invention on the planet, but it descended into quiet as their lids dropped and she wondered why she couldn't think of anything more insightful to say.

It had felt like only seconds that she rested her eyes, but Leah and David jumped to a start, the fire alarm beeping in the kitchen. The both looked at each other, their eyes big with surprise.

"Oh no!" he laughed.

They ran into the kitchen, David throwing on one of Nan's oven mitts and yanking the smoking, sizzling peppers out of the oven. Leah opened the windows and the back door, but it seemed to let more cold air in than smoke out. She fanned the air, while David took the peppers outside and set them on the brick walkway. As they both stood in the freezing kitchen, the smoke billowing around the ceiling, they broke into laughter.

"Maybe we should've just had the marshmallows," he said.

Leah rolled under the duvet to view the time, the gray morning barely giving her enough light to focus. It was still early—six o'clock. She closed her eyes and lay back on the pillow, the feel of the linens so familiar and comfortable that, at first, she'd almost forgotten about her troubles. This was the bed she'd slept in when she needed the security of family, and a retreat to ease her mind.

After the kitchen incident, Leah had talked to David until they could both barely keep their eyes open for a second time that night. They talked about everything and nothing at the same time. David had such a gentle way about him that she found herself both lost in his stories and waiting for what he was going to say next, and equally enthralled by the affectionate curiosity she saw in his eyes when she talked. Neither of them mentioned the elephant in the room. Every time the conversation would swing toward the house itself, one of them would change course.

She pushed the duvet off her legs and sat up, covering her mouth to stifle a yawn, having no idea why she'd woken so early until her tummy rumbled. They'd ended up not eating a thing last night. She made the bed, brushed her teeth, and washed her face. Then, with a quick comb through her hair, a change of clothes, and her things all packed, she grabbed her bag and headed downstairs, trying not to creak too badly on the way down.

The house was cold, as it usually was on winter mornings, the heat swirling in uneven waves down the hallway. She ran her hand along the curl of wood at the bottom of the banister. When she was little, she used to trace the curl all the way to the center. Shifting her bag on her shoulder, she stepped onto the hardwoods, the shiny boards slick beneath her socks as she walked. She rounded the corner to the kitchen, and threw her hand to her chest.

"Oh!" she said, nearly running David down, her bag making a smack on the floor when she dropped it. She picked it up.

"Sorry." He backed up and let her enter the kitchen. "I was just coming up to tell you I'd made breakfast." He was smiling that smile she remembered from last night as he looked down at her. "It's nothing big. Just pancakes and coffee."

"That sounds nice." She hung her bag on the back of the kitchen chair.

There was an easy silence between them as they both filled their mugs and dished up their plates. David had cut a few strawberries for topping, or she could opt for the bottle of syrup on the counter. She chose the strawberries and then took her breakfast to the table, setting her food on the placemat.

David joined her. "This is Nina's recipe."

The idea that he was using Nan's recipe made her feel possessive of Nan's things in the light of morning, and she finally felt strong enough. "Can we talk about the house a minute?" she asked, changing the direction of the conversation.

"Of course." He set his fork down, folded his hands, and put them under his chin, leaning on his elbows. She had his complete attention. "I would actually like to discuss our options," he said. That formal phrasing rubbed her the wrong way again.

"And what do you think our options are?" she asked, running her finger around the top of her mug to expel the nervous energy that was building up inside. Something told her he wasn't going to see eye to eye with her plan.

David took a deep breath, his broad chest showing beneath his sweater. "Well, there's the option I'd choose…"

She waited, still, her stare bearing down on him, willing him to give her something she could live with.

"I'd like to buy you out."

Realizing her mouth had dropped open, she clamped it shut and tried not to look as incredulous as she felt. He had to be kidding. But it was clear by his face that he wasn't.

"You want me to just hand over my half of Evergreen Hill?" Her words had come out sounding hurt, despite her best attempt to keep emotion out of it.

He shook his head. "Not 'hand over.' Sell it for a reasonable price."

She gritted her teeth, knowing she was about to ask what she'd accused him of asking. She couldn't afford to match his offer and was being forced to beg. "What if I want *you* to give up your half?" She stayed sitting still, although it took every ounce of strength she could muster not to jump up and walk away from the table. "I want to run the business like Nan did. I want to pass the house to Sadie when I'm gone. It's what Nan and I always planned."

David got up, walked to the window and peered outside, although Leah wondered if he even registered the view. His shoulders were tense. "Well, that's... a problem." He turned to face her. "Because I don't want to sell. And I'd like to clear the exterior buildings, build a swimming pool for the summer months, and make this a private residence."

Leah could feel her dreams slipping away. He'd ruin historical property! "Well, that will *not* be possible. Both parties have to agree," she said, trying to keep herself calm. It worked both ways. How had this gone so wrong? She should've started out by asking why he felt Nan had changed her will, not jumped straight to the conclusion—she'd known they wouldn't concur but now all the laughter of last night seemed wasted, and that hurt too. "I have a family connection to this house that spans decades!" she said, standing up in her frustration.

David walked over to her side. He looked down at her, sincerity in his eyes. "So do I. In fact, my connection might be stronger. As you may know, Lydia Forester was my grandmother."

Images of Lydia Forester swam around in Leah's memory. She pictured her, draped in glamorous kaftan dresses, sipping cocktails with perfectly lipsticked lips. She remembered Nan always asking if anyone had seen her, then rolling her eyes good-humoredly and turning instead to Lydia's daughter, June. Leah's memories of June were much clearer.

While Lydia would have nothing to do with the business side of things most of the time, it was June who was always at Nan's side, helping her. June was always outside at the weddings, running things back and forth to the kitchen. Leah used to slide around the ballroom floor in her socks while June set up for events and, every now and again, June would grab her hands and spin her around. Just like Leah, June had loved the business side, telling Leah that one day, maybe she could grow up and have a job like that. Leah was only six when Nan bought the house from Lydia.

"Your grandmother sold it to Nan because she didn't want the burden of the house anymore. That's what Nan told me," Leah said.

David sat back down and Leah took a seat in front of her breakfast.

"That's true," he said. "My grandmother grew up in this house. It had belonged to her parents. When she couldn't handle it financially and didn't want to run the business anymore, she sold it to Nina.

"But my mom grew up here too," he continued. "She was thirty-four when my grandmother sold it. My mom was devastated. She'd lived here her whole life. As I got older, and especially after my grandmother passed, Mom and I talked a lot about this place. It was magic for her, just like it is for you. My mother wished she could've done more to save it when my grandmother couldn't afford it anymore. She felt guilty for not working harder, getting a job, doing something to bring in the income. She had these amazing stories to tell of her childhood, and she impressed upon me how important the house was for her and how sad she was that I wouldn't have it growing up—I'm guessing that's just how you feel about Sadie. So when I was in town, looking for a place to live, I decided to come and see it again, and I made a very unlikely friend in Nina. I can see why my grandmother liked her so much."

Until that moment, Leah hadn't seen the compassion on his face when he spoke about the house, the complete seriousness of his connection to Evergreen Hill. He'd barely scratched the surface for her of how this house came to be Nan's, but she already felt the length of the story just by looking into his eyes. She'd known, vaguely, the ins and outs of the sale of the house, but the emotions involved hadn't ever occurred to her. She and David weren't much different from the sounds of it.

Leah was unable to speak. She'd had grand plans for this place. It was a chance for a new life for Sadie and for her. Her mind was racing as David got up and made them more coffee. When he sat back down, she was trying to think of a compromise. They could both live there. Maybe there was somewhere unobtrusive where he could put a pool. They could fence it off and landscape around it to give him privacy. He could live in the guesthouse and she could use the main part of the house for events.

"You know," he said, "my mother told me that none of her family back then agreed with my grandmother selling the house, but nobody had enough money to help her."

She took a bite of her pancakes, now cold, as the fire cracked in the other room. The smell of soot and the scent of the house took her back to late nights with Nan, when she'd guided Leah through some of the hard times. She wished Nan were there right now, to sort out this mess.

"The whole time my mother was growing up, my grandmother had promised that this house would be hers. Then the bills started mounting and my grandmother—always the creative—thought she'd open it to the public. Having functions here would help her pay the bills with little investment. What she hadn't planned for was its success."

Leah knew all about its success. And if she wasn't allowed to bring that back to life, she'd have no choice but to sell out. Surely that wasn't what Nan had wanted.

David took a bite and looked down at his plate. "My grandmother never wanted to open Evergreen Hill," he said, before looking over at Leah. "She only did that because she needed money. You know she told your nan everything—they'd been friends since they were kids. She'd confided in Nina, telling her all about her problems because Nina was such a great listener. When she'd heard Nina's idea to run the business, she couldn't pass up the opportunity to make the money. But that wasn't who my grandmother was. I was eleven years old when she walked in one day and told my mom she'd sold the house. She said it was sucking all her time and energy, and she wanted to get out of here, travel, spend the rest of her years enjoying herself.

"I didn't move here to run the plantation and I can't just hand over my half of the inheritance. Why would Nina have willed it to me if that's what she intended? I moved here hoping to be able to buy the house for my mother. I still remember her crying when my grandmother sold the house. She cried all day. She cried again when we packed our things, but I remember, she always smiled at your nan because she didn't want her to feel guilty. It wasn't her fault."

So the house had been taken from June at the age of thirty-four when all she wanted was to raise David the way Leah wanted to raise Sadie. It really was the same. She rubbed her eyes in frustration.

"Nina told me never to have regrets," David said. "And if I let go of this house, I will regret letting an opportunity to give it back to my family slip through my fingers."

Leah couldn't deny that, and the irritation that caused was driving her crazy. After all, though, it had been Lydia's choice to sell it, right? "If the business was so successful, why did Lydia want to sell it to Nan? Couldn't she just let Nan run it and go travel like she wanted to?"

David shook his head. "My grandmother was struggling to keep it all running smoothly due to its success. She wasn't great with the business side of things so she offered to have your nan move in and run it for her. When Nina arrived, she whipped everything into shape, and that's when it really took off. My grandmother, thrilled to have enough to satisfy her free spirit, started spending too much. She began taking lavish trips, and buying extravagant things. My mother begged her to tone it down, but pretty soon, she didn't have enough money to pay for the house. And you know the rest."

Leah nodded. Nan had saved every penny she'd earned, and was happy to do the legwork, applying for historical grants and business loans and running fundraisers in the name of supporting local history.

"Wow," Leah said. She took a sip of her coffee. Even though her guard was still up, she felt like she understood David a little better now. "I do remember Lydia, just a little bit. I remember her smile. She had this wild, long hair, but she pulled it up into a loose bun, wisps falling down around her face. She would sing all the time."

"Oh yeah," he said with a smile as the memory surfaced for him. "She used to write her own lullabies and sing them to me at night.

See, she was creative, artistic; she saw the house's potential and once it was at its best, she was bored again. She was always chasing something to settle that creative urge."

Leah sat silently, all of this setting in. It made her feel less angry, but more hopeless. She could see now why Nan would have wanted him to have a share in it. Maybe Nan hadn't anticipated the trouble it would cause; she might not have known David's plans, and Leah had never been open with Nan about the state of her own finances. She took another sip of coffee.

Leah had more to say. She wasn't ready to leave the conversation—not by a long shot. She set her mug down and turned toward David as he leaned back on his chair. "Think about your story, David. I'm just like your mother the day your grandmother told her she'd sold the house. This is the only place I've ever called home. I have the chance to make a living doing what I love while also providing the best life for Sadie. The only way I can afford to do that is to open the house back up. I'm a single mother, and I've worked in a florist's for the last five years, paying college fees on top of everything. You think I have the money to maintain this house if I don't run the business here? I've been studying for years to prepare for this. Nan and I had it all planned out. I even had a move-in day. June twenty-first.

"I want to meet interesting people, hear their stories, put pictures of them up in the hallway like Nan always did. Even years later both she and I could recall personal stories about the people on that wall. To me, that was real education—meeting all those people, sharing the home's history. I want that for me and my daughter."

David sat quietly, his breathing steady, his face revealing his own frustration. "What are we going to do?" he asked quietly.

"I have no idea." She looked up at him and tears swelled in her eyes, one escaping down her cheek. She wiped it away. The way he was looking at her startled her enough to pull her out of her sadness. It reminded her of a time when a big storm had passed through when they were kids—the sky was pitch black and the power had gone out. Everyone was asleep but Leah, and she was too scared to leave her room, hidden under her covers. David came in with a flashlight and crawled under them with her. He dumped a handful of butterscotch candies on the bed between them. They sat under the covers together, their heads pushing the sheets up like a tent. He read her books and they ate the candy. Ever since that day, the taste of butterscotch reminded her of that night. Every time the thunder clapped, he'd look at her the same way he was looking at her now, concern in those big eyes.

"I acted insensitively. I should've found out how you felt before I suggested buying your half. I apologize. We'll figure something out."

She looked down at her half-eaten pancake, lying cold on Nan's floral-patterned plate. Nan was all around her—everywhere she looked—yet she felt at the same time like she was nowhere near. Leah needed her grandmother. She needed her guidance. Nan had always told her how to handle the big stuff that came her way, but now she wasn't here, and Leah felt lost.

Neither of them talked, and she swam around in her thoughts about the situation, coming to the conclusion that they were completely at odds. There *was* no solution.

Chapter Five

Sadie, Jo, and Ethan were in the front car of the children's Christmas train at the outdoor mall, while Louise, Roz, and Leah were piled into the car behind them, a man dressed up as one of Santa's elves driving the large red-and-green locomotive. Leah rubbed her mittens together to try to get feeling back into her icy fingers. The whistle blew to alert passengers that the ride was about to begin.

Every year, The Girls brought their kids to this mall. They would have hot chocolate, ride the train, and take advantage of the before-Christmas deals that some of the shops offered. They hadn't planned to come today, but Leah had called them the minute she'd gotten home, desperate to talk to Roz and Louise about her predicament. She hoped they'd have some kind of suggestion for her.

The train lurched forward, the sound of Christmas music filling the air. Roz steadied herself as the car rocked, shifting the carrier bags by their feet.

"So, tell us," Roz said. "What did he say?"

"David wants me to sell him the plantation." She still couldn't believe the words as they came out of her mouth.

Louise's face was serious, pouting as she shook her head in disapproval.

The kids all laughed at something but Leah barely noticed, waiting for what Roz was about to say. She knew her friend would tell it to her straight.

"And what are you going to do?" Roz asked.

"I don't know."

"Yes, you do! You're going to refuse to give it to him." Roz leaned forward, the train taking a turn around the cascading outdoor fountain. Two kids were standing there, throwing coins into it. "You can't give up that easily."

"She's right," Louise agreed.

Leah held on to the frame between the two open-air windows to steady herself, her other hand holding the handle of her shopping bag. "So what do I do?"

"Move in there," Roz said, her voice direct, as if it were a command. "Dig your heels in. Don't let him make a move. Eventually, he'll get tired of hanging around in the house with you, and if he knows you aren't going anywhere, maybe he'll let his half go."

She nodded, more to calm Roz than to agree completely. She was still mulling over what to do. Sadie laughed in the car in front of them again, tipping her head back, a giant smile on her face, and Leah decided to push her thoughts about the house away for now. She wasn't going to solve it today, and this was their yearly tradition. She wanted to just have fun. Roz seemed to sense her change in direction because she smiled at her.

Leah leaned into the kids' car through the open window between them, her eyes darting back to The Girls to let them know something was up. "Why don't we all go to the chocolate shop next?" she asked as the train headed toward the stopping point. The kids cheered above the jingling Christmas music and the chugging of the engine. Leah laughed. "I'll take that as a yes."

When the train had docked and they'd gotten off, the three kids ran down the sidewalk toward the chocolatier, Leah, Roz, and Louise hurrying along behind them until they reached the towering glass doors. Roz grabbed the brass handle and pulled, releasing the glorious scent of chocolate into the air. They'd taken the kids before, so they knew what to do. They walked carefully through the tables that were piled high with golden Christmas boxes of candy in every size until they reached the store-long glass chocolate counter.

Leah stopped beside Sadie at the first display and peered in at what seemed like miles of truffles. Double chocolate raspberry, carrot cake, tiramisu, chocolate éclair—the list went on and on.

One of the clerks came over and smiled at them. "Lots of choices," she said brightly. "See any that you'd like?"

"I'll have the strawberry cream," Sadie said, bouncing slightly on her toes, her little sneakers squeaking slightly on the shiny white tiled floor. "What are you going to have, Mama?"

"I've narrowed it down to a few hundred," she teased. "Let me see…"

"Wait! I'll bet I can guess which one you're going to get. I've already seen one I know you'll love." Sadie cupped her hand at the side of her mouth to allow the clerk to see what she was saying but keeping her guess hidden from Leah.

"I'll take the butterscotch walnut truffle," she said with a laugh.

"Your daughter was right!" the clerk said, surprise on her face. "She knows you well."

Sadie smiled that big playful smile of hers that always made Leah laugh. They paid for their truffles and joined the others on the edge of the shop. Leah handed the golden foil bag to Sadie and sat down at a small, round table.

"Remember we were going to bring Nan here?" Sadie asked. "I wish we could've."

"Me too," Leah said. "What kind of truffle do you think she'd have gotten?"

"Maybe cookie dough because she liked to bake cookies." Sadie looked thoughtful as she took a bite of her own truffle.

They sat for a minute enjoying their candy—just Leah and Sadie at their two-person table, the others behind them at their own little bistro tables, chattering.

"Did you find out about Nan's house?" Sadie asked. "Are we going to live there?"

"I'm working on it," she said with a gentle smile.

Leah punched the numbers on her calculator and wrote down the amount of what she guessed it would cost for her to run the business on a scratch pad on her lap as she sat in the dim light of the living room. She'd tried all kinds of scenarios: limiting the business to outside events; having events in only part of the house; opening the grounds during a specific season and closing it the rest of the time. Maybe she could get David to understand.

Sadie had gone to sleep early, exhausted, and Leah had some time to think through her plan. Leah was going to Evergreen Hill and she'd finally decided that Roz was right. She wasn't going to budge until David surrendered the property, even if it took years. She knew she was legally liable for half the house bills, and if she couldn't pay, he could take her to court. But once she'd finished her degree, she could get a better job and maybe she could take out a loan until her earnings increased.

She'd cancelled a few of her shifts at the restaurant, finding replacements for them. For the rest, she would commute, as they were during evening hours.

With everything in place, Leah called David, and he picked up on the first ring. "Hello?"

"Hi. It's Leah."

"Yes, I know…" He was silent for a moment and it was as if he wanted to say something; she could almost feel it through the line.

"I have a proposition for *you*," she said. "You can live in one part of Evergreen Hill and I'll live in another part. I'll run my side as a business and pay you rent on the rooms of the house that I'll occupy."

"Leah…" he said. "I don't want to be quarantined in half of my home. I don't want a business like that running in my home at all. It's a headache that I don't want to deal with. I hate to think of strangers lurking around the grounds."

"Don't you think Nan would have wanted us to find a compromise?"

"Maybe, but that won't work for me. I can't have busy events going on, hordes of kids, cars parked outside."

"Why not? I'm trying here."

David sighed down the phone. "My mother's not doing so well at the moment. To get better, she needs peace and quiet."

Leah's heart lurched at that news. She didn't want to put any unnecessary burden on June. But they both still had good points. "I'm coming to stay until Christmas. We were supposed to have family Christmas there anyway, and no one has changed that plan," she blurted. "I'll be there the day after tomorrow." She wasn't asking him; she was telling him. It didn't matter that he didn't want to share his house. It was half hers, so she could live there if she wanted to. "We can talk about reopening the house when I get there."

David took in a frustrated breath big enough that she could hear it on her end of the line.

"As you know, your grandmother wrote a holographic will," a man named Tim Campbell said as he flipped through the paperwork. Roz had suggested she see a lawyer to find out where she stood. She'd found an attorney who would see her this morning before work. Then, armed with the knowledge he provided, she'd drive the two hours tomorrow to the plantation. Leah had literally called every name in the book until she found the only person who fell for her story and agreed to consult for free, on the basis he'd get the work if it went to court. She clasped her hands together nervously as she sat in the cold leather-backed chair across from him, his desk meticulously tidy, nothing between them but a gold pen set.

"That's a will that is entirely written by hand, in her own handwriting. In this will, she's named both you and David Forester as the beneficiaries." He shuffled a few more papers around and clipped the stack together.

"She already had a will drawn up. She'd always said she was going to give Evergreen Hill to me."

"That was prior to the handwritten will." Mr. Campbell tapped the date on the paperwork Leah had given him to review.

"Is that definitely legal?"

"In Virginia, yes." He smiled a half smile, his face focused and businesslike. He was older than Leah, with round glasses and a bow tie.

She took in a tense breath. It wasn't like Nan to put anyone through an ordeal like this. "So, what can we do?" she asked.

"We could contest the will."

Leah felt the swell of hope, and she shifted forward in her seat.

"Tell me about your grandmother. Was she on any medications, or did she have an illness that would've caused her to be not of sound mind when drawing up the will?"

"She was totally fine. Then she called one day with what sounded like the flu. The next thing I knew, she'd passed away." Her voice broke a little and she cleared her throat. "I think she was worse off than she let anyone know. She had to have been to rewrite her will so quickly," she said quietly, her unable to rein in her thoughts. Nan's friend Muriel had mentioned at the funeral that Nan had known something about her health but hadn't shared the full scope of it all. That was typical of Nan.

He nodded politely. "How about any undue influence by another person?"

A cold knot formed in her chest, sending prickles up her neck. If David had manipulated Nan, Leah would never, ever forgive him. Even though it was highly unlikely, given what she knew about David, just thinking it made her anxious. "David Forester might have been staying with her at the time that she wrote the will. I'm not sure definitively if he influenced her in any way, but could his presence have persuaded her?"

Mr. Campbell pressed his lips into a straight line, his gaze falling back onto the paperwork. "Contesting a will requires a lot of hours in court, and it can carry a hefty price tag. We'd have to prove that your grandmother did not know what she was doing when she wrote that will. You have to be sure because there is a presumption that anyone who sits down and writes out a will by themselves is competent." He looked back up at her, his face showing pity.

Leah's shoulders slumped in defeat.

"Dual-owner properties can be difficult. Essentially, both parties must consent to the terms before any changes can be made. I'm certain that Mr. Forester's lawyers have worked through this with him as well. Can you think of any circumstances under which he might be persuaded to sell?"

She fixed her eyes on the shiny leaves of the philodendron sitting on a bookshelf in the corner of the room behind him. It had a green pot with a red Christmas bow. The window next to it offered a view of the city street: a lone person walking past with his bike, his breath billowing into the cold air; and a streetlight with the city's celebratory holiday banner attached at the top.

She wouldn't be able to afford to buy him out. "Not at the moment," she said finally.

"You can force him to sell," he said more directly, "by filing a partition suit. But the court will appoint commissioners to recheck the title and place all the property up for sale. The only problem with this is that anyone can bid on it, so you never know what can happen. And property can go for more or less than appraised value. You wouldn't want to put yourself in a position where someone else outbids you."

"I don't want to do that," she said, her heart up in her throat.

"All right. You're sure there isn't anything *you* can propose that will make it impossible for him to say no when you suggest single ownership?"

She didn't have money to hold in front of him, nor did she know if it would change his mind. She could hardly rearrange her finances to hire a lawyer.

She shook her head.

Mr. Campbell reached into his desk drawer and pulled out a file folder, placing the paperwork inside. "I'll just get someone to make a copy, if that's okay with you, and then we'll have to think about it. My best suggestion would be to have another talk with Mr. Forester to see if you can change his mind. If you'd like me to talk to his lawyer, I can, but we'll need something to offer first."

Mr. Campbell stood up, so Leah followed suit. He held out his hand. "It was a pleasure meeting you," he said. "I'll walk you out to the lobby and we'll get this paperwork copied on the way. Take it home, think it over, and call me if you think I can help."

"Thank you," she said, feeling deflated.

"I wonder if he's just trying to swindle you out of everything," Roz said, as she took a handful of red roses and shimmied them into a vase. "Would you give me that baby's breath, please? He's a con artist."

"I don't know…" Leah passed the clump of little white flowers her way. She pulled the end of a red velvet ribbon, its spool spinning wildly on the dowel. She snipped it off and tied it around the vase Roz had been working on. "I'd wondered about his motives myself, but he really seems like an honest guy. He seems… nice." She thought about the mock-serious expression he'd had as he'd recited Bill Murray's lines during the donut and coffee scenes in *Groundhog Day*, and she had to suppress her smile.

"They always do!" Roz got up and helped herself to a complimentary peppermint from the dish on the counter. "I wouldn't trust him."

Her expression made Leah laugh. "You're being protective. You're always paranoid when it comes to your friends. His motives really aren't much different than mine."

"You're doing it again. Don't let him convince you that he's anything other than a bump in your road to Evergreen Hill. You can't let yourself become friendly with him. You're too nice, too forgiving. You don't want your heart involved when you're making this kind of decision. You have to be on your game. This is your whole entire future we're talking about—and Sadie's."

She sat there, silent, chewing her thumbnail. "You're right." Leah thought back, and she wondered now if being at Evergreen Hill had idealized the night for her, and maybe he wasn't as nice as she'd originally thought. There was something about that place that made people happy. The snowy woods, the burning fires, the fresh evergreens at Christmas—she'd had it all. But, when it came down to it, she and David would probably be facing each other across a stark boardroom table sometime soon, not that she could afford it, and all those warm feelings would be stripped away. She needed to keep her focus.

"Did the lawyer help?"

"I don't think so," she said.

"What are you going to do?"

"I have no idea. For starters, I'm doing what you said—moving in and having family Christmas." She smiled at Roz. Louise always attended Leah's family Christmas—she wouldn't have it any other way—and this year she'd convinced Roz to come too. "I'm taking Sadie and we're leaving tomorrow, but it's a long commute to work from there."

"Could you find a job that's closer to your nan's?" Roz asked as she set the vase of roses in a box with five others, preparing for the delivery van.

Leah cupped her hand, dragged the broken petals and bits of leaves to the edge of the table, and threw them away. "I'm going to have to. But it's not like I can get one immediately. I'll start looking as soon as possible. The taxes alone on that house are going to kill me, and I'm still paying rent in Richmond. Even if there's a miracle, I don't know how I'm going to do it."

"You know I'm here if you need me."

That was the great thing about Richmond: Roz would be there whenever she needed her. There weren't many people on whom Leah relied; she handled most things herself. But Roz and Louise were the two people who always came through for her. She knew neither of them could afford to help her with the bills, but they'd be there for her, emotionally, and in the end that was more important. Somehow, with their help, Leah would get through this. One way or another.

"I don't understand how to do this," Sadie said, frustrated. She was sitting at the kitchen table, doing her homework, the eraser on the end of her pencil chewed flat.

"Let me see," Leah said, walking over. Her hands were covered in hamburger from preparing the patties for dinner. "Ah, well you can't take seven away from four, so you have to borrow from the tens."

"What do you mean?"

"The three is in the tens place. You'll need to borrow from that."

Sadie's confusion was obvious, her lips set in a frown, the space between her brows creased. "I don't think my teacher told us about how to borrow. I don't know what you mean."

"Hang on. Let me wash my hands and I'll show you." She went over and turned on the sink.

"I don't think that's right," Sadie said from the table.

"Yes, it is. Don't worry. I'll show you."

"I'm getting confused. I don't think that's how she taught us."

Leah finished scrubbing her hands and rinsed them at the sink. She grabbed a paper towel, and with a deep breath, she looked down at Sadie's homework. There were ten problems on the page. Sadie had rubbed a hole under number one. She'd been getting extra math tutoring at school, but the tutor quit, and the teacher was overloaded with too many kids in the class. Leah started to explain again; this time, more slowly, showing her with light pencil marks on the page.

Sadie looked up at her, her face guilty and worried. "I'm sorry I'm so slow," she said. She picked up the other pencil that was on the table and brushed away the eraser dust she'd created on the page, trying to focus on what her mother had written, her pencil poised to write—but the stillness of her hand told Leah that Sadie still didn't understand what to do next.

Leah felt awful looking at her daughter. She wanted to make it all better. "You'll get it," she said and offered her most reassuring smile in an attempt to ease Sadie's fears. The more she struggled with math, the more she withdrew from practicing it, and practice was the only thing Leah thought might help her. "Why don't you take a break?" She feared Sadie was getting lost in the crowd. She needed to get her daughter out of that school and into a better one—something smaller with fewer kids per teacher and more resources.

She finished cooking the burgers, turning them to low on the stove. Then she poured a cup of milk, put one of Louise's Christmas cookies on a small plate, and went to Sadie's room. When no one answered after a knock, she pushed the door open. Sadie was face down on her purple bedspread, her daisy pillow balled up under her.

Leah set the glass of milk on the bedside table and lowered herself down beside her on the bed. "Sadie," she said, tracing her daughter's face to push the hair off of it. "Would a cookie help?"

Sadie shook her head, sending the hair back over her face.

"It's Louise's," she said, trying to persuade her.

When Sadie didn't move, Leah sat there beside her and looked around at her tiny room. They'd done the best with what they had, and every week, Leah brought home a bouquet from work that she would make with unused flowers from that day. Sadie always had a fresh bouquet next to her bed.

"Why don't we have dinner and then we can make ice cream sundaes for dessert? Are you hungry?"

Sadie sat up slowly. "I can't do that math," she said, her face full of worry.

"I'll write a note on it for your teacher." Leah had written a note on the last three homework assignments, and every time she did, she knew that the teacher would barely have enough time to get around to her. Sadie hadn't progressed at all since the last reporting period. "Maybe after we eat, and you feel better, I can show you how I do the math."

"I don't think it's the way my teacher does it."

Leah didn't want to speak badly of the teacher. She'd never do that. But she wanted to tell Sadie that it didn't matter what her teacher said, Leah could show her, and she'd know how to do it for the rest of her life. "Perhaps we could tell your teacher that we did it my way instead. I'm sure she'd be fine with that."

"I wish Mrs. Stevenson was still at school."

Mrs. Stevenson was the third tutor to quit, and they were only halfway through the year.

"Me too," Leah said, forcing a smile. As she fretted over Sadie, her protective motherly instincts kicked in and a thought slithered through her mind that hadn't occurred to her before: there was another way to get Sadie out of her school, rather than moving to Evergreen Hill. If Leah sold her half of the plantation, she could afford to live in an area with better schools. But were there any schools with as good a gymnastics program? She tried to ignore the thought, wishing she hadn't just twisted the idea of selling into a positive one. Both she and Sadie had their hearts set on Evergreen Hill. How could she contemplate giving in without a fight?

Chapter Six

After a discussion with Roz, Leah had decided to leave Sadie with her to finish out school for the last few weeks until Christmas break. She pulled her car to a stop in front of Evergreen Hill and got out, the icy air pelting her cheeks as she went to the back of the car to get her bags. David opened the door and came down the walk to help her. He picked up the heaviest one.

"Hello," he said, a guarded look on his face.

"Hi."

With the rest of her bags in hand, she started to walk up to the house, saying nothing more. She'd allowed a few paces between her and David as he lugged her bag over the icy ground. The air between them was so heavy she could feel it settling on her shoulders. All she wanted to do was get inside to be close to Nan. Whenever things bothered her like this, Nan was the one who could comfort her. She wanted to go upstairs and lie down on Nan's bed, curl up with her pillows and wait for the right answer to all this.

Before she could process what was happening, she tripped, and, unable to recover, she was falling. Suddenly, she felt as though she were going to pass out, the pain in her ankle causing her to crumble to the ground.

"Are you all right?" she heard from behind her as David abandoned the bag and jogged to her side. He squatted down and put his arm around her back. "What hurts?"

Leah squeezed her eyes shut in an attempt to alleviate the throbbing. "It's my ankle." She'd stepped in a hole that had been camouflaged by newly fallen snow. "I don't think I can walk."

"Okay," David said, his eyes roaming the space around her as he assessed the situation. "I'm going to stand you up very slowly. Just put all your weight on your good leg and on me. Then, I'll give you a piggyback ride to the house. I'll come back for the bags once I get you inside."

He put his hands under her arms and gently pulled her up. She wobbled slightly, but he caught her. While helping her to maintain balance, David turned his back to her and guided her arms until they were in a position that she could grab on to his shoulders. She hopped into place.

"I've got you," he said, tilting forward. "Just lean onto my back and I'll grab your legs."

She moved toward him, wrapping her arms around his neck, the clean smell of his shirt and his unique scent—like lavender and nutmeg with a dash of cedar—causing heat to spread over her cheeks despite the cold. She let him take her weight as he grabbed the backs of her thighs to lift her up, and she swallowed to keep her composure.

She didn't want to think about the fact that he was going to haul her all the way up to the house. Truthfully, though, her ankle was hurting so much that she couldn't think much more than that. He began to walk through the snow. Immediately, the pain in her ankle as it swung with his movements was nearly unbearable. With every step, she winced.

"I know it hurts," he said, as if he'd read her thoughts. When he said it, another memory slid into her mind. She'd gotten stung on the leg by a bee, the bright red welt and the excruciating burning alarming her. She'd sat down, her hands cupping the wound, tears springing to her eyes. David had been hitting baseballs in the yard—she could still remember the tinny sound of the ball as it hit his metal bat. The ball sailed into the air, *PING*, and off it went across the yard, one ball after another. He dropped his bat and sat down next to her. "I know it hurts," he'd said once he'd seen the sting. She'd totally forgotten that until he'd done it again just now.

"We're almost there."

Leah came back to reality.

"I'm going to set you down now so that I can open the door," he said, gingerly lowering himself until her good leg touched the step. He held on to her so that she wouldn't fall. She hopped around a bit despite his attempts to steady her, the pain starting to give her a headache. "Hold on to this," he said, helping her over to the railing leading to the door. She took hold of the oversized, iron handrail.

David opened the door and then came back to get her. He carried her into the kitchen, then went to the freezer and pulled out a bag of frozen peas.

She slid off her boots and lifted her leg, the hard dining chair not offering much comfort. "I think I've sprained it. It hurts so much," she told him.

"Let me get you a pillow to put it on." David hurried out of the room.

Leah grimaced, carefully pulling off her sock. Her ankle was starting to swell already, and the sock was getting tight. She placed the bag of peas on her leg, more pain shooting through it.

"You might want to lie down and prop it up with pillows. I can carry you," David said, concern in his eyes. "I have a first aid kit upstairs with a compression bandage. And you need to keep those peas on it for at least twenty minutes."

David lifted her up in his arms. He was winded from all the carrying, but he continued without a word until he had her in the room next to her room, where he put her on the bed. Awkwardly, she tossed a pillow down by her foot and wiggled it under her ankle while David went to get the first aid kit.

When he returned, David slipped his hands under her leg and started to lift, the pain nearly taking her breath away. "I think it's a pretty nasty sprain." He held her foot with one hand and pushed the pillow onto the floor, sitting down on the bed where it had been. Then, his hands so steady, he lowered her foot onto his lap. He unclipped the bandage, pushed the leg of her jeans up, and started to wrap her ankle.

"You might have to see a doctor," he said.

"It's fine, I'm sure. I probably just need to elevate it and—" She grimaced when he had to lift her ankle higher to get the bandage under it.

"At least to get something for the pain, and you probably could do with a pair of crutches."

"Please stop fussing over me. I said I'll be fine," she snapped, feeling agitated but knowing it was because she was upset with the situation. "Sorry."

Her tone caused David to stop and make eye contact. He got up and carefully put her foot on the pillow that he'd picked up off the floor.

She had so much emotion pent up that something like this, which she could normally just shrug off as bad luck, sent her into a tailspin.

"I understand."

"I don't think you do," she said quietly. "It's not about the ankle."

"I'm sorry. I'm not sure how to handle all of this. Honestly, when I saw your grandmother had given me half of Evergreen Hill, I assumed she wanted to honor you and include you. I never thought you'd want to live here. I thought you had your own life in Richmond. I thought I could buy you out and you'd be happy to take the money. I'd assumed that was what Nina had planned all along. I've sold off some real estate I had... I was going to offer you a million dollars."

A million dollars? Leah sat in silence, the words settling in her mind. A million dollars was a lot of money. It would definitely buy Sadie's gymnastics lessons. It could pay off a mortgage for Leah—she could own a home. She could live debt free and still have money to set aside for Sadie's college education. And what was her alternative? She couldn't afford to buy him out, and she doubted he'd ever just give his half away. The more she thought about it, the more she realized it really was her only option, and, while it wasn't what she wanted, it would be a positive change in hers and Sadie's lives.

Leah sighed. "That's a very generous offer."

Chapter Seven

"A million dollars?" Roz screamed down the line. Leah pulled the phone away from her ear. She'd stayed in her room, telling David she needed time to rest and think things through. She didn't want to make a decision like this without having time to consider all sides. He'd left her alone and, when she heard the sound of his car door shutting outside and his wheels against the gravel, Leah had called Roz.

"He knows how much a million dollars is, and how hard it is for me to pass up."

"He's being a big bully!"

"Don't tell Sadie, please," Leah said. "I want to spare dragging her through the whole thing. I'd like to check in on her after we talk."

"They're in Jo's bedroom, playing. She can't hear us. Tell me what you're thinking."

Leah wanted to pace the room, let out her nervous energy, but her ankle was still aching, and she couldn't get up. She could feel the frustration settling in her shoulders. She twisted awkwardly on the blue-and-yellow striped bedspread, the stripes distorting as the fabric moved under her. She rubbed her face with her free hand.

"If I took the money, I could find a venue in Richmond. I could start my business and do it in my own time—it wouldn't be rushed. Right now, I'd be having to pay the bills while I'm still taking classes."

Roz waited silently; she was letting her get it out. "Are you finished?" she asked, and Leah smiled—she'd known exactly what Roz was doing. "Don't be crazy," she said.

Leah didn't say anything back. She was too busy thinking. Was she being crazy? If she took the money, it would give her the chance to do everything she wanted, just somewhere else. She could find the perfect place near Roz and Louise, and she could still afford to move so Sadie could have a better school. Maybe it wouldn't be the perfect future she and Nan had planned, but it would be an amazing start.

"Hello-o!" Roz's voice cut through her thoughts. "When you get quiet like that, you worry me. Don't settle. You've worked too hard; you've made too many plans. Don't let them all go now."

Indecision swam around inside her.

"Look. I'll get Sadie so you can tell her hi. Then call Louise. She knows how to sweet talk you into the right decision."

Leah laughed as Roz called Sadie to the phone.

"Hi, Mama!" Sadie's voice came through a little muffled as she got situated with the phone. "Are you having a good time?"

The innocence of her question made Leah smile. "Yes, thank you," she said. "Except that I hurt my ankle."

"Oh no! Is it okay?"

"It'll be fine," she said as she tried to move her foot, pain running through her ankle like an electric current. "Tell me what you and Jo have been up to," she said, steering the conversation away from her and any possible questions about the house.

"I did a back handspring on Jo's mat in her spare room!" Sadie said, her voice going up at the end in excitement. She'd been practicing her tumbling any chance she got. One night, Leah had even pulled her mattress onto the floor to let her have a soft space to practice.

"Did you keep your arms straight?" Leah asked, still smiling at the sound of her daughter's voice. Sadie had been struggling with one arm bending slightly when she did her handsprings.

"Yes! Jo said they were the best handsprings she'd ever seen!"

"It sounds like you all are having fun." She tried to straighten the bedspread underneath her but with her ankle was unsuccessful.

"We are, Mama! What are you doing over there at Nan's?"

"Oh, not much at the moment. I'm just sitting around…" She ran her fingers through her hair, straightening the curls before they bounced back into place. She hadn't bothered to straighten her hair today, more worried about getting to Evergreen Hill to talk to David, and now look at her. She was locked away in her bedroom, not facing anyone. But there was no use in facing him until she had an answer for him.

"That doesn't sound like much fun. I thought you were going to decorate and stuff for family Christmas."

"I haven't started," she said, not wanting to mention that it hadn't crossed her mind once since she'd used it as the excuse for coming up without Sadie. Sadie had wanted to come with her, but Leah had told her that she'd be bored while she decorated all day. She'd come up with it on the fly. "Well, I'll let you go so you and Jo can play. Have a good night, okay?"

"I will, Mama. You too!"

"Tell Roz I said bye."

"Okay."

She hung up the phone and cast her gaze over at the dresser she'd helped Nan paint. It was a light shade of yellow, to match the com-

forter, the original wood showing through. They'd gotten paint everywhere when they'd refinished it. It had taken both of them to carry
it out into the yard. Nan had insisted on putting down a tarp, but it
had been breezy that day, the wind coming off the river, and the tarp
kept blowing across the yard before they could set the dresser on it.

They should've known right then that it probably wasn't a good
day to paint. Nan had set two flimsy trays on the tarp beside the
dresser once they'd gotten it in place during a lull in the wind. She
dumped yellow paint into them and handed a brush to Leah.

"Let's take the drawers out first," Nan said. As she took a step, she
put her foot right into the tray, submerging her canvas shoe. "Oh!"
she cried, jumping out of it, only to bump Leah who was stepping
over to help her.

Leah tripped, trying not to have the same fate, and fell, her bottom going right into the paint.

"Well, don't we look like a couple of amateurs," Nan said, her
laughter rising into the air around them. "The paint is supposed to go
on the dresser, not us."

Nan turned Leah around so she faced the river, backed her up, and
started to push her slightly back and forth. It took Leah a minute to
realize what she was doing, but when she did, she couldn't stop laughing. Nan was painting the dresser with Leah! Joining in, she bent over
and wiggled her bottom along the drawer.

With a grin, Leah looked at the drawer now, and only because she
knew what had happened, she could see a darker spot on it, and she
knew it was because they'd had to blend the paintbrush strokes and
the marks her bottom had made. She'd tried to work harder to hide
the mark but Nan had insisted they leave a little spot so that they
could remember. In the end, they'd done a great job both leaving

a reminder and making it look unified enough that no one would notice. Now, it sat, pristine, with its glass drawer pulls and matching mirror on the wall above it, a collection of glass vases in one corner of the dresser top. It was simply perfect.

Her phone rang, and she looked down at the number, recognizing it immediately. "Hi, Louise," she answered.

"Hi. Roz said I had to call you if you didn't call in the next two minutes. Is everything okay?"

"She's being dramatic," she teased. "She wants you to talk some sense into me." Leah explained David's offer.

"I can't imagine that's what your grandmother would have wanted."

"I know." She rolled over, wrapping herself in the bedspread.

"But true joint ownership won't allow either of you to have what you want."

"That's what I keep coming back to." She pulled the top of the bedspread over her head in frustration, wishing that the little cocoon she'd made would just swallow her up and spit her back out when none of this was an issue. Back before David had come, when Nan still saw Evergreen Hill as the place where Leah and Sadie would throw lavish parties. She could close her eyes and see those big white tents, the sound of music filling the air all the way to the woods, a glass of champagne in her hand as she plopped down on the bench outside to rest her sore feet. It wasn't hard to imagine Sadie running down the long path between the trees, coming home from school, her backpack bouncing with every step, that smile on her face that had the whole day's events inside it, just waiting to come out.

"A million dollars really would turn your life around," Louise said, bringing her back to the present moment.

"Yes. It would."

Chapter Eight

When David came home, Leah met him in the living room. He was unpacking a new printer, fiddling with the plastic manufacturer's cover that had been sealed for shipping. "David," she said, pulling his attention away from his purchase. "I need to talk to you."

He stood up and set the printer back into its box.

"It's about your offer," she said, feeling the sadness over letting go of her last connection with Nan. "I think I'd like to take it."

David's head tilted slightly to the side, surprise in his eyes, and for an instant, she felt the stab in her chest at how little she'd fought for Evergreen Hill. But her mind had won out over her heart, and she knew it was the only way. She tried not to think about what it was going to be like to actually let go of this place or how she'd break the news to Sadie.

"I have one request, though," she said, feeling the emotion welling up. "I'd like to still have family Christmas."

"Of course," he said. "You should have Christmas in the house with all your family and we'll make it the very best Christmas ever."

She nodded, unable to speak for fear she might start to sob.

* * *

Once she'd stopped crying, Leah was frustrated. Nan knew her better than anyone else. Why had she put her in this position? Pushing through the pain in her ankle, she went into Nan's room and closed the door. Starting with the tall dresser, she opened the first drawer and dug through the clothes, running her hand along underneath the garments. Nothing. She pulled out the second drawer—sweaters, shirts… She felt around some more and came up empty and shut it. Next drawer. This time, she pulled everything out, lumping it onto the floor, her irritation bubbling up. But seeing Nan's things askew on the floor gave her pause. She knew Nan wouldn't have wanted to see a mess like that. Carefully, she folded every item and replaced it in the drawer.

By the time Leah had checked all the drawers, the nightstands, and under the bed, she was losing hope. Nan, who always wrote notes and letters, who wrote her will by hand—had nothing to say to her granddaughter from this room. Maybe she'd have been okay with Leah selling her half. Without Nan here to guide her, she had to go with her head and trust herself. But she was going to check every nook and cranny to be sure there wasn't something that would lead her in a different direction. Leah went to the closet and opened the door: clothes hanging in neat rows above shoes in their shelves. The pain in her ankle was so great that she had to sit down. Nothing. No clues anywhere.

Leah managed to avoid David the rest of the evening yesterday. She hobbled downstairs quietly, late at night, and got herself something to eat, then took it back to her room, locking the door. She didn't want to see him. She really just wanted to go home, but his offer to have one final family Christmas was what was keeping her here.

This morning, she'd managed to get to the kitchen and back before he was up. She sat on the bed with a bowl of cereal, her swollen ankle propped on two bed pillows, and her phone in her hand. She felt like she couldn't move from that room. She was paralyzed by the situation. After a taking a bite of her cereal, she set the bowl beside her and texted Roz.

He's a selfish bastard, Roz replied, after Leah had told her the deed was done.

While Roz always erred on the harsher side of things, Leah, too, was disconcerted by it all. She texted back: *He has lived without this house for thirty-odd years. Why does he think his connection is stronger than mine?*

Roz's response floated onto her screen: *He doesn't deserve it, Leah.*

After she'd finished her conversation with Roz, she lay back on the bed and stared at the ceiling, her mind completely blank. She let the familiar scent of the bedspread and pillows comfort her. She noticed the large, ornamental crown molding at the ceiling. It had been painted over many times, the white paint settling in the nooks and crannies of the design, but the original hand carving of it was still visible. She thought about the time it must have taken to carve all that wood, and the precision needed to make the pattern uniform along the whole thing. Usually there was a beam of light from the window that shone along one of the corners, illuminating the joint where the two pieces came together. It was hidden somewhat in the gray winter morning light. She'd wanted to put caulk up there but just never mentioned it.

There was a quiet knock on the door, and she sat up. She wasn't ready to see David yet. She had nothing to say. But then, a small envelope shot under the door and came to rest on the hardwoods next to the area rug. When she could hear the footsteps moving away, Leah gingerly pulled her bad leg across the bed to the edge and stood up. She limped over and picked up the envelope, recognizing Nan's handwriting immediately as she read David's name on the outside. It was the same lacy stationery that Nan had used to write Leah's letter. She took it over to the chair in the corner of the room and sat down.

Her hands were shaking as she pulled the paper from the envelope and unfolded it. *Dear David* she read. *You will not understand this now, and I'm sure it will be a complete shock to you since we've never discussed it, but I feel it in my heart—I'm giving you half of Evergreen Hill. You will share it with my granddaughter, whom I'm sure you remember, Leah.* She went on to read a similar statement about regrets, her heart in her throat.

There had been no confusion in Nan's mind when she'd rewritten the will. It was clear now. David hadn't had a part in it in any way. David's stories about growing up at Evergreen Hill and his mother's sadness about losing it must have affected Nan the way they had Leah. Nan must've thought Leah had enough income to make the joint ownership work—after all, Leah had never mentioned her money worries to Nan.

With no reason to be set against him, Nan saw just what Leah had that first night: David was kind, funny, and thoughtful. Nan, always seeing the bright side of everything, probably figured they'd work something out.

In the end, it was nobody's fault but her own that she had hidden her financial problems. David was a good guy. He deserved something nice for his mother, and his connection to the house was undeniable. Leah sighed. She knew her anger with him was rooted in things not working out the way she'd planned, rather than based on the facts of the situation. Nan had wanted them both to have Ever-green Hill but their visions for its future meant joint ownership just wasn't an option. David was giving her a huge amount of money. He was being generous.

Chapter Nine

"Did you keep in touch with her?" she asked David once she finally felt like she could talk, the reality setting in. She needed answers about Nan. She wanted to understand Nan's side of things. She looked down at the coffee she'd made, waiting for his answer, her leg propped up on the kitchen chair beside her to keep the swelling in her ankle at bay.

"I hadn't seen Nina since I was young. I was only reunited with her about six months before she died." He stirred his mug of coffee and brought it over to the table, sitting down across from her.

"Six months?"

"Yes." He took a sip of his coffee, the silence settling in the air between them. The kitchen was particularly cold this morning, but it seemed to be the right spot to talk. She didn't feel very emotionally comfortable at the moment either. She traced her finger along a grain in the table—David's table.

"That seems so brief to have inherited half the plantation," she said, more thinking aloud than to him. Worried her mug might make a ring, she set it on the placemat like Nan had always done.

"That must seem... I don't know how that seems, but I didn't have a hand in this. My inheritance was entirely Nina's idea. It was as much of a surprise to me as, I'm sure, it was to you."

"And how is it that you're staying here?" she asked.

"I'd stopped by to see this place when I was looking for somewhere to live in town. I'd found a house, but it wasn't going to be ready for six months. I mentioned it to Nina, just in conversation, and to my surprise, she suggested I live here and rent a room until the house was ready."

Things were starting to come together in Leah's mind now.

"She was planning to introduce me to everyone at your family Christmas."

"Oh," she said, wondering what that day would've been like if Nan was still here. "Were you at the funeral?"

"No. I was in Chicago on business," he said, his expression downcast. "I was training someone to take my place when I left my job. By the time I got back I had to be filled in by the neighbor, Mrs. Jenkins. I was floored." He looked down at his hands.

Muriel Jenkins had spoken to Leah at the funeral. They were good friends, and Nan often had her over for lunch. It was Muriel's turn to host, but Nan hadn't shown up, so she went over to Evergreen Hill to check on her. The door was unlocked, and she let herself in. That was when she'd found her in her chair. Just like she was sleeping.

Leah nodded, and they both sat for a moment in this new reality. Nan had surprised her a lot in the last few weeks.

"What do you think Nan meant about regrets? She said it to both of us, but to me she was always such a positive, forward-looking person."

David nodded. "Do you know anyone named Samuel Patterson?" he asked.

Leah shook her head.

"She didn't mention him ever?"

"No. Why?"

"Nina got me to send a letter to him for her."

"She did?" she asked. "What kind of letter?"

He set his mug of coffee down. "When I got back from Chicago, I found two letters in my room: one was the letter I slipped under the door. The other was addressed to Samuel Patterson. It was just a thin envelope like mine, already sealed and stamped with a note asking me to please mail it for her."

"Do you know what it said?"

He shook his head. "Like I said, it was sealed—not that I'd have looked."

"Do you remember the address on the envelope she left you to send?"

"I'm sorry. I was really upset that I'd missed her funeral, and the house was so empty without Nina, I didn't pay attention to those kinds of details. I was sort of on autopilot, still in shock."

"I totally understand. Did she ask you to mail any other letters?"

"No. Just that one."

She looked around the room, not really processing her view, but thinking. At the funeral, Muriel had mentioned how sudden and unexpected Nan's death had been. She hadn't mentioned any sort of note or letter, and given how close she was with the family, and how much she usually shared with them, she probably would've said something. Even Leah's mother and uncle hadn't received any kind of letter—her mom had told her so in an attempt to help relieve her grief when she'd called her on the way to Evergreen Hill. She'd said, "You know your nan thought the world of you if she took the time to include her own words with your inheritance. She loved you so much."

So as far as Leah knew, Nan had written three letters, and one of those was to this mystery person.

"I'm so curious about what was in that letter. She wrote everything down. She must have an address book somewhere. Where was she writing it, do you know?"

"I wasn't here. Maybe at the writing desk in the parlor? I saw her writing things there sometimes."

"You're right." She got up, careful not to tweak her ankle as she walked gingerly toward the hallway, David right alongside her. They entered the grand parlor, which had been used by Mr. Truman, the original owner, for weddings and family gatherings. Nan had used it as an indoor space for corporate meetings as well as weddings if the weather didn't permit the use of the grounds. At one end, she had a rosewood piano, a book of music still propped up from the last time she'd had someone play. Nan always kept books of period music, and when there were events, she'd hire someone to play in the background.

Along the far wall, sitting on an oriental rug, was a complementary upholstered rosewood sofa with matching chairs flanking the space. At the other end was Nan's writing desk along with an enormous glass-doored bookcase.

Leah pulled the handle of the narrow drawer on the writing desk and peered inside. She thumbed through the vintage magazines that were there.

"Any luck?" David asked, leaning over her shoulder.

"No," she said shaking her head.

"How about that bookcase? Would it be in there?"

Leah opened the door, its hinges groaning with their age. The glass was original, with imperfections giving it a wavy look like the kitchen window. She took a peek at the spines of the books that were there. "These are all period books," she said. "Nan would scour second-hand bookshops and antique stores to find just the right ones—I remember. She hasn't put anything in here that's younger than nineteen hundred." She turned around. "Where would she have put an address book?"

Again, Nan wasn't giving away her secrets.

When David had gone upstairs to finish a little work, Leah decided to call her mom. "Have you ever heard of Samuel Patterson?" she asked after a quick hello.

"Wow. I haven't heard that name in a long time. He was a friend of your nan's when we were little."

"A friend," she clarified. It was a statement more than a question because she thought Nan would've mentioned a friend who was important enough to receive a letter like that. "How long did Nan know him?"

"She worked for him at a college when we were young. I was in elementary school. By the time I was around eleven, we'd moved to Evergreen Hill, and she'd left the job. Why?"

She told her mother what David had said and was surprised to hear that her mother knew nothing else at all. After she'd gotten off the phone with her, Leah called her uncle, but he had a similar story to her mother's—someone she'd worked for. He did remember instances where they'd gone to dinner or stayed out together, but he'd always figured it was something to do with work.

She decided to check the boxes that she'd once seen in the attic, to see if she could find any more clues. She'd always wondered what was in them. Perhaps, if this Samuel hadn't been in Nan's life for a while, she'd have moved things up there. But when she opened them, Leah found only old hats and handbags, a couple of boxes of vintage magazines—she thumbed through them—and another box full of old film reels. She took them out, one by one, and read the descriptions, but none of them seemed to be something that might have this friend in them—old weddings Nan had thrown on the property, a tour of the servants' quarters, and the construction as they banked off the property from the James River.

Leah went to bed that night still wondering about Samuel. If she'd been able to see Nan at the end, would Nan have told her anything about him?

Chapter Ten

When Leah awakened the next morning, it was as if her brain had been on pause. She sat up quickly in bed, realizing she hadn't checked the closet in Nan's room to see if there was any sign of her connection to Samuel Patterson. Leah hobbled down the hall and went straight in before she'd done anything else.

She opened the closet again and rifled through the clothes. She got on her knees, careful of her ankle, and inspected the shoes in their racks, and when she did, she noticed a small trunk at the very back. Curious, she leaned in and scooted it forward until she could open the lid.

Inside, she found all sorts of things—books, picture frames with photos of various family members, scrapbooks from when Leah's mother and uncle were young, some baby items. But what caught her eye was an enormous stack of letters, tied together with a blue satin ribbon. She reached into the trunk and pulled them out, setting them in her lap, holding her breath.

She flipped through the envelopes—they were all addressed to Nina Evans and their return addresses were all the same name: Samuel Patterson. Leah clapped a hand over her mouth, her heart pounding. She shut the lid of the trunk and slid it back into place. Then she closed the closet door and tucked the letters under her arm. She might have never heard that name before, but Nan must have wanted to keep the memories since the letters were in there. She couldn't wait to see what they said.

She took them back to her room and sat down on the bed, untying the ribbon that held them together. Nan had put them in date order by their postmark, she'd noticed. She opened the first letter and read:

Dear Nina,

I wish I knew if you were all right. It keeps me up at night. I miss you terribly. Things aren't as hard as you think they are. I can make them easier. Why did you leave me without a word? It has broken my heart...

She looked up, her mind racing. Who was this person? She continued to read the letters, but the more she read, the less she understood what was going on. This Samuel Patterson had clearly had romantic moments with Nan. In one, he'd even said he loved her. Yet she'd never mentioned him.

As quickly as she could, pushing herself through the throbbing in her ankle, too excited to worry about the pain, she hurried out into the hallway, noticing the door to the sewing room, where David worked, was shut. She limped down to it as fast as possible, the letters bundled under her arm, and knocked quietly on the door.

"Come in," he said.

She pushed the door open. David was sitting at Nan's sewing table, beneath her bulletin board full of unusual fabric squares, their ragged edges waiting to be stitched together. He was wearing glasses—she'd never seen him wear them—and facing his laptop.

"I'm so sorry to interrupt your work, but, when you get a chance to take a break, I found out who Samuel Patterson is." She waved the letters in the air.

David stood up immediately and walked toward her. Then he stopped and really looked at her, the corner of his mouth going up in amusement. It was only then that she realized she was in her red Christmas tree flannel pajamas, and she hadn't looked in the mirror since she'd gotten up.

"Should we read them over breakfast?" he asked.

He was dressed, showered, shaved. She wanted to run her hands through her hair, rub her face, straighten her pajamas, but she didn't want to be obvious. From the flush she felt across her neck she was pretty sure David already knew what she was thinking.

"That would be nice," she said. "I'll just… freshen up."

"I got some muffins at the market when I was out last. We can have those. Coffee or tea?"

"Coffee, please."

Leah raced to get ready, just dying to read more of the letters and find out about this man whom Nan had kept a secret all these years. She tugged on her curls, pulling them back into a loose ponytail, and then washed her face and added some powder and lip gloss. When she'd changed and was generally presentable, she grabbed the letters and headed downstairs.

This time, she was surprised to find that David had set out the plate of muffins on the coffee table in the sitting room by the fire, and he'd already made her coffee the way she liked it. Holding the letters, and feeling like Nan had given the two of them a little nudge, she sat down, feeling quite a bit more relaxed.

He sat down beside her and handed her the mug. "Thank you," she said with a smile. Then, over coffee, she filled him in on the letters she'd read. She set the rest of the envelopes between them.

"May I?" David asked, taking the top one.

"Of course."

He pulled the paper out, gently unfolded it, and started reading silently. Leah watched his eyes moving across the text. "I could give you the life you've always wanted," he read aloud. "I'd be good to your children—they're angels..." He read on and then looked up, his eyes wide. "I can't believe this."

"I know! Who is this guy?" She took the next one and opened it, scanning the text. "We only have one life... I understand if you've chosen your own path, but please know that I'm here for you whenever you need me..."

They continued to read the letters, each one telling them so much about the love this man had and the memories of Nan that he held so dear, but at the same time, they didn't contain specifics, and the questions were mounting. "I'd really like to meet him and hear his story."

"We could try to look up the address on my computer."

"Oh!" she said, excitement swelling. "We could!"

David went upstairs and got his laptop. He started it up and sat back on the settee, close enough for Leah to view the screen. Once he had the search engine up, she held out the envelope so he could type in the address. Nervous energy pinged through her fingertips as he hit search.

"It's a list of phone numbers!" she said, immediately pulling out her phone. They scrolled through the list—hundreds of Samuel Pattersons. Any of them could be him. They narrowed it a bit by age and possible location. She picked one, dialed the number and put the phone to her ear. A thrill prickled her spine. "It's ringing."

David shifted on the settee, hanging on every ring as she put the phone on speaker.

"Hello?" a woman answered.

"Hi. I'm looking for Samuel Patterson," Leah said, making eye contact with David and seeing as much excitement in his eyes as she felt in hers. He smiled at her.

"I'm sorry. There's no one here by that name. I think you have the wrong number."

She let out the air she'd been holding in her lungs. "Okay. Thank you," she said and hung up.

"There are so many," David said, scrolling through the rest of the numbers.

Leah's shoulders slumped as she felt the opportunity to know this man slipping from her fingers. "Maybe once everything has settled down after the holidays, I'll make a list and try them all."

"I'm sorry," he said. "I wish I'd ripped that letter open when I'd had it."

Leah laughed, despite herself.

The melting ice off the roof was the only sound between them as Leah contemplated what might have been. She didn't know what she had expected from calling Samuel, or what she would've done next, but she wished she could learn that part of Nan's life right now, and not have to wait any longer.

"I wonder if she would've said anything to Muriel about him. They were great friends." Leah thought about how much more she told Roz and Louise than she told her family, because she knew they wouldn't judge her. "I might ask her over for dinner tonight. Would that be okay with you?"

"Of course. I'd love to see her again."

"What should we cook?"

"Why don't we call her and see if she's available? Then we can go shopping and cook something from one of Nina's millions of recipes. If anyone knew how to cater to someone, it was her."

Leah couldn't help but think how creative and considerate a suggestion this was. "That sounds like a perfect idea. It'll be so good to see her! I haven't seen her since the funeral and I miss her. She's a great lady, isn't she?"

"Yes," he said, smiling.

"I'll give her a call."

Muriel had been delighted to hear from Leah. Leah had asked her what recipe of Nan's was her favorite. It had taken some coaxing to get the answer, as Muriel didn't want to impose at all, but she'd told Muriel she'd pick the dessert if Muriel picked the main dish, so, finally, Muriel relented and asked Leah to cook Nan's chili and cornbread. "It's world famous, you know?" she'd said. "Your nan won over a group of international students with that chili."

"Oh, I remember them!" Leah had said. They'd come on a tour of the southern U.S., and they'd stopped at Nan's to see a preserved plantation. They all looked beat down and exhausted as they shuffled through the hallways, pairs of them talking in their native tongues, barely any of them able to speak much English. But without saying a word, Nan started handing out little chocolates and glasses of ginger ale.

Nan beckoned for them to come into the kitchen, and they all piled around the table. Those who couldn't sit stood nearby. She got out a large pot and some vegetables and, with a lot of hand gestures, told them she was going to feed them. She put on music—American pop music—even though she never listened to it, and she started dancing around as she chopped vegetables and added beans and beef to the pot. She already had the cornbread made from the night before, so she heated it in the oven, sliced it, and plated it piece by piece, dabbing a dollop of butter on the top. She handed it out while Muriel, who'd volunteered to help that day like she often did, refilled their glasses. The smell of the stew as it cooked seemed to be intoxicating, the whole group chattering and laughing, raising their glasses to each other.

Leah, Nan, and Muriel had sat with them that cold evening, and even though they couldn't speak much to each other, there was happiness all around. Nan could just bring it out in people.

Having made a list of ingredients, Leah stood alone in the kitchen, considering going to town alone—and with a very sore ankle. All the reminiscing about Nan had brought her emotions to the surface and she didn't really know if spending time with David would help anything. She needed space. Leah tapped the folded list against her empty hand, debating. She was going to have to get used to the idea that things would be different from here on out. She had to start accepting the situation. She made her way up the stairs to get him.

"So what do we need for the chili?" David asked, pushing the shopping cart slowly down the aisle so Leah could keep up with her sore ankle.

"Let's make a double batch," Leah suggested. "I texted Roz this morning. Sadie's coming the day after tomorrow and I'll want to spend every minute with her, so I'd rather not have to cook. We can just warm up the chili." She handed him the list and he turned the cart toward the vegetable aisle.

"I can't wait to meet her. I've heard so much about her from Nina. She just adored Sadie."

She took a moment to look at him, to take in how kind and genuine he was. "They were nearly inseparable. Sadie idolized Nan; it used to be the running joke that if I wanted Sadie to do anything, all I had to do was ask Nan to tell her to do it." She smiled. "One time, I was dying to get Sadie to try cucumbers. I knew she'd love them and they'd be so easy to pack in her lunches. I was always snacking on them but she'd never try them. I told Nan, and, one day, out of the blue, when Sadie was visiting, she started chopping one. She asked Sadie to help her arrange them on a small platter with some other cold vegetables. 'I love the way you stacked them just so!' she said to her. 'You're a natural at presentation.' Then, as calm as ever, Nan said, 'You know, Sadie, cucumbers are one of my favorite snacks. Feel free to get one if you'd like.' That was all she said. Then Nan picked a slice off the platter and popped it into her mouth. And, do you know, Sadie did the same thing?" She laughed at the memory.

David grinned at her, laughing too, as he got two onions to put into the cart. Their shared laugher must have made him feel playful because he juggled the onions, tossing them higher and higher into the air. But the last time, he missed, and one of the onions hit the edge of the cart and bounced away, rolling through the legs of an incredulous shopper.

"So sorry," David said, trying to stifle his laughter as the lady stared at him. "Lost my onion." He stepped lightly around her and bent down to pick it up, Leah laughing uncontrollably. There was something about him that made even shopping seem more eventful than usual. She enjoyed talking to David, and she was happy to be able to have this time with him.

The smell of vanilla and caramel filled the air, the warmth from the oven making Leah's face feel flushed. She'd poked the cake with a toothpick to see if it was ready and then set it on the counter to cool. Nan had always said when the toothpick came out clean the cake was done. Feeling festive, she had Christmas music playing while she baked, and she noticed the flour handprints, just like Nan's, on the apron she was wearing.

The cake had been cooling a good twenty minutes while she freshened up for dinner. She'd straightened her hair, done her make-up, and put on one of her fitted sweaters and a pair of jeans, dressing it up just a bit with some teardrop earrings. She slid the cake onto Nan's glass cake stand, scooting it into the center to prepare it for icing.

David came into the kitchen. His face was clean-shaven, his hair just wet enough to give away that he'd recently showered. He had on an oxford shirt and a pair of jeans, and Leah couldn't help but want to look at him, he was so attractive. She smiled, willing herself to keep busy with the container of icing. She picked at the foil safety seal.

"You look really nice," he said, and when she looked up at him, his expression seemed to mirror her own thoughts about him. "I've never seen your hair like that before."

She smiled, hoping her cheeks didn't blush too much. At least she could blame it on all the heat from the oven. "Thank you," she said.

"So this is Nina's famous caramel cake?" he asked, standing beside her. She continued to pick at the foil on the icing container until he reached over and gently took if from her hands, pulling the foil off in one motion. He handed it back to her.

"Well, it's not as famous as her chili," she teased. She dipped the icing spreader into the tub of caramel icing and dropped a large glob of it on the top of the cake, spreading it evenly along the surface. She added more and, just as Nan had taught her, she made little waves of icing toward the sides, where she added enough to make a thick layer around the edges, all while David looked on. When she'd finished, she took a clean rag and dragged it around the cake plate to give it a clean look. Then, with her icing bag, she made little stars around the edges too and added a caramel drizzle on top to finish it off. She put the glass cover over the top and stacked three small white dessert plates with silver spoons next to it.

The old doorbell rang. "That will be Muriel," Leah said. They walked to the door together to greet her.

Leah opened the door, and just as she always had, Muriel stood with a gorgeous bouquet of flowers. Amidst a bundle of greenery were buttery cream ranunculuses, their petals like abundant folds of silk, bright red poppies, and red-and-white peonies that looked like Christmas peppermints.

"It's good to see you," Leah said, letting her in. She kissed her on the cheek. "Those are gorgeous!"

"Well, you should know," Muriel said with a smile as she returned Leah's kiss and then handed her the bouquet. "You are quite stunning yourself! Look at you!" She offered a quick wink and turned. "Hello, David. Lovely to see you."

Muriel took off her long, black trench coat, the dark color of it complementing her fair complexion and wavy silver hair. She started toward the closet but David stepped in and offered to take her coat.

"It smells divine in here," she said. "Just like when Nina used to cook that chili. She would be proud."

"I hope you're hungry. It's all ready and warming on the stove."

"Dear, let's get right to it. I'm starving."

David led them down the hallway to the kitchen, Muriel's boxy heels making clacking noises on the hardwoods. She was in good shape for her age. She'd been a runner when she was younger and now she walked quite a bit. Leah removed the paper from around the bouquet and arranged the flowers in the empty vase on the table.

"Please. Have a seat," Leah said, pulling out a chair for Muriel. "I'll bring everything over to the table. What would you like to drink?"

Muriel sat down, the seat nearly swallowing her tiny body. She crossed her legs at the ankle and put her hands in her lap. "An iced tea if you have it."

"Of course we do!" Leah said with a knowing grin. Nan always had sweet tea on hand and Leah continued that tradition even at her own house. She pulled out Nan's Waterford crystal pitcher, made of clear glass except for the bottom, which was etched in latticework. She'd always loved that pitcher. This afternoon, in preparation for dinner, Leah had made a fresh batch of tea and dropped rounds of lemons into it. She tried to pour it just so, to keep the lemons from dropping into the glass as she poured the tea over the cubes of ice.

"May I help in any way?" Muriel asked.

"Oh no. I'm just fine." Leah dished out three hearty bowls of steaming chili and David took them to the table.

Once they were all settled, Leah having set a long platter of cornbread in the center, and had enjoyed a little small talk, Leah decided it was a good time to ask about Samuel.

Muriel's lips were set in a pout, her head shaking back and forth. "No, dear. I've never heard of anyone named Samuel Patterson before."

"Did Nan ever mention an old flame or anything like that?"

Muriel straightened the napkin in her lap. "No," she said wistfully. "She was such a fabulous individual, I often wondered why she'd never settled down. I assumed that it was because she'd never moved on after your grandfather died, but I never pressed her on it."

Leah told her a little about Samuel, and Muriel seemed to enjoy hearing that someone was in love with Nan.

"She was an easy woman to love," Muriel said. "Knowing her, she was so busy being everything for everyone else that she neglected herself."

Leah wondered about Nan. What had it been like for her once everyone had gone home and she was snuggled in her bed all alone at night? Had she been missing someone? Had she missed Samuel? It looked like Leah might never find out.

Chapter Eleven

All morning and into the afternoon, David had been upstairs working. Leah had popped into town, doing a little Christmas shopping in some of the specialty shops, and now she was resting her ankle. She decided to text Roz to ask if Sadie could give her a call.

"Hi, my sweet girl!" she said as she answered the call from Roz's number.

"Hi, Mama! How is your foot?"

"It's my ankle and it's okay. It's getting better every minute. How are you?" She twisted on the settee, braving the pain as she lifted her foot up onto one of the throw pillows.

"I'm great! We made a gingerbread house and then ate all the candy off!"

"I hope you didn't get a bellyache!" she said, laughing.

"No. It wasn't that much candy. They don't give you much in the boxed ones you buy in the stores. It wasn't anything like Nan's."

She didn't do it every year, but when Nan made a gingerbread house, she went all out, baking real gingerbread, cutting it into perfect house shapes, and buying bags and bags of gourmet candy from the local candy shop. She'd let Sadie pick out all the flavors last time, and Sadie still talked about that gingerbread house.

"Well, you were polite and thankful to Roz, right?" said Leah, thinking of the cost of those boxed houses at the store. She made a mental note to try to slip Roz ten dollars the next time she saw her, although she doubted Roz would accept it.

"Yes, Mama. I always say thank you when she does something nice."

"Good girl."

"I wish we could've made it at Nan's house with all the candy!"

"Me too." She took in a deep breath and rolled her head on her shoulders, a pinch forming.

"Maybe next year when we live there! We could have them up early for family Christmas!"

"I definitely want to spend Christmas with Roz and Jo," she said, avoiding the subject of the house. Her skin prickled with the reality of her choices. With the money, perhaps she could rent something in town, close to Evergreen Hill... But the more she thought about it, the more she realized that she couldn't handle being that close and not living at the plantation.

"Mama?" Sadie said, breaking into her thoughts.

"Yes?"

"You got quiet."

"Oh, I'm sorry. I didn't mean to. Something distracted me. I'm glad you're having a great time with Roz and Jo. Why don't you let me speak to Roz now?"

"Okay. Love you!"

"Love you too!"

She heard Sadie calling for Roz and, after a moment, she answered.

"Thank you for making the gingerbread house with Sadie," she said.

"It was fun! And a good way to keep them busy in this weather. How are you?"

"I'm okay."

"Any headway with the con artist? Have you reconsidered?"

Leah allowed a little chuckle but sobered when the actual subject of the house entered her mind. "Roz, this isn't how I expected things to turn out, but in the end, Sadie and I will benefit from selling him the house. Think about all the ways our lives will change with this money. I don't even have to spell it all out for you. I know you understand. A *million* dollars…"

"When you first said a million, I was blown away. But how much is that house worth? The way you and Louise describe it… I don't know. Is it *that* generous? In the end, you have to do what makes you happy. You know what's right for you, and no one else can make that decision except you."

The fire in the sitting room had fizzled, and Leah checked the back door where Nan kept logs, but couldn't find any. Without a fire, the house would get extremely cold downstairs. She went to look for David to ask if he had any cut, praying that he did.

At the top of the stairs, she could hear clicking at the end of the hallway, so she walked toward Nan's sewing room. The door was only open a crack. Gently, she opened it wider.

"Sorry to interrupt," she said.

He stopped typing, slipped off his glasses, and turned toward her.

"Are there any more logs for the fire?"

He clicked a few more keys before looking at her again. "Are we out?"

"There weren't any at the back door. Have you put the logs somewhere new?"

He leaned on his elbows, rubbing his eyes. "No," he said.

"Are you all right?" She walked into the middle of the room, concerned.

"I'm just behind. It's no one's fault, but I have to get this done today." He swiveled around in the chair to face her and smiled. "There might be some salvageable wood under a small tarp behind the servants' quarters building."

"I'll get it. You can finish your work," she said.

He looked down for a moment, consideration on his face. "I'll try to get to a stopping point in a second and then I'll get you the wood."

Leah grinned. "It's fine. I can get it. How many times do you think it was just me and Nan up here?"

He smiled back. "But I'm here now and I like chopping and collecting the wood. It's not something I've been able to do much, living in the city." He turned back toward his computer. "I'll meet you downstairs in a second," he said, typing madly as he spoke.

Leah quietly let herself out and closed the door behind her.

The servants' quarters building was a small brick structure at the back of the long yard, quite a walk from the main house. Nan had used its undersized rooms as a museum, displaying old photos and memorabilia in glass cases, although she'd never finished the actual restoration of the building. She'd gotten help from private donors to fund it, and it was on her to-do list. As a lover of history, Leah had spent a lot of time there, learning about life at Evergreen Hill during its time as a tobacco plantation.

The plantation had originally belonged to the Truman family in the eighteenth century. Tobacco was the heart of Virginia back then; the climate was ideal for its growth, and, by the eighteenth century, it was one of the primary cash crops in the state, along with cotton. Victor Truman made his income in the tobacco trade, but he died with no descendants and the house fell into disrepair. Nan had told her once that Lydia said her parents could barely afford it at the price they'd gotten it, but it was so magnificent in its grand but understated way that they'd decided to sink every penny they had into it, including a large family inheritance.

Leah, glad that her ankle was hurting less today when she walked, trudged through the snowy yard and stopped when she reached the servants' quarters. When the building came into view, her mouth dropped open. A tree had fallen on the roof of it, crumpling the slate shingles like gingerbread cookies. Her heart pounded as she wondered how long the items inside had been exposed to the elements. Temperature and humidity levels had to be controlled or the artifacts could be damaged beyond repair.

She slipped the key into the lock and opened the door to assess the situation. The trunk of the tree was wedged in the corner of the room; water damage on the wall had caused the paint to peel. The glass cases were still intact, dusty, the original wood floors not swept. With the radiators off and a gaping hole, plugged only by the tree, in the ceiling, it was just as frigid as it was outside. Leah could feel her pulse pounding in her head as she frantically checked the items.

She used the sleeve of her coat to clean the top of one of the cases, revealing a preserved dried tobacco leaf, two hand-carved smoking pipes, and a small tin cigarette case. Her breath dissipated into the icy air in front of her. She ran her mitten along the entire case and then clapped her hands together to remove the dust. There was a small plaque describing the first tobacco planted by Europeans in 1609, and the struggles they had. The items in that case seemed to be okay, although she wouldn't really know until she'd had someone inspect them.

She checked the next case. All the artifacts in that one had belonged to the Truman family. She peered in, checking the color of one of the work shirts Victor Truman had used in the fields, the dark yellow stains of tobacco still evident. It seemed okay. She checked the teacup that had belonged to his aunt, Mildred Truman, the delicate flowers as pristine as the day they were painted. Her eyes moved along the items frantically—a brooch and a hair comb worn by Victor's mother, white gloves with the Truman initials next to the button clasp, a small pair of spectacles. All the items would need to be checked over, but they seemed okay.

The next case, this one larger, had samples of the wood that had been used in the house, remnants of the old ships. Accompanying it was a plaque with the history of the ships that had sailed from England to Virginia in those early days, detailing the hardships they faced crossing the Atlantic and the trade routes they'd taken. The other relics were also things from those early days—the original blueprint of the house, drawn by hand and sketched on yellowing paper, the edges worn completely away, the first tobacco seed bags that had been found on the property and preserved, an example of one of the stones used in the foundation, imported from England as ballast and sold in the New World, and a brick from the brick supply that made up the structure itself, cut and molded in the American colonies.

The last case was devoted completely to farming tobacco—tons of sketches showing the original plot of the land, maps of the shipments that were made, and information about farming techniques such as curing the leaves from the rafters of barns. She remembered Nan telling her how every single tobacco plant had to be checked every day because tobacco fleas would infest them. It was a meticulous effort to harvest tobacco, but the crop in Virginia was one of the sweetest, and reaped a solid income for those who could do it. London was importing millions of pounds of it every year, just from Virginia, so Mr. Truman covered every square inch of the property with tobacco crop. Leah could smell the sweet aroma in the wood there. It still lingered in the structures that had held the harvest.

Mr. Truman had spent every day in the fields. He never married; people said that he was married to his money. She remembered thinking, as a girl, how sad it would be to go through life with no one. But now, wiser, she thought she understood him a little better.

"I wonder when this happened," David said from behind, causing her to jump. "Sorry. I didn't mean to startle you." He walked up beside her and peered up at the tree. "I told you I'd help you. You shouldn't be in here with that ankle. It could be dangerous."

"I think it's fine." She checked the items closer to the damage again, and they all seemed to be in good shape, but it didn't squash her worry.

"From outside, the tree looked as though it were dead. I wonder if the snow just got too heavy for its brittle limbs."

"I hope it hasn't been like this very long. These items are priceless." She wanted to spring into action to take care of it before it caused any further damage. She knew it was an unplanned expense and would require some time to coordinate the removal of the items and their repair, but Leah felt like a protective mother. Then she remembered that this was David's burden now, and he was planning to knock all these buildings down. The thought settled heavily in her stomach. "That wall's in bad shape," she said.

"Yeah," he agreed with a huff of breath, and he looked up at the tree.

Maybe he wanted to demolish the building, but surely he knew the importance of all of these artifacts? "We'll have to get these items transported to the main house before anyone messes with that tree," she said, refusing to acknowledge the fact that he might bulldoze the structure. She cleaned off another case with her sleeve and beckoned him over. "Look at these," she said, trying to get him to understand how important the story of this place was. She tapped the glass above the exhibit of a satin baby blanket; presumably the one Mrs. Truman had wrapped a baby Victor in the day he was born. Beside it was a white dress, his christening gown. This wasn't just a tree damaging a building. It was a narrow escape from losing pieces of history.

He leaned forward to view its contents. "You know, I remember this," he said, peering down at a picture of Mr. Truman. "My grand-mother told me that this man didn't live extravagantly like many thought. He had to turn his profits back around to the farm to fund it. He was dirty, his hands worn and calloused. He wasn't a gentleman at all."

"I know. It's so odd, isn't it?" she said, relieved that he had some knowledge of the history here. "It's such an odd thing, because the house itself, with the hundred-year-old oak trees outside, the James River in front of it—it seems every bit a gentleman's retreat.

"His life was a far cry from the house's existence now, though." Talking about the house's history—one of her favorite topics—was relaxing her a bit. "In its height of business, when I was in high school, there were parties and weddings rivaling Gatsby. Champagne would flow faster than the river. It was an amazing atmosphere—candlelit lanterns, white gauzy fabrics on outdoor tables, games of polo in the fields. It was something to see."

As she swam out of her memories of it, she focused on David, her dreams slipping away with the reality of the situation. He was looking at a painting of someone in the Truman family—maybe an aunt. Nan had searched all over Virginia to find relics of the home's owner. She'd found this one in an estate sale. It was a bust painting of a woman, her black hair parted perfectly down the middle and secured at the back, a subtle smile on her lips, her green eyes direct, her posture rigid. "We called her Aunt Ellie," she said. "We didn't know her name; it's written on the back, but the first name is smudged and it could've been Elizabeth, Elsie—we don't know. I decided to call her Ellie and it stuck. We were pretty sure it was a family member because there's another painting in the main house that looks just like her."

"That makes total sense now," he said. "I used to sneak butterscotch candies up to my room."

"I remember that," she said, grinning at the thought.

"One time Nina caught me. She pointed to the painting by the stairs and said, 'Aunt Ellie's watching. She tells me everything.' Then she winked at me. I still remember it because I felt so guilty. After that, I hid them in my pockets and scooted around the corner of the stairway away from that woman in the picture. I was terrified of her," he said, laughing.

Leah laughed right alongside him. "She got that from me! That woman in the painting always scared me. I thought she was watching me. It looks like her eyes follow us. I still don't like to look at it. It creeps me out."

"I don't look at it either. Maybe we should move the other one in here! Get it out of the house."

They both stood together in the freezing cold of that room, Leah glad that they could have that memory together. David was smiling just slightly, the gesture reaching his eyes and causing them to squint a little, revealing evidence of laughter in the small lines at the corners.

"Let me show you where that wood is. I brought the wheelbarrow so we can take it back up to the house. Then we'll make some calls to have the relics moved to a safe location and get this tree off the building."

She nodded, plowing through the thickness of shared experiences in the air between them, and followed him out, her ankle only aching just slightly from standing so long. Then, David grabbed the wheelbarrow and she plodded through the snow to the back of the building where there was an enormous pile of wood, hidden beneath a blue tarp that was covered in snow.

David lifted it off, shaking it out, and set it aside on the ground. "The wood is dry," he said, as he grabbed a log and set it in the wheelbarrow.

Leah helped, dropping a few logs in.

"I've got it," David said, but she insisted she could help.

"Do you still like butterscotch candies?" she asked while they filled the wheelbarrow.

"Not as much as I used to. Why?"

"I was just… wondering if you liked the same things you did as a kid. Do you still watch baseball?"

"Yes," he smiled. "Can you imagine a kid like me losing interest?" He clapped his hands together and grabbed the handles of the wheelbarrow, lifting the back of it to push it across the yard.

Leah laughed. "Not really. Not a kid as crazy about baseball as you were. I think you wore a different baseball jersey every day."

"I remember a lot about you."

He was five years older than her, and Leah suddenly felt embarrassed at all the things he probably remembered. He'd seen her in diapers, playing make-believe in her princess dress and pink glitter heels. He'd seen her that time she'd refused to take a bath and had run naked down the stairs. "Really? What do you remember?"

"I remember picking blueberries with you in the fields out back. You kept wiping your fingers on your shirt, and by the end, it was full of purple streaks. You were probably only four. You loved it." He smiled at her.

Leah swallowed. "I don't remember."

"How about the time you climbed the tree with me and you couldn't get back down? Do you remember that?"

"Oh, yeah! I'd forgotten about that! You stayed up there with me and helped me, branch by branch, until I made it safely to the ground."

"We waited in the middle for ages. You were too afraid to go any further. I thought my hands would cramp, I was holding on for so long, but you didn't feel like you could go, so I had to wait until you'd spent enough time on that branch to feel comfortable enough to take a chance and move again."

"You were so patient with me."

"I liked you. You were always kind and so happy all the time."

Leah tried to calm herself as she looked at him. He was right. She was happy all the time back then. Growing up, she'd thought she had endless opportunities in front of her, the whole world at her fingertips. And was that Leah really gone? Life had hit her hard a few times, but she'd always gotten back up, dusted herself off, and tried to do the best she could. Surely she could do that now. After all, she was about to get a huge chunk of money, enough to completely turn her life around. Couldn't she get excited about that and just enjoy her last Christmas at Evergreen Hill?

When they got to the house, Leah tried to help unload the wood but David refused to let her, telling her that she needed to rest her ankle. Against his wishes, she did grab a couple of logs, bringing them in while he had an armful. It was the best she could do, and she wasn't going to just stand there and do nothing.

They tossed the logs onto the fire and took off their coats, the warmth making her shiver.

"I'll need your help figuring out who to call to transport the items into the house," David said. "We can put them in the ballroom for now."

"And we'll need to find a company who specializes in historical properties to do the repairs." She wasn't going to mention that she remembered his wish to knock down the building. And it had occurred to her that there would be laws about maintaining historical buildings, never mind actually demolishing them. Maybe he wouldn't get his way on this point. Even still, she waited to see how he responded with a pattering heart.

"One thing at a time," he said. Her heart dropped, but she picked herself up. It wasn't her house anymore. It wasn't her business.

Chapter Twelve

By the next evening, Leah was exhausted from moving furniture in the ballroom and coordinating with the local historical society to transport the items into the main house. She'd insisted on helping them actually move every piece, although she couldn't move the heavy ones due to her ankle. It had taken all day, but the servants' quarters were finally emptied and she could breathe a sigh of relief now that the items were secure. Whatever happened with the servants' quarters, Leah could make sure the artifacts went to a safe home. She'd spoken to a woman from the historical society who'd been positive the local museum would be very interested in acquiring the entire collection. Leah had made a note to tell David.

The smell of potatoes and gravy pulled her into the kitchen, where she found David.

"I'm making you dinner," he said. "I know you must be tired. And you've got to get your weight off that ankle."

"It's not so bad today." She sat down and propped her leg up on another chair. It was still a little swollen. She'd been so focused on caring for the relics that she hadn't stopped to realize how much she was using her ankle. It was twinging a bit, but it seemed to be much better.

"I've got a roast in the crockpot and I've made biscuits, green beans, and potato casserole with cheese." He wiped his hands on the kitchen towel and pulled a bag of peas from the freezer. With a smile, he came over and placed them on her ankle, his hands lingering tenderly. It was just a second, but she'd caught it.

"Really, I'm okay," she said, surprised at how many dishes he'd prepared.

"I wish you would've just let the company move everything. They're professionals, you know."

"I know, but they don't have the emotional attachment to them that I do, and I worried they wouldn't take the same care that I would."

"Well, they're all safe now. You can relax and eat." He poured a glass of wine and brought it over to her. "I've checked the networks and *It's a Wonderful Life* is on tonight. I thought perhaps you'd like to wind down a bit and watch it with me."

Suddenly, the memory of him juggling those onions came back to her, and the lightness in her chest that she'd felt when she'd laughed at him then did too. "I'd love to," she said, taking a drink of her wine. And she meant it.

"How was your day?" she asked while he made them each a plate, the warm, buttery aroma heightening her awareness of hunger. She hadn't allowed David to help move anything, promising him she'd be fine and the team was with her, knowing he had to work.

"It was busy. I'm coordinating a few new contracts, and taking on a little more business than usual, but I need to get my name out there so things can get rolling. You know, I've been running my own company for years on the side while working for other corporations. I'd always wanted to see if I could go off entirely on my own. It was Nina who finally got me to take the plunge."

She smiled at that as he set a plate down in front of her and went to the other side of the table.

"We've both had a big day," he said.

Leah gently took the peas off her ankle and lifted it off the chair. She twisted forward and scooted closer to the table. "This looks amazing," she said, scraping a bite of potato casserole onto her fork. "You said you couldn't cook." She smiled up at him.

"Well, I have to admit, I got the recipes off the Internet." He smiled at her in return and that warm feeling she had for him came rushing back. "And I have popcorn for the movie. I'm a pro at making that," he said with a wink.

"Sadie and I have movie night once a week. I really enjoy it, although, I must say, I'm excited to watch something that isn't for the seven-and-under crowd."

David let out a little huff of laughter, his features warm and content. "Whenever you mention her, I imagine you when you were young. Does Sadie look like you?"

"A little. Her hair is blonder and not as curly. She's more focused than I was as a kid. She worries about adult problems, she seems comfortable in a room full of women even though she's only a child." Leah took a bite and swallowed, thinking about Sadie and wishing her daughter could have siblings to give her more of a childhood. But she did have Jo and Ethan, and she also had her friends at school. That was the best Leah could provide, given the circumstances. "You know, Nan taught her how to quilt. Sadie spent hours with her, quietly listening and making stitches as Nan showed her, step by step. I remember watching them one day, once Sadie had gotten the hang of it, and they were both stitching, the quilt across both of their laps, their hands moving exactly the same. She was so much like Nan…"

"I'll bet she misses her."

"Terribly. I feel so guilty because I'd started working a lot this past year, and Sadie had asked several times to come for a visit but I just didn't have the time. I should've come."

"There was no way to know."

"Yeah, but I should've come anyway." Leah wondered why it was so easy to say things like this to him—things she'd been holding in since Nan's passing.

"Did you know Cary Grant was supposed to play the role of George Bailey, but Jimmy Stewart got it?" she said, pulling Nan's quilt up over them as they settled in front of the TV. David turned the channels until he'd reached the movie.

"He'd have been great, I'm sure, but I can't imagine anyone other than Jimmy Stewart in the role."

"I agree." She pulled the tub of popcorn onto her lap. "Scoot in; we can share," she said, nodding toward the popcorn.

It was dark outside and the only light in the room was coming from the fire, and the old black-and-white movie. She tried to ignore the emptiness in the corner, where a Christmas tree should be.

"This movie always makes me cry," she warned him.

With a grin, David reached over to the end table and lifted a box of tissues into view, then set them back down.

"You've thought of everything," she said.

Leah snuggled down a little and the movie got started. She'd watched it a handful of times. It was a nice break from everything. David reached into her lap and grabbed a piece of popcorn, the salty, butter scent of it lightening the mood further. She reached over to the coffee table to get her glass of wine that David had brought in with them, and settled in to watch the movie.

"The part I wait for is when the guardian angel shows up," David said. "It's as if I'm holding my breath just waiting for things to get better."

"That's the only part I remember!" she said with a laugh.

Leah didn't remember finishing the movie. How'd she get in bed? She moved, although she was so warm and comfortable, she didn't really want to. Then, suddenly, she was aware of an arm around her and her eyes flew open, her body completely still in response. That warm pillow wasn't a pillow; it was David's chest. They were still on the settee, cuddled up under the quilt, the popcorn and empty wine glasses on the coffee table, the television off, the remote on the floor next to her.

Leah noticed the way their legs were intertwined, the feel of his hand as it rested on her waist, the slow movement of his chest under her head as he slept. The air outside the quilt was icy cold, the fire having long burned out. Her nose was cold but the rest of her was completely toasty as she lay on David. There was something so perfect about the way it felt to be near him that she couldn't think of anything else. He inhaled sharply, moving a little, his hand moving up her waist in almost a caress, and she held her breath.

"Oh!" she heard and tilted her head to find he was looking at her. He hid a smile and they untangled, but not too quickly. She wondered if he meant to stroke her side so softly as he withdrew his arm.

"Sorry I fell asleep," she said.

"You were tired." He pulled the quilt up around them.

This is weird and awkward and surprisingly thrilling at the same time, she thought. "I hope I didn't snore," she said instead, trying to break the tension she felt. It seemed like it was just her, though, because David laughed, his arms finding their way to her again.

"You were as quiet as a baby," he said with a smile. "Are you hungry?"

"I'll cook," she said, wriggling out of his embrace. "You did dinner last night."

"Why don't we go out?" He sat up.

His suggestion took her by surprise, but the thought sounded wonderful. "We could go to that little diner on the corner of Main Street in town," she said.

"I know it. That sounds perfect."

"Give me twenty minutes."

While she'd gotten ready, she'd called Sadie to check in and see how she felt about coming to the plantation today. Sadie had started to talk about the house and Leah had been able to steer the conversation elsewhere, but she couldn't stifle the worry about telling Sadie that she was selling her half and she knew she couldn't put her off forever. She had no idea when the right time would be because there just didn't seem to be a right time. Since she wasn't getting Sadie until the afternoon, Leah had suggested they take the farm truck to get breakfast. Its tires were large enough to get through the snow and ice without slipping. She opened the truck's heavy door and got in on the driver's side. While David had insisted on driving, she'd refused to let him, telling him it had been a long time since she'd driven it, and she enjoyed it.

She remembered Nan driving this two-toned green and cream truck, the windows down, letting in the heat of the bright summer sun, her hair twisted up into a bun with wisps escaping in the wind, her tiny body dwarfed by the large vehicle as it bumped along the dirt road. She would drive them out to the fields near the tree line where she'd planted her blueberries. Leah always ended up eating more than she collected.

David got into the truck on the other side and shut the door. The wide bench seat in the front could easily hold four adults.

Hoping the dusty upholstery didn't soil her wool trousers, she punched the clutch with a heeled boot and cranked it into gear. The engine strained against the cold as the truck bumped along the path, now completely hidden by snow. She wouldn't have known where to drive were it not for the line of bordering trees that led to the main road. She clicked on the wipers to clear the drizzle on the windshield.

The long country roads gave way to the narrow Main Street, which divided the town into two halves. There was only one stoplight, and until recently, it had just been a blinking caution signal. She pulled up to the red light and hit the brake. She was so happy to have another chance to come into town. Downtown looked lovely in the winter. The streetlights all had evergreen wreaths on them, their bright red bows dusted with snow. Most of the stores had trimmed their large, rectangular shop windows with twinkle lights, some even creating window displays that had Christmas trees. A few shoppers bustled by, one woman clutching her coat together at the neck, a carrier bag from the local dress shop in the crook of her arm.

After turning down a side street that bordered the diner, she pulled the truck along the curb and turned off the engine. The old ignition key dangled from a weathered chain, the keychain ornament that had been attached long gone. She dropped the key into her handbag and opened the door, stepping carefully onto the icy curb. With a slight slide, she began to rethink the idea of the boots, worried about her ankle, but it was too late. Fashion over utility it was. That was what Roz had said when she'd bought them. Leah had wanted the flat boots, but Roz had insisted that the heels were the better choice. Today, she'd wanted to look nice.

David had gotten out and was offering to help her across the sidewalk. Even though she didn't need any assistance, she took his hand. The masculine feel of his fingers against hers was very different than she remembered from when they were kids.

He opened the door of the diner for her and allowed her to enter. The tiny place, being one of the few open for breakfast, was buzzing with people. The sizzle of the grill and the chatter created a warm atmosphere. They hung their coats along a wall with a row of brass hooks.

David pulled out a chair for Leah at a small table decorated with a silver pot of rosemary inside a ring of miniature pinecones. He scooted it to the side next to the crystal salt and pepper shakers and took a seat across from her.

A waitress with a yellow pencil behind her ear and a smile that showed off her cheekbones materialized. "Will this be one check?" she asked.

Both David and Leah spoke at the same time. He'd suggested one check and she'd said two. David spoke again, clarifying for the waitress that it would, in fact, be one check. "And we'll both start out with a coffee," he said. The waitress handed them each a menu.

Leah took a moment to look around. She hadn't been here in so long, and the place had changed since she was a girl. The door opened and two more people entered. As it shut she noticed a wreath of greenery with a sign that said *Merry Christmas, y'all!* The couple hung their coats on the coat rack beside hers. There was a glass case at the end of the room, near the register, that had rows of desserts—a tall coconut cake with green holly and red berries on the top; another one, white with caramel drizzle, and gingerbread cookies in the shape of snowflakes jutting out from the top. There were cranberry cakes, German chocolate cakes, pecan pies, and more varieties of Christmas cookies than she'd ever seen in one place. She made a mental note to bring Sadie here.

The waitress returned with silverware wrapped in red-and-white linen napkins, the print resembling candy canes. She set their coffees down, along with cream and sugar in porcelain containers. David told her they'd need a few minutes to decide, and Leah had to pull her eyes from the white lights and the three Christmas trees in various sizes that were filling one corner, their ornaments all color-coordinated in silver, red, and white.

"I've never been here at Christmas," she said over her menu.

"I've never been at all. But your nan talked about it. What's good to eat?"

"The red velvet pancakes are really good. They drizzle them with a cream cheese icing syrup. They also serve a walnut-bacon pancake that's out of this world. But if you want a more traditional breakfast, their eggs and sausage are great. They serve them with enormous buttermilk biscuits."

"I was hoping your suggestion would narrow the choices down…" He smiled. "The menu is overwhelming."

"Why don't we get a couple of dishes and share them?"

"That sounds like a great idea."

When the waitress returned, they settled on a few pancake options and bacon and eggs with biscuits. After a refill on their coffees, Leah heard a familiar "Hello" from behind and swiveled around to find Muriel, wearing a skirt that fell mid-shin and long coat, shopping bags hanging from her arms.

"I was buying a few last minute gifts for the family," she said, dropping them at her feet. "You remember Phillip?"

Muriel's husband threw up a hand as he reached them after making his way through the small crowd.

"Hi, Phillip," Leah said with a smile. She remembered everything about him—his tall frame, his balding hairline, the way his smile filled up his entire face whenever he greeted someone. When Leah was a kid, Muriel and Phillip had often come over to visit. Phillip would lift her up so high she swore she'd be able to reach the chandelier. She'd always wondered if it would hold her if he let her swing on it, but before she could try, she'd fly through the air and land back on her feet. She stood up and greeted him with a quick hug then sat back down. "It's nice to see you." She turned to David. "Have you met Phillip?"

David stood up for a moment and shook his hand, introducing himself.

"Look at you," Phillip said, shaking his head at Leah. "A young lady now. It's been too long." While Muriel often came for visits, Phillip was a pilot and spent many weeks away. It was always a treat when he was around. He'd usually show up with something from his travels: a new candy of some sort or cans of drink from the airline. Once he'd even brought her a new baby doll from Paris. But he was so kind and fun to be around that he didn't even have to bring anything.

"Yes, you're right."

"Muriel's had me out shopping all morning," he said, his voice teasing. "I hope we can get a table. Otherwise you might find me over your shoulder stealing bites. What did you order?"

"A little bit of everything, it seems."

"Perfect! I'll just pull up a chair." He winked at her, and she laughed, so glad to have run into him. "John and Elaine might stop in. We saw them in town," he said. "I know John was trying to get Elaine to come in but she kept shooing him away—the sugar, you know." He threw a smile over at David as if he knew the story.

Leah smiled and turned to David. "Elaine refuses to eat sugar. She says it's evil. However, she married John who has a sweet tooth the size of Texas. When they visit at parties, he slips over to the sweets table and sneaks bites."

Leah and Phillip both laughed at a shared memory but Phillip was the first to tell it. "Remember how he always said he was going to spike her coffee with sugar because it would only take one taste and she'd never go back?" he said.

They both laughed. This is what Leah loved so much about living here: she seemed to find a friendly face anywhere she went.

"Well, I'll let you all enjoy your breakfast." He pointed toward Muriel who was waving madly from an empty table. "Looks like Muriel found us a seat. It was good to see you!"

"You too!" Leah said.

When she and David were left alone, and the waitress had stopped by with more cream, David looked at her, a smile on his face, and said, "You look very nice this morning."

"Thank you." Waking up with David had made her feel less like a mother and more like a woman. It had been a long time since she'd put in the extra effort. She remembered the feel of his arms around her and quickly tried to shake the thought.

"So! Are you all ready for Christmas?" *Where did that come from?*

He grinned at her in a way that made her wonder if he could sense her thoughts. But then he gave her a legitimate answer. "I actually have a little shopping to do. I'd like to buy my mother a Christmas present."

The waitress returned with an armful of plates, setting down eggs and bacon, a basket of buttermilk biscuits, and more pancakes than the two of them could eat: blueberry, butter pecan, cinnamon walnut, and chocolate chip.

"Oh. Well, we could look for something while we're in town," she said after thanking the waitress.

"If you wouldn't mind. It might be good to get a woman's opinion."

"What are you thinking about getting your mother?" she asked, browsing a table of specialty teapots and mugs in the housewares shop two doors down from the diner.

"I want to find something sentimental that would lift her spirits." He looked back down at the table, pursing his lips in concentration, his expression making it clear that the teapots weren't hitting the mark.

She didn't want to pry, but she couldn't help but be curious. "Lift her spirits?"

He glanced up and nodded.

"Is she sick?" Leah asked, forgetting all about the teacup that had caught her attention.

He waggled his head and his gaze went darting around the room. "In a way." He sighed and rubbed the back of his neck. "She's grieving. Her best friend died suddenly, and she's struggling to recover."

Leah caught her breath.

"It was a long time ago now, over a year, but she just hasn't been able to pick herself back up again."

"No. Of course not." Leah could almost feel tears welling, her thoughts immediately with Roz and Louise, imagining life without one of them.

"Well, everyone else seems to think she's just being difficult."

Leah shook her head. "I don't think so. That's a big blow to someone."

He looked her in the eye. "I agree with you. I think she needs the time and the space to heal. She needs taking care of." He looked away again.

"I'm sorry. It must be hard, worrying about her."

He nodded. "It's kind of exhausting."

Leah reached over and gripped his hand. "I'll help you find something perfect."

They searched around a little while, splitting up as they found various things to look at. Then, Leah noticed a perfect little box, the surface of it highly polished to a shine. She opened it and a song tinkled from a music box inside. It took a minute before she realized what it was; the gritty voice of the singer was like some sort of time machine, taking her right back to the days she'd spent with Nan when she'd been only Sadie's age. She hurried over to David.

"Look!" she said, opening the box. "Does this song mean anything to you?" She opened it and Louis Armstrong's "Dream a Little Dream" played on the music box.

David's expression was unreadable for a moment, and then realization slid across his face. "That's perfect," he said, taking it gently from her hands. "My mother used to play that song all the time."

"It's Nan's favorite song too."

"Really?"

"Yes. When she used to play it, she'd take me by the hands, swing me around, and we'd dance to it. I wonder if she did that with your mom?"

"It's possible." He shut the box. "You've just found mom's present!" He leaned down and kissed her cheek, his spicy scent making her dizzy for a second.

"I'll help you wrap it," she said, taking in a breath to get her head straight.

He took her hand and they went up to the register to pay for June's present.

Afterwards, while Leah warmed up the truck, David ran to the gift shop a few stores down to find some wrapping paper and ribbon. When he got in to the truck, he tossed the bag between them on the seat, and she noticed the roll of pretty green paper protruding from the top. "That's a nice choice," she said. David admitted he'd asked the sales lady to pick something out for him.

As she pulled away from the curb, he turned to her. "I hope it's okay, but I asked my mom to come to Evergreen Hill. I organized everything a long time ago."

Leah nodded, pulling up to the stoplight. "Of course." She almost added "it's your house now" but caught herself. "When's she coming?"

"The day after tomorrow. I should've told you sooner."

Leah glanced over. She could see the worry on his face and knew it was hard for him just to talk about her. "It's no problem, David. It sounds like she needs this." The light turned green and they headed home.

"Would you put your finger on this ribbon to hold it in place while I tie the bow?" Leah asked David as she put the finishing touches on June's present. She was cross-legged on the sitting room floor, the heat from the fire warming her. She moved a pile of balled-up wrapping paper scraps with her free hand to give David some space.

He complied, kneeling down beside her, one hand on the coffee table, the other on the present. She tied the bow, nodding when he could remove his finger.

"Thank you." She snipped off the ends of the ribbon at a slant, and held up the package. It was wrapped in the hunter-green paper with a bright red ribbon and, hanging from the bow, a small silver bell ornament the sales lady had found for David.

"That's great, thank you for wrapping it," David said. "While you were busy, I got the number of a tree service to get the tree taken care of, and they're going to put a tarp over the roof of the building for now."

"I'm so glad to hear that." She wanted to look through Nan's files to see whom she used for restoration. They'd need an expert to fix the roof but the only one with enough money to pay for it was David. She wondered what would come of it, but decided not to press the point.

"I got us something at the gift shop," David said, a grin on his face. He picked up his mother's gift and put it under the tree. "Why don't you have a seat and I'll bring it in."

Leah sat down on the edge of the settee and put her hands on her knees as he left the room, wondering what he was going to bring in.

He returned quickly, carrying a single card of some sort. He held it out to her.

"What is this?" she asked, turning it over in her hand. It looked like some sort of ad for a picture book.

"I've already paid for it, so we can get right to business. It's a company that takes your snapshots and text and turns them into a story in a bound hardback book. I thought maybe you'd like to take some pictures at your family Christmas or maybe of the artifacts from the servants' quarters—memories you'd like to keep." He smiled at her, his eyes soft, that kind look that she was so used to seeing now on his face.

She put her hand on her chest, tingly warmth in her limbs. That was the most thoughtful thing he could've ever given her, and it had been a complete surprise. She felt the prick of tears. "Thank you," she said.

He must have been able to read her gratitude because his face lit up with pride. "You're welcome."

"I want to take some pictures right now," she said, pulling her phone out of her back pocket. "Would you walk around with me while I take them?"

"Of course. It'll be fun. What should we photograph first?"

"There's so much! I want to have memories of the house as Nan had it. So, let's start with the fireplace." She walked over, lined up her phone and snapped a picture, tapping it to check its quality. "Oh, that's pretty." She took one more just to be on the safe side.

They walked into the kitchen where Muriel's flower arrangement sat in Nan's vase in the center of the table. Leah straightened the placemats and took another photo. "Look how beautiful the flowers look," she said, turning her phone to David. "Nan always had flowers like these in that vase. I'm so glad Muriel brought some. I was thinking how empty it looked."

When she made eye contact with him, she could've sworn she saw affection in his eyes when he looked at her. He was smiling, and she wondered what he could be thinking.

"What else should I take a photo of..." She tapped her chin.

"You don't have to have this many, but I bought you a hundred pages. It just occurred to me while we were in the kitchen that, if you'd like, I can scan in all of Nan's recipes and they could go at the back. But that's just an idea."

"That's an amazing idea," she said getting excited.

She took pictures of Nan's room, of the quilt squares in the sewing room; they went outside and took photos of the house, the tree-lined drive, and the James River. Her camera roll nearly full, David then helped her load the photos onto his computer, and he said when she felt like taking more to let him know.

"I can't thank you enough for this," she said, and without warning, she put her arms around his neck and hugged him. The hug lasted a little longer than normal, and she had to use all her strength to pull away.

Chapter Thirteen

Roz rented part of an old Richmond row house that had been "renovated"—the term being used loosely—into apartments. What the owner had really done was thrown up a few thin walls, closing off parts of it until it resembled four separate dwellings—two downstairs and two upstairs.

The street was generally shabby, but it was a few blocks over from the magnificent, stately city homes that made the issue of *City Style Magazine* every Christmas, and from Roz's bedroom window she could get a glimpse of the camera flashes at night through gaps in the buildings as photographers captured the essence of wealthy southern holiday decorating for their various publications.

Roz's apartment was only accessible from the cobbled alleyway, lined with cars and trashcans, in the back of the property. But the long, crooked hallway that stretched from her door wound around to the front of the building and she had a nice bay window overlooking the front street from her living room. She'd always put her Christmas tree there, covered in colored twinkle lights and peacock feathers strung together to look like giant, multicolored snowflakes—only Roz...

Leah smiled when she noticed Roz's Christmas tree painting from their girls' night propped up on her mantle alongside a silver candelabra with purple candles.

She settled in on the sofa next to Louise as Ethan went screaming past them with his play sword, chasing Sadie and Jo who squealed with delight. "I'm making macaroni and cheese for lunch… from the box," Roz warned from the small slab of linoleum thrown down in the corner of the room to mark off the area that had been termed "the kitchen" in the listing that she'd read aloud to Leah before she'd signed the lease. There were exactly three cabinets, a drawer, a stove with an oven, and room for a small fridge.

"I had a sandwich at the little bistro on the corner before I came," Louise said. "I would've waited, but Ethan was hungry and I didn't know if you were planning on all of us for lunch. But thank you for offering."

Sadie ran in and hid behind the long curtains flanking the bay window at the front. Ethan came barreling in after her, out of breath. "Has anyone seen Sadie?" he asked, his head swiveling manically from side to side. He dropped down to the floor and searched under the couch. Just then there was a tiny giggle from the curtains and Sadie came flying out, running down the hallway before Ethan could catch her.

Roz plopped down between Louise and Leah, an enormous bowl of bright orange macaroni and cheese in her lap. She swirled it around with her fork.

"What are the green flakes in there?" Louise said, leaning over her.

"Broccoli." She turned to Louise with a dramatic flair. "The box came with a packet of added broccoli bits. I have to get my green veggies in. Health conscious and all that, you know…"

"I'm sorry I can't stay long," Leah said. "I have to get back to Evergreen Hill."

"How are you feeling about everything?" Louise asked. She pressed her lips together delicately—her listening face.

"I'm getting used to the idea," Leah said quietly. "But I don't know how I'm going to break it to Sadie. I want to get her up to Evergreen Hill as soon as I can today so she can spend as much time as possible there before Christmas."

"Nah, you just want to get back to David." Roz leaned around Leah to talk to Louise and whispered, "She thinks he's hot."

"I should've never told you that I thought he was nice." Leah shook her head. "And I've never used the word 'hot' to describe him."

"No," Roz said. "But your cheeks are giving you away."

Louise giggled.

"Did you get my pillow?" Sadie asked. Her face was flushed from the heat that was blowing full blast from the car vents. Leah'd had the engine going for quite a while to keep it warm in the freezing temperatures.

"Yep."

"And my book?"

"Yep." Leah shut the trunk of her car, the engine growling as it worked overtime. She'd emailed Sadie's teachers and told them that she planned to keep her out of school for the last three days before winter break, but she'd be sure to practice her math. Then she'd asked if they could email any other assignments they'd like her to complete.

"How about my sketchpad and my colored pencils?"

"Got 'em. They're in your backpack." Leah opened the door of the car to put a few more bags next to Sadie.

"I feel like we're forgetting something," Sadie worried as Leah climbed in and adjusted the rearview mirror.

"Well, if we did, it's only a few hours away. We'll invite Roz up for dinner and she can bring it to us. She has a key to our house, so she can water our plants for us. If you left something, she can get it."

"Okay."

Leah shut the door as Sadie fastened her seatbelt, eager to get out of the cold. She turned the radio on to Christmas carols and pulled out of the driveway.

Once they got on the highway, Sadie wanted to play the license plate game. It was her favorite game during long trips. Before she'd gotten too sleepy—probably from playing so hard with Jo and Ethan—they'd found North Carolina, Georgia, Michigan, California, and Iowa.

After that, Sadie had slept most of the trip, giving Leah a chance to think about how she was going to tell her daughter about the house. It was really weighing on her because she just didn't know how Sadie would react. She'd been so sad when Nan died, and this would be another large blow. She thought about calling different gymnastics programs and using the money from selling her half to enroll Sadie as surprise to help soften the disappointment, but she just didn't have enough time before the subject would come up—she was sure of it. Sadie would probably be asking the minute they got there.

She woke up as they neared the plantation. When they'd arrived at Evergreen Hill, and began the drive down the long road leading to the house, Leah took a peek at Sadie in her rearview mirror. She had her forehead pressed against the glass of her window, her eyes on the James River. The water was gray and choppy in the winter rain that had started spitting against the windshield the second half of the trip there.

"I wish Nan was here," Sadie said after turning back around to face the front. "These trees always tell me when we're close. Nan used to wait at the end of them for us. Remember?"

"Yes. The trees have been here for hundreds of years. I saw that the tree swing's still out back. Maybe if it stops raining, you can swing."

She rounded the small curve and came to a stop in front of the house.

Sadie hadn't returned her comment because she was too busy leaning between the front seats to see, having taken her seatbelt off as soon as they were off the main road and on the property.

"Can we sled down the big hill if it snows some more?" The grounds had snow, but not enough to completely cover the grass. It wasn't deep and the old sled, if it was still in the shed out back, wouldn't make it down the hill; the metal rails would inevitably create divots of grass, slowing it down too much to sled.

Her excitement made Leah chuckle. "Well, let's get inside first and then if it snows, absolutely." She pulled the car to a stop.

"Can we just go in without Nan?" Sadie asked, tipping her head up to view all the way to the top of the house. "Oh! Is that David?" Sadie opened her door. Leah had given her a heads-up that things were a little different now that Nan wasn't here, and David would be in the house too.

David was standing on the front steps, a grin on his face. But Leah's attention was pulled to the wreaths that were hanging from the windows, and the larger one on the door. He'd put little lanterns on the front steps and there was some sort of Christmas flower arrangement on the porch. Were those poinsettias?

"Hello!" Sadie called, waving. "We're here! I'm Sadie." She started toward him.

"Sadie," Leah called. "Be careful!" Sadie hadn't seemed to hear. David started walking toward the car after he let Sadie inside.

"Hi," he said, when he reached Leah.

"Hi. You decorated."

"Yes. I wanted you to have a great Christmas here, so I did what I could in the time I had. I got all this from the Christmas shop in town."

Leah didn't know what to say. She was touched by this gesture. She looked up, noticing the lights he'd hung along the roofline. "Thank you," she said, feeling like it wasn't enough to express how she felt.

"You're welcome." He offered her a tender smile. "Need some help?" He reached past her, pulling the two large suitcases from the trunk and shutting the lid. Leah grabbed the few smaller bags from the back, and Sadie's teddy bear, and headed up to the house beside him.

"She seems excited," he said, glancing over to her as they walked. The suitcases were heavy, but he carried them with ease.

"Yes. It's been ages since she was here, and she misses it."

David opened the door and let Leah enter first. "I wanted to decorate inside but I couldn't find the decorations."

They came into the living room, where Sadie was already snuggled up under a quilt with the TV on.

"Sadie, would you like something to eat?" David asked.

"Not right now, but thank you." She lay down on the settee, her eyes heavy. She was fighting to keep them open to watch the television, the long car ride having gotten to her, despite sleeping on the way.

"Are *you* hungry?" David asked Leah. "I made soup. It's just canned soup that I warmed up—broccoli and cheddar. But I also have eggnog."

"The soup smells good," she said. "And eggnog sounds like a great starter."

After lunch, David had gone upstairs to do some work and Leah had curled up with Sadie on the settee until she'd woken from her little nap. She always did that after the drive to Nan's.

She and Sadie were discussing the different kinds of pancakes she could get at the Main Street diner. Sadie had been listing the pancakes she'd like to try for the last minute or so.

"They have any kind you could think of!"

"What about brown sugar pancakes like Nan made?"

"Yes."

"Okay," she said with a devious grin. "I'll bet they don't have this one: gummy worm pancakes."

Leah laughed. "I think you might have found them a new recipe to create."

"No," she said, her thoughts evident in the way she stretched out the "oh" in the word. "I wouldn't want to eat those. They don't sound very yummy. But cotton candy does! That's another new one!"

Leah grimaced as she laughed. "Cotton candy pancakes? Just the sound of that makes my tummy hurt."

David came in wearing his coat and boots and holding a saw. Both Leah and Sadie stopped, mid-sentence, and looked up at him.

"Hi," he said as he looked between the both of them, an odd expression on his face. Was it excitement? "I have an idea."

"Any idea involving a saw is slightly worrying," Leah joked.

David let out a huff of laughter. "I think we should have a Christmas tree. Don't you?" he said to Sadie, pulling the quilt off of them.

"Let's go out back. We'll cut a tree like Nan always did. How does that sound?"

Leah couldn't stand how bare Nan's house looked. With the family coming in, she owed it to Nan to put the house together just like she would for the holidays.

"Yes!" Sadie said, standing up with excitement. She hopped around, clapping her hands.

"Okay! Let's get our boots and coats and hats on then!" Leah said, jumping up behind her.

Once they were both bundled up, Leah, David, and Sadie went outside, headed for the expanse of woods behind the house. There were so many trees to choose from.

"How good are you with a saw?" Leah asked, as they trudged through the last bit of slushy, snowy grass before entering the woods.

David looked at her, amusement on his face.

"Nan always used to put a tree up after we got here," said Leah. "We'd go out in the woods and cut one down like we are now and then spend all night decorating it."

Sadie stopped to consider one of the small spruces in her path but then must have decided against it, turning away and walking further into the woods.

"I remember that from when I was here as a kid," David said, his cheeks rosy from the icy air.

"I think the best Christmas trees are this way," Sadie said, leading them through the woods ahead.

"This used to be a little clearing," David said as they walked through an area now overgrown with trees and brush. "I remember making a fort here when I was young."

Leah remembered that fort. Back then, the low branches of the evergreens surrounding the clearing had made it feel as though they were encased by walls of spruce. David had pulled two logs into the center that they'd used as seats, and they'd divided rooms by making lines in the forest floor with rocks they'd found.

Sadie stopped in front of a spruce and Leah looked down at her for approval.

"This might be our tree," Sadie said. It was a sweet, little evergreen, about five feet tall, its branches spaced as evenly as possible for a natural tree.

"It looks perfect." Leah peered under the bottom branches to view the trunk. It was manageable. "Do you think you can cut this?"

David bent down and took a look. "I think so. You sure this is the one you want?" he asked Sadie.

Sadie danced around. "Yes! I love it."

Leah held the tree steady as David dragged the saw across the base, back and forth. The cold whipped around them, and the frosty air had made her fingers go numb, but she didn't say anything. She was glad that Sadie had put on her mittens. Pretty soon, the tree began to tip. David caught it with his free hand and finished sawing. The tree came loose from the ground, its branches rustling.

David held it up. The width of the tree made it awkward to tote, she could tell, but he wobbled forward with it. "Are you okay dropping the saw back off in the shed?" he asked.

"Totally fine," she said, reaching out to take it.

David looked over at Leah from behind the tree. "If your fingers look anything like your cheeks, you're lying."

She giggled and started walking back through the yard beside Sadie until they had to part ways briefly so she could return the saw.

When they all had gotten back to the house, Sadie was in charge of watching the tree, propped up against the wall, while Leah headed upstairs. David followed. She stopped at the door at the end of the hallway that led to the walk-up attic. When Leah opened it, the freezing air gave her a shiver, her body still not recovered from being outside. She grabbed a pair of Nan's shoes that she had always kept just inside the door and told David to wait right there.

The staircase was dark, so she clicked on a light switch that was mounted to a stud between columns of thick, wiry insulation. Climbing the stairs, the grit scratched beneath her shoes. The attic was full of furniture and the old boxes she'd looked through. She ran her hand along a full-length mirror that needed a good painting, wondering if it had been Nan's next project. At the back of the room she found the Christmas boxes—all labeled. She got the big one and tugged it across the floor. It was dusty, making her nose itch.

Gently, she wedged it between her body and the stairs, sliding it down toward David. When he came into view, he took a large step forward and grasped both sides of the box, lifting it easily.

"I've got it," he said, hauling it out into the hallway.

Leah kicked off Nan's shoes and shut the door, the warmth of the main house blanketing her skin. She followed David downstairs and into the living room, where he gently placed the box on the floor and opened the lid. Sadie came over and sat down next to him.

He peered inside, lifting a small piece of paper that was tied to a bundle of lights, and his brows furrowed. "What are all these little notes?" he asked, reading the one in his hand as Sadie scooted toward him on the floor, rooting around in the box.

Leah smiled, knowing exactly what they were. "Nan wrote notes to herself every time she packed something away so that it would be easier to decorate the next year."

David read the one attached to the lights. "'This particular strand will go best on the spruce by the oak tree in the yard because that tree is so tall. The other strands of lights are shorter.'" He smiled. "Efficient."

"That was Nan."

Leah bent over Sadie and rummaged around in the box until she found the tree stand. "The note says to keep the tree under six feet or it starts to wobble."

"Absolutely," he said straightening his face out to look serious.

After pulling out the tree skirt, the lights, and a smaller box of ornaments, Leah moved the rocking chair to the other corner of the room, creating an empty space in the spot where Nan had always put the tree.

David secured the tree in the tree stand, asking Sadie to tell him when the tree was straight. When he had it, Sadie offered a thumbs-up, and he tightened the silver screws until the tree was standing on its own. Sadie went into the kitchen and got a cup of water to put into the bottom of the stand.

They'd left it for about an hour to dry out a bit before they put the lights on.

Leah took a step back to look at the tree, planning where to put the lights, but as she did, she noticed the snow outside in the dusk of early evening. She clicked the wall switch nearby, illuminating the back deck. "It's starting to really come down." The flurries had begun to fall while they were in the woods, but they hadn't noticed at first, the many trees providing a canopy for them.

"It's not supposed to accumulate, but it is nice." David handed Sadie a mug of hot chocolate he'd made after coloring two pages in Sadie's coloring book at her request while they'd waited for the tree to dry. He passed another mug to Leah.

She wrapped her fingers around her mug and looked back at the tree, trying to avoid what had popped into her mind. She was really starting to like David. She pushed the thought away. Things were getting too complicated.

David took a spool of lights out of the box and unwound it, stringing it along the floor. To check the bulbs, he plugged it in, and the whole floor lit up in white sparkles. Sadie gasped, the lights reflecting in her eyes.

"They work," he said with a smile, sitting down on the floor next to the box, by the coffee table.

Leah set down her mug, picked up the end of the lights, and began to wind them in and out of the branches and down the tree until it was covered, Sadie standing on the other side, reaching up on her tiptoes to get them as high as she could. As she wound them around the tree, it was starting to look just like the ones Nan had done over the years. She felt the emotion rising up again as she remembered the times they'd sat around a tree just like this one and opened presents, Nan smiling from the nearby chair. When they unwrapped their presents, Nan would listen, ask questions, nod and smile.

"Would you hand me the tree skirt, please?" she asked, swallowing her emotion back down.

David pulled a plastic bag from the box and removed the folded deep red velvet tree skirt. Another note floated to the ground. Leah walked over and picked it up.

The skirt is fraying on the edge. Don't forget to sew it.

The hair on Leah's arms stood up. David was fiddling with the ragged edge of the skirt, the dark red fabric draped across his lap. It was as if her grandmother were right there talking to them. Her presence was everywhere. "I'll need to sew that," she said, eyeing the fray and raising the note in the air.

"I think Nan's sewing kit is in that cabinet at the other end of the sofa. She always liked to sit there when she mended things," Sadie said, skipping over to the cabinet. She and Nan had spent many days sewing in this room.

Sure enough, it was there—a box, padded in a flowery print with a handle and shiny silver closure. Leah sat down on the floor and opened it. It was full of brightly colored ribbon, spools of thread in every shade, and two pincushions—one with needles and the other with pushpins. She pulled a needle out and grabbed the spool of thread that was closest to the cranberry color she needed.

"I'm glad you know how to sew," David said as he walked over and sat down beside her, handing Leah the tree skirt. "We could've probably just hidden this part at the back of the tree."

"Nan wrote herself a note because she wanted it fixed. It would bug me if I put it under there without taking care of this seam." She pulled the thread through and looped it around.

It only took a few stitches. "There," she said. "All done." She returned the sewing kit and carefully put the tree skirt in place, fastening it at the back.

"Your grandmother wrote where she places each ornament?" David said, holding another piece of paper in his hand, the bag of ornaments in his lap. "What if she changed her mind?"

"I suppose she wouldn't have."

Sadie offered a look of agreement from across the room. She twirled and then did a little leap in the large open space between the fireplace and the coffee table.

David went back over to the box. "So, here's the big question: Will Leah Evans choose her own locations for the ornaments or will she adhere to tradition? This says a lot about you. Choose carefully," David said with a grin that reached his eyes.

Leah rolled her eyes at him playfully. "Why don't I place the ornaments the way I'd like them and then we can see how near I was to Nan's suggestions? I'm willing to guess I'll have it pretty close."

David dangled an ornament between his fingers. It was a silver angel with crystal wings. "Ornament Number One," he said, peeking at Nan's paper and then hiding the writing from Leah as she came closer to take the ornament from him.

She studied it. "Nan taught me that ornaments go from smallest at the top to largest at the bottom. This one is pretty small. I'm guessing… here." She hung the ornament at the top of the tree.

"Would you say that is 'top center' or 'upper middle'?" He leaned against the sofa.

"Top center." She looked over at Sadie for agreement.

She was doing a handstand, her toes perfectly pointed, her legs straight as arrows. "Top center!" she said from upside down.

"Correct!"

"Ha! Give me another one!"

"Sadie, you're really good at that," he said, his attention pulled away for a second. Sadie's handstand was flawlessly still, her arms strong, her body completely in line.

"Thank you," she said, bringing one leg down until her foot was on the floor. She righted herself. "I love gymnastics."

"Show me what else you can do," he said.

"Okay!" Sadie said, her little eyebrows rising in excitement. There was plenty of room, the center of the sitting room floor left open except for an enormous area rug and a small coffee table near the settee.

Gracefully, she raised her hands above her head and tilted backward, leaning slowly, her back arching until her hands found the floor. Even in her jeans, she was so limber that they didn't obstruct her movements. She kicked her leg, the other following and flipped over, landing in an upright position. Her feet still moving, she slid down into the splits. Sadie raised her hands again as if to signal the end of her routine.

"Wow, that's great," David said, clearly impressed. "You have a lot of talent, Miss Sadie."

"Thank you!"

"I take her every year to see a big gymnastics competition in town here."

"Mama! We're going this year, right? David should go with us!"

"Well, if he wants to," she said, unsure.

He was looking at her, happiness in his eyes, a small smile playing at his lips. "I'd love to." He had his arm propped along the sofa, his legs crossed, and for an instant, she wished she could cuddle up against his sweater and feel his arms around her.

"Yay!" Sadie danced around and then did a cartwheel. "Now, back to the ornament game!"

David smiled wider at Leah, clearly amused by Sadie. He held out five glass candy canes. "Put these on the tree where you think they go, and I'll get us something else to drink," he said, standing up. More hot chocolate, Sadie?"

Sadie nodded.

"How about you?" He turned to Leah. "Hot chocolate, or should I open a bottle of wine?"

She studied the ornaments as she took them from his hand. The glass candy canes made a tinkling sound, dangling from her fingers. There was something about the atmosphere that made her want to celebrate. She was decorating Nan's tree, giving life to the house, and putting Nan's stamp back on things. "I think we should have wine since we're decorating the tree. Nan would be so thrilled to know that we're carrying on the tradition another year."

"Wine it is then. Make sure you get those candy canes in the right place," he said with a wink, and held up the paper. "I'm taking this with me."

Leah had put Sadie to bed and now she and David were settled on the settee in front of the fire, both of them completely relaxed under Nan's quilt, the empty glasses and bottle of wine on the coffee table, the tree sparkling in the corner. When she'd first arrived, her grief had overwhelmed her, but now, the more she relaxed in Nan's space, the closer she felt to her, and the more at peace she was.

"Do you remember how we used to do everything together?" David asked.

"Yes," she said.

"You always wanted to do things your way," he teased.

"And you let me." She smiled up at him, noticing again how attractive he was—the square of his chin, the way his smile reached his eyes. He grinned back at her. She'd enjoyed him so much tonight and it was starting to confuse her more as the night went on.

"Sadie seems to have your independence. Is she a lot like you?" he asked.

"Sometimes. She loved Nan like I did. But she's different in many ways."

"And her father? Is she like him?"

It was just a question but it sent a wave of hurt through her. So far, Sadie had asked simple questions that Leah had been able to answer, but she was waiting for the big one: Why did my daddy leave? "She's like her father in that she worries about things a lot. He was like that."

"Was?"

"He left when he found out I was pregnant. He said he wasn't ready for that kind of commitment." She let out an indignant huff. "At the time, I'd told him it wasn't a choice the commitment. But, from his seven-year absence, I suppose I was wrong. Apparently, for him, it was a choice."

David took in a breath and let his gaze fall onto the quilt that covered them. "I can't imagine doing that."

"Leaving your unborn child?"

He looked back at her. "Well, yes, but he also left you. He was leaving the both of you." Leah tried not to hear what he was really saying.

"Well, I can manage on my own."

"I'm sure you can. But wouldn't it be nice to have someone there to go through it all with you?"

"Nan was there. And my parents helped when they could."

"That's how my mother was for me, growing up. She was my rock. It was just the two of us, like you and Sadie, and I could always tell her anything."

She realized just then that she and David were talking as freely as if they'd never separated. It had taken Leah years to know Louise enough to feel comfortable telling her things like this. It was slightly worrying to her how easy it was and she wondered if she was getting too close to him. She didn't want to put anyone in Sadie's life who might not stay, and she knew she couldn't let herself fall for the man who was taking Evergreen Hill from her. Maybe he was doing it nicely, but it didn't change the fact that he was. And wouldn't he wonder if she was interested in him because of the house? It couldn't work, and so she had to stop dipping her toes in the water. With Sadie, safe bets were the only bets she'd consider.

Chapter Fourteen

Leah rolled over and blinked to view the clock. She squinted to see the time, the crystal analog face the size of a quarter. It was the only thing on the little yellow table except for a lamp with a simple white base and a blue shade to coordinate with the room.

It was early, the sun still tucked away behind the horizon. Gently, so as not to disturb Sadie, Leah sat up and padded across the hardwoods and into the bathroom, shutting the door behind her. She got herself ready enough to go downstairs, pulling her hair up into a loose ponytail, washing her face and brushing her teeth. Then she went to make some coffee.

"Good morning," David said in a hushed voice. He was sitting at the table, his computer to the side. He had on jeans and a T-shirt, his hair slightly messy, and stubble on his face. "I've made coffee." He got up and went to the counter, his eyes still on her.

"Oh great. Thank you. I was coming down for that," Leah said. When he turned away from her, she straightened her top and tucked it into her pajama bottoms in an attempt to look less frumpy. Then realizing what she'd done, she pulled her shirt back out. She wasn't going to allow herself to worry about how she looked. But as she watched David at the counter, noticing the muscles in his back through his

T-shirt as he got coffee mugs from the top cabinet, she tucked it back in again. Little Davey was all grown up… "I'm glad I'm not the only one awake at this hour."

"I had work to do." He looked over at her and smiled, but she could tell he was tired. "I'd like to show you something."

She waited, wondering what it could be.

They went into the living room and Leah sucked in a breath of surprise. The candles on the mantle were lit, the stockings hung, greenery draped on the tops of the doorframes and tied back with the big bows that Nan had always used. She looked at David.

"I followed your grandmother's notes. Anything she didn't tell me, I guessed at. How did I do?"

"You did very well," she said, the words catching on her emotion. "What made you decorate?"

"You haven't had the Christmas here this year that I'm sure you're used to, and I knew Sadie had noticed. I wanted to give you a great Christmas here, and I didn't want her to be uncomfortable in any way. I thought it might make things more festive. But I'm not finished," he said with a grin. "It's still dark outside. Want to see?"

He offered his hand. Without even a flinch, she took it. He led her to the back door and turned the handle.

"Should we get our coats?" she asked.

"No. We won't stay out too long. I just want to plug this in," he said, opening the door. It had started to snow again, the white flakes filling the air like a frozen mist, disappearing into the drifts of snow that were forming, covering everything as far as she could see. He dropped her hand and pushed the plug from an extension cord, which was running discreetly along the edge of the porch, into the socket. Like some sort of Christmassy dream, the woods lit up, every spruce tree as far as she could see covered in glistening white lights, creating a winter wonderland. It was just like she remembered as a kid.

Tears brimmed in her eyes. Maybe it was the Christmas spirit, or the love that she felt when she looked at those lights, but she threw her arms around him and buried her face in his neck, his scent filling her lungs. With one hand wrapped around her, he pulled them inside, shut the door and then embraced her, his cuddle tenderer than she expected. They stayed that way, neither of them moving. She couldn't deny the chemistry she felt.

"I didn't know you liked the lights that much or I would've done them sooner," he said into her ear. "It's my peace offering."

She pulled back to look at him, but she shouldn't have because he was looking at her in a way that made it nearly impossible to stop the zinging electricity between them.

"That must have taken you ages!" she said, pulling away from him and clearing her throat. The winter chill he'd let in made her skin prickle with cold.

"Well, like I said, I got up early. I had work to do. This work." He smiled.

"It's gorgeous," she said, looking back out the lights through the window. "Leave them on. I want Sadie to see them."

"Mama!" Sadie said as she ran to the front window in her red footed pajamas. Leah had gone up to get her to show her the trees out back, too excited to wait for her to wake on her own. Sadie pressed her nose against the glass, the edges of it frosted with ice and newly fallen snow. The fields were covered in snow as far as they could see— rolling hills of white—but it just kept coming. The sun was hidden by the snowstorm, the sky turning from black to gray with the early morning light.

"I want to show you something that David did for us." Leah took Sadie by the hand and led her to the back window as David looked on with a grin. The trees were still lit, illuminating the woods like a winter version of heaven. Sadie gasped, the joy on her face enough to make Leah feel a flutter in her chest.

"It's so pretty! It's just like how Nan used to do it!" She ran over and gave David a giant hug. What struck Leah most was the way he bent down and hugged her back, and suddenly, she longed to have someone like him in Sadie's life.

David had spent the rest of the morning pulling the large plow down the drive with the farm truck to clear the snow. Leah had never seen anyone use it other than the groundsmen that Nan had employed, and she was surprised by his ability to use the equipment. He'd been buzzing around the house all morning, and she could tell as the day wore on, he was a little on edge while he prepared for June's arrival.

Leah put linens on the bed in the spare room that June would be using. David had gone to the airport to pick her up.

"Somebody's here, Mama," Sadie said as she leaned on the large front windowsill. She'd spent the morning looking through different windows around the house at all the snow that had fallen. Leah went over to the window.

David was opening the door of the passenger side of his car so June could exit. She emerged, looking almost like Leah remembered her—her thin frame, her shoulder-length hair tucked behind one ear. She looked older, but it still seemed as if she'd stepped right out of Leah's memory. David popped the trunk and pulled two bags from the back. He stepped up beside her and they started toward the house.

Leah opened the door.

"Oh my gosh!" June said, throwing a frail hand to her chest. "Leah Evans." She shook her head, a smile on her face. Leah noticed how much older she looked now that they were up close. Her eyes seemed tired despite her bright expression. She reached out and gave Leah a hug then pulled back. "Wow," she said with emphasis. "You look so much like your nan did at your age. It's unbelievable."

That was the biggest compliment Leah could've gotten because she'd always thought Nan was beautiful in pictures of her when she was younger. "It's great to see you," she said, stepping aside so they could enter.

Sadie rounded the corner and June's jaw dropped. "My goodness," she said in almost a whisper. "It's like going back in time." She squatted down to level herself with Sadie. "Hello," she said.

"Hi. I'm Sadie. That's my mama."

June smiled. "Yes, I can tell. You look just like her."

David shut the door and carried the bags upstairs. Leah was about to offer June something to eat, but she was standing still, her eyes moving all over the entryway, the smile slowly disappearing. June tilted her head back and peered up at the chandelier. "It has been a while," she said, more emotion on her face than that simple phrase allowed. "It's good to be home."

"Would you like something to eat?" Leah finally offered.

"Thank you, dear. I'd love something to eat."

"Okay. With all the snow we got last night, I was going to make lasagna now for a warm, hearty late lunch but we can have some nibbles before. Does that sound good?"

"That would be wonderful, dear."

Leah noticed how June's energy seemed so different from the June of her memory. Back then, she was always laughing, always fluttering around, never sitting still. She seemed slower now, her actions more deliberate.

"Mama, can I get some of Nan's quilt squares and sew like we used to do?" Sadie asked.

"Yes. Do you remember where everything is in the sewing room?"

Sadie nodded. "I wonder if she still has the basket of squares she used to save just for my visits."

"Knowing Nan, she probably does."

"She likes to quilt like Nina did?" June said with interest as they headed down the hallway. She ran her fingers along the entry table as they walked by it.

"Nan taught her how."

"I remember your grandmother would sit in the chair in the sitting room, a beautiful quilt draped over her legs as she sewed the next square, her concentration almost beautiful in itself, like an artist at work."

"That's how Sadie got started. She'd watched Nan sewing one day and asked her how she did it. She was only probably five or so. Nan was so patient with her, teaching her step by step how to stitch. Sadie looks forward to visits to Evergreen Hill so she can do it." They reached the kitchen.

Leah pulled out some cut vegetables and arranged them on a tray. Then, quickly, she mixed a little sour cream and mayonnaise together in a bowl and added a few dried herbs to make a quick dip. She set it all out on the island. As June grabbed a slice of green pepper, Leah retrieved a pan from the cupboard and set it on the stove. She rooted around in the drawers for the spatula. "You used to cook for us a lot when I was little, didn't you?"

June nodded. Leah waited for her to say something, but she didn't, so she carried on and pulled a cutting board from under the counter. She placed an onion on it before walking around the island toward Sadie, who'd come in with a small square of quilt. "May I see what you've made?" Leah asked.

"I'm making a quilt for my baby doll," she said, holding up the small rectangle of fabric. "Do you like it?"

"You remembered all your stitches," she said, so thrilled that Nan's work with her wasn't lost.

"It was easy to remember them," Sadie said. "I'm not finished. I just wanted to show you."

"Will you show us again when you've finished?" Leah asked.

"Yes!" Sadie ran off down the hallway.

"She is just lovely, Leah," June said.

"Thank you," she said, returning to the onion and peeling the outer layer off. She chopped the onion in half and lay the flat, cut sides on the cutting board. "Would you like to cook with me?" she asked, wondering if June still loved cooking like she used to.

June sat still and seemed to be thinking carefully. She blinked then slowly nodded. "I'd love to, thank you." She got up and made her way over to the cutting board on the island. With perfect precision, June made cuts in the onion until she had minced it. She used the knife to scrape the pieces into her hand and dumped them in the pan. They sizzled as they hit the heat.

Leah added the ground beef and began to mix it with the onion. They worked silently, side by side and something in Leah told her to just allow the quiet between them.

"It smells delicious in here," David said, entering the kitchen. He walked over and gave his mother a kiss on the cheek. "You're all unpacked."

"You didn't have to do that, dear," she said.

"It's fine. What are you two cooking?"

"You're smelling the onions. They always fill the house with a delectable smell," June said.

"It's about to smell better once I get this garlic into the pan," Leah added.

"Did you know that whenever your grandmother made anything with ground beef and garlic, she always roasted the garlic first in the pan?" June said.

"Really?"

"Oh yes." She looked thoughtful for a moment and then went over to the cupboard where Nan kept all her baking items—rolling pins, cookie cutters, drying racks. "I'll bet…" she trailed off, pulling Nan's recipe box out of the cabinet. She flipped through the little cards, intently searching for something. Leah continued to stir, her eyes on June.

Then suddenly, June pulled a card from the box and laughed quietly. She turned it around and walked closer to Leah. In Nan's slanted handwriting, on the recipe for lasagna, the first direction was, *ROAST the garlic. Trust me.*

"Why did she write 'trust me' if it was her recipe?" Leah asked with a giggle.

"Because she cooked everything from her head but she wrote the recipes, she told me, for anyone else who may need them."

"What if she never gave them to anyone to use?"

"Clearly she didn't. It's still in the box. Should we use her recipe?"

"Let me get another pan for the garlic. We'll roast it before we put it into the ground beef." Leah turned the heat down on the meat to hold it until the garlic was finished roasting.

"You two are having too much fun," David said. "I'm going up to do some work. But let me know when it's done! I'll give it a taste test for you."

"I'm sure you will, son," June said, shaking her head at him. Her hair had fallen forward a little. She tucked it behind her ear. Leah opened her mouth to start a conversation, but she stopped herself. June seemed happy enough considering, and Leah could sense talking would change that.

"When can we go sledding?"

"Right after we finish eating, if you'd like," said Leah, setting Sadie's lasagna on the table.

"Are you talking about the big hill down the drive? How will you get down there?" David asked, turning toward her briefly as he got forks from the drawer and set them beside each plate, handing one to Sadie. "There's quite a bit of snow."

The trouble with this place was that it was so far off the road; it would take an army to shovel the private path if it got too deep for the tractor, and they wouldn't get any help from the road crews. Once they were snowed in, there was nothing they could do. Last night's snow accumulation had come as a surprise, and now, she wondered if anyone would be able to get out.

"I suppose we could try the farm truck," Leah said. "Good thing you plowed the drive."

"Will you come with us?" Sadie asked, dancing over to David.

David peeked over his shoulder at Sadie. "I used to love sledding here. I haven't been in a very long time."

"Then come!" Sadie had gone back to her lasagna and crawled into the chair, sitting on her knees.

Jenny Hale

"I suppose I could," David said. "If it's all right with your mom."

"It's fine by me." Leah smiled, remembering the times they'd sledded down that hill together.

After lunch had settled, Leah suggested that Sadie do her math practice before going sledding, but when Sadie didn't want to, Leah didn't press the issue. She didn't want anything getting in the way of Sadie's perfect last Christmas at Evergreen Hill. She figured maybe she could offer to help her at another time.

"I'm going to get to go sledding instead of doing math!" Sadie said with a grin.

"Oh, come on," David teased, "you know you'd rather be doing math." He sat down beside Leah on the settee as she collected her snow gear—boots, hat, scarf, and gloves. She made a pile by the fireplace so they'd be warm when she put them on.

Sadie's eyes grew round. "I hate math."

"*Hate* is a strong word. What don't you like about it?"

"I don't get it. It's too hard." A glove slipped out of Sadie's hand as she dumped her plastic overalls, designed for skiing, into the pile by the fire. David leaned down and handed it to her. "Mama packed one sheet for my homework to come here. I tried three times in the car, but I couldn't do it. I'm not good at it."

"What if you are? What if you just don't know the secret?"

Leah was transfixed, watching how effortlessly David handled the conversation. It was clear that he'd found a topic of interest with Sadie, and the way Sadie was looking at David, she might just trust him.

"What's the secret?" Sadie asked.

"How about I show it to you later. We can work on your homework together."

"Okay," she said a little uncertain.

"Right now, let's get ready to go sledding."

"I'm too scared," Sadie said as she looked at the large hill in front of her. It was on the edge of the property. The sky had cleared after the storm, leaving it a cloudless electric blue. A blanket of white stretched out before them, down the hill, the trees that outlined the space casting long shadows on the pristine surface of the field. The air was still frigid, the wind cutting through them harshly. Sadie was tugging at her scarf to cover her mouth. With a gloved hand, she pushed her hat up unsuccessfully to get it out of her eyes, her multicolored, striped cap pinning the strands to her head. "It's really steep."

Nan had said last year, when Leah had suggested it, that they should possibly wait for Sadie to get older before sledding on this hill. She'd worried about it being too high for her. In her old age, Nan was much more cautious with Sadie than she'd ever been with Leah. The problem was, they weren't going to have another chance, once David owned the house outright, and Leah thought that if she'd just give it a chance, she'd love it, and it would be a memory she'd cherish.

"The sled is big enough for someone to ride with you," David said, trying to ease her fears. "Would you like one of us to sit behind and hold on to you?" Leah didn't want to admit to herself that she liked the way he talked to Sadie. David was so calm and gentle with her—a natural with kids.

Sadie looked past him at the hill, those brown eyes so unsure.

"Would you like to watch someone do it first? Your mom and I can go down and you can see how fast the sled goes. How's that?"

Sadie nodded and took a large step backward, leaving boot prints in the snow.

The sled was a flat bed of wooden slats sitting on bright red iron rails with a rope handle. David sat down first at the back, leaving a spot in front of him for Leah. Gingerly, she climbed on and leaned back until she could feel his chest against her, his chin on her shoulder. When they were little, they'd sat the same way, but she'd had room to stretch her legs all the way out.

David reached around her and grabbed the rope, his arms nearly embracing her. His face was right next to hers. She kept looking forward to keep from bumping noses with him. She usually didn't like it when men put their arms around her; it made her feel confined. But with David, she felt safe.

"Here, put your feet up on the sled," he said in her ear, causing a shiver to run down her arm. "Are you cold?" he asked.

"I'm fine." She yanked her feet up, noticing then that the pain in her ankle was nearly gone.

David dug his heels into the snow and inched them closer to the edge of the hill. "Ready to watch, Sadie?" He turned around and looked her way.

Sadie nodded. She had her hands in the pockets of her navy blue coat and she was bouncing for warmth. "Are you scared, Mama?" she called out.

"No, I think it'll be fun!" Her mind went again to David's arms, still wrapped tightly around her.

Sadie was giggling uncontrollably.

"Okay. Here we go, Sadie!" David pushed off and pulled his legs around Leah's as they went speeding toward the bottom of the hill.

Leah's stomach flew right up into her chest and she let out a loud squeal, causing David to laugh. The hill stretched on forever and once the initial drop was over, they were gliding, flying through the snow, his strong arms holding her, his breath in her ear. When it finally ended, she didn't want him to let go. Unexpectedly, her mind went to Nan and Samuel. Had Samuel ever made her nan feel this way? If so, how had she ever let him go?

David hopped right off the sled without lingering even a second, and she had to get herself together.

"See, Sadie," he called up, "it's not that bad!"

Leah stood up, focused on the sled. She turned it around by the rope handle, and started up the hill.

"I think I'm ready!" Sadie called to him. She was smiling, her face so trusting of him that it took Leah aback. She was standing at the top of the hill, bouncing and creating a little spot in the snow from her movements. Leah couldn't help but notice how perfect this moment between the three of them was.

"You can do it!" David said once he'd reached her. He positioned the sled at the top of the hill and held it steady. "Want anyone to go with you?"

"I've got it," she said, getting on the sled and pulling the rope handle up to her waist. The rails of the sled made little tracks in the fresh snow where she'd wiggled to get on.

"You sure?" David had the tread anchored down with his boot.

"Yes! You can let go!"

David let go and Sadie went sailing down the hill. It was as if Leah were watching an old movie of herself. She remembered how Nan would stand at the top of this very hill, clapping her gloved hands, her poised demeanor not breaking for a moment, but that smile and the look in her eyes giving away her playfulness.

"You're a natural!" she said as Sadie pulled the sled up the hill.

"Thank you for your patience with her," Leah said. "That was amazing how you thought to have us go first."

"Ah, it wasn't my idea. My mom and my grandmother had to do that for me my first time sledding down this hill. It's a monster of a hill, and it can be intimidating. I just did what I was taught."

She thought about how his and June's connection to the house really was strong, and while she was going to miss it, she was glad it would be taken care of by people who shared its history and truly valued it.

They'd stayed out sledding until Leah couldn't feel her hands. When they'd come back, Leah had seen June hurry back up the stairs as if she were avoiding them, and David had bounded up after her to check on her. He came back into the kitchen, pulling his sweater off over his head and Leah gave him a nod. "Who wants hot chocolate?" she asked, pulling a candy cane from a box in the pantry and stirring a fresh cup with it. She added a decadent dollop of whipped cream and shaved chocolate to the top.

"I do!" Sadie said, now wearing her pajamas, her wet clothes from sledding hung over the radiator.

"What's that you've got there?" David asked, sitting down beside her.

"It's my sketchpad. I don't know what to draw."

"Hmm… How about your Christmas list? Have you made one yet?"

"Oh yes! I used to make one with Nan!" She opened her sketchpad and started numbering down the page. She wrote next to number one, *a box of pencils*. "For writing stories and drawing," she explained. Then, number two: *a new hairbrush*. "Mine doesn't get the tangles out like it used to."

David chuckled. "Anything else?"

"Maybe one more." *A new book to read.*

After delivering the hot chocolate, Leah went into the hallway to take care of the rest of the snowy clothes. They were making an enormous puddle on the hardwoods.

"Those are all very nice presents," she heard David say. "But what would your dream gift be if you could ask for anything?"

"I never write those down," she said in a whisper, but Leah could hear it.

"Why not? It's Christmas. You might get it."

Leah felt an ache beginning in her temple. She'd always had to try to stretch her dollar just to make the tree look full of presents. She'd wanted to get those big gifts for Sadie, but she just hadn't been able to. She started mopping the floor. But she stopped when she heard Sadie answer David.

Still in a whisper, she heard her say, "I only put things on my list that I know my mama can afford. It wouldn't be very nice to ask for something she couldn't buy me."

"But what about Santa Claus?" David said.

Her voice was so low that Leah had to strain to hear it. "I think he's real, but I'm not sure. I don't get the big things that my friends get, so I think Mama buys them. I don't know why Santa doesn't come."

Leah held on to the mop and took a deep breath. Sadie's answer broke her heart.

David hadn't responded right away, and Leah wondered what he must have been thinking. "Well, I think the magic is real. Just for fun, what would you ask Santa for if you could have anything?"

Sadie giggled. "A kitten."

Leah breathed out, relieved she hadn't asked for a laptop or a trip to Disneyland, and pleased she'd asked for something so sweet. In fact, while she'd avoided the cost of pet food and vet bills until now, once she'd sold her half of Evergreen Hill, there would be no reason to scrimp and save like that. And actually, now, she could probably afford a trip to Disneyland if Sadie ever wanted one. She peeked in to see Sadie.

Sadie leaned over the paper, her pen with the fluffy, pink ball at the end hovering near where she'd written the other items on her list. She looked up at David. "Maybe I'll write a kitten."

"I'm sure you were plenty good this year. And most of the time, things aren't just given to us. We have to work for them. If Santa Claus doesn't give you a kitten, it's not the end of the world, but wouldn't it be fun to at least ask?"

Sadie's eyes lit up.

Sadie flipped to a new page and carried on. "Number one," she said as she wrote the letters, "kitten." She looked up at David. "Did Santa come while you lived here as a kid?" she asked.

David smiled. "You know, I think he did."

"I'm worried," she said, her little eyebrows puckering in trepidation. "What if Santa looks for me but doesn't know where to find me?"

"I wouldn't worry," he said with a grin.

"But what if he thinks I'm still in Richmond?"

"I think he's always known we've spent Christmases here before," Leah said.

"But it's different this year," said Sadie, suddenly looking sad, and Leah knew she was thinking about Nan.

"He knows because he's always watching. His elves are everywhere. Sometimes, they even leave little trails of glitter. There's probably some in here right now. You'll have to look and see if you find any."

David's answers were so perfect, so effortless, that Leah almost believed it herself. When he looked up at her, she couldn't help but smile, despite her own fears.

"I don't think he'll bring me my kitten," Sadie said, her face dropping. "And that's okay."

David's gaze flickered over to Leah and then back to Sadie. "Well, you'll just have to see."

Leah thought about ways she could get out and get a kitten on or very near to Christmas Eve. She wouldn't want Sadie to find it before, but not much would be open when she needed to buy one. Maybe she could call around and find a private residence selling them, and she could pick it up at just the right time.

"Number two," Sadie said, "I'd like a gymnastics mat."

A kitten she could manage right now, knowing the money was on its way, but Leah wouldn't have *that* kind of money this Christmas unless she signed the contract of sale immediately—not for the quality mat that Sadie's talent required. But then she thought, what was she waiting for? She'd made her decision and, Christmas or not, there was no use in delaying the contract any longer.

"David, may I see you for a moment?" she said, beckoning him into the hallway. She looked at him a moment, deliberating one last time. But really there was no other way. "I'm ready to sign the papers for the sale of Evergreen Hill," she told him quietly.

David looked at her, and she thought she saw concern behind his eyes. "Okay," he said. "I'll have my attorney email them over."

Leah jumped with a start as she realized she'd fallen asleep. After agreeing to sign, she'd needed to lie down. To her relief, she'd only been asleep for twenty minutes.

She'd gone downstairs but stopped in the doorway of the kitchen. David was sitting beside Sadie and they were hunched over a piece of paper together.

"So when you have to go to the tens place, it's called 'regrouping,'" he said to her, his pencil moving on the paper. "Do it like I showed you. If you have three pieces of candy, can you eat seven?"

"No," Sadie said, turning her head into Leah's view to look at him, her eyes trusting.

"So regroup the candies in the top number. Isn't forty-three the same as thirty and thirteen?"

Her eyes got big. "Yes! Thirty plus thirteen makes forty-three! I see!" She bent down over her paper and started writing.

"Now look at the ones place. If you have thirteen candies, can you eat seven?"

Sadie wriggled up onto her knees to be as tall as David and wrapped her arms around his neck. "Thank you." She buried her little face in his shoulder. With a smile that changed his whole face, David hugged her back, and in that moment, like a perfect snapshot, Leah got a glimpse of what David would be like as a father—his strong arms protective, his doting smile, his gentle demeanor. Leah hung back, getting herself together.

Chapter Fifteen

"Don't sign the papers, Leah," Roz said down the phone. After Roz had inquired about Sadie, she'd asked about the house and with Sadie safely downstairs watching television, Leah had told Roz everything. "As much as you tell me how great this money will be, I just don't believe that you're ready to give up the plantation. Why don't I come for a visit so we can come up with something else?"

"We're still planning to have family Christmas. You know I wouldn't leave you out of that. Let's discuss it then."

"By then it'll be too late!"

"Roz…" She knew her friend meant well, but tactfulness wasn't her strong point and she worried about what her friend might say to David. She had made up her mind, and she knew Roz would only make her doubt her decision. But then, Roz always had Leah's best interests at heart, and even just thinking about it like that made doubt swell in her stomach. "You have to be on your best behavior."

"Of course, chickadee! No biggie. I need to feel things out so I can help you know your next move. I've got to work tomorrow, but I'll come the day after."

Leah smiled and shook her head. To be honest, she couldn't wait to see Roz.

* * *

"Do you want to hear something that will make you very happy?" Leah said to Sadie after they'd eaten dinner. She'd already told David when they'd been cooking, so it wouldn't be a surprise to him.

Sadie nodded excitedly.

"I spoke to Roz, and guess what. She's going to come for a visit in a couple of days!"

Sadie threw her hands in the air and squealed with happiness. "Is she bringing Jo?"

"Yep!"

"Yaaaaay!" Sadie cheered. "I think we should make snow cream for dessert to celebrate!"

"I can't remember the last time I had snow cream," David said.

"Should I go out and get us a bunch of snow?" Sadie asked, already running to the hallway to get her coat and hat. Leah grabbed a bowl from the cupboard and handed it to Sadie. Then Sadie flew out the door.

June, who had sobered a little as the meal went on, had excused herself and gone upstairs for the night.

"Do you think your mom's okay?" Leah asked once she and David were alone.

"She struggles," he answered frankly, joining her at the island as she cleared dinner dishes. "She isolates herself a lot. She quit her job because she just couldn't cope with her grief. She and Christine—her friend's name was Christine—did everything together. She was that one friend my mom would call family."

"I understand that kind of friend."

"When she quit her job, she told me she was being pleasant on the surface, but inside, being around everyone was slowly eating away at her until she snapped and quit. I told her never to do that around me—never to pretend."

"Look at how much I got!" Sadie said, coming in and tracking snow across the kitchen to show them. She hugged the giant bowl as she wobbled it onto the table.

"Wow, that's a lot of snow," David said, abandoning their conversation. "What do we need to make the snow cream?"

"Milk, sugar, vanilla, and a pinch of salt," Leah said, putting the ingredients onto the island. She put the ingredients into a bowl and whisked them together. "Would you get a measuring cup, please?" she asked David.

David handed it to her, both of them giving in wholeheartedly to the task at hand.

"David, will you eat some?" Sadie asked.

"Of course," he said, pulling a chair over to the island so she could climb up and see a little better.

Leah handed her the measuring cup. "Remember how we did this last year with Nan? I need eight scoops, one at a time." She continued to whisk very gently as Sadie dropped lumps of snow into the mixture. Before long, it was a bowl of creamy, icy goodness. "What should we put on top, Sadie? There are sprinkles, M&Ms, or mini chocolate chips in the pantry."

"Mini chocolate chips and M&Ms!"

"That sounds tasty," David said.

"Do David's bowl first, Mama! I want him to try it!"

Leah set out three bowls in a row and filled them each to the brim. "I have a can of whipped cream in the fridge. Who wants some?" She laughed when both David and Sadie raised their hands. She got it out along with the chocolate chips and M&Ms. "Everyone can top their own bowl. How about that?"

Sadie shook the can of whipped cream and pointed the spout at her bowl, but her hands were small, and the can was too big to maintain control. She pressed, the spout slipping from under her finger and sending a blob of whipped cream onto the counter.

"Oh!" both Leah and Sadie said at the same time. Leah wiped the counter with a towel. "Maybe I should do the whipped cream," she said with a laugh. Sadie handed her the can.

"Remember that time Nan got us to try to catch M&Ms in each other's mouths?" Sadie doubled over laughing, nearly falling off the chair.

"She did what?" David asked.

"I tried to throw an M&M into Mama's mouth and then I gave her one and she tried to get it into mine."

"Did anyone actually catch one?"

"Yes! We both did!" Sadie turned to Leah. "Mama, try with David! See if he can catch one."

Leah reached her hand into the bag, unable to hide her grin.

He looked at her, unsure.

"What? You don't trust me?" she said, her grin widening.

"Do it! Do it! Do it!" Sadie called out.

"Okay, fine."

David opened his mouth. Leah tossed an M&M, hitting just under David's eye. With a laugh, he caught it in his hand and popped it into his mouth.

"My turn," he said.

With mock annoyance, Leah handed over the bag. Sadie was now sitting cross-legged, eating her snow cream and watching like a spectator. She'd already added the chocolate chips.

"Okay. Ready?"

Leah opened her mouth, and in a split second, the M&M came sailing in. Surprised, she closed her mouth, and chewed.

"One point for David!" Sadie cheered. "My turn!" she said, standing up and opening her mouth while still holding her bowl. She grabbed a handful of M&Ms and plopped them into her mouth, falling down to the chair, giggling.

"I need to redeem myself," Leah said. "Hand over the candy."

"Oh no. You're not getting another chance at my face," he teased, holding the bag in the air.

"Hand it over or I'm coming over there to get it. I can do it! Can't I, Sadie?"

"She can. You ought to give her another chance." Sadie took a bite of her snow cream, what was left now a soupy mush with floating chocolate chips in the bottom of her bowl.

David handed the bag to Leah. "One shot," he said and then dramatically grabbed the counter for support, making Sadie laugh.

Leah rolled her eyes. "Open up!" she said in a sing-songy voice. David complied. She aimed. She shot. And to her surprise, she got an M&M right into his mouth.

"One to one!" Sadie giggled. Then she switched her bowl with Leah's and took another bite.

"Hey, that's my bowl!" Leah teased.

David walked around to her side. "It's okay. You and I can share." He scooped some fresh snow cream into his bowl. "Would you like M&Ms on it or have you had enough?"

"One can never have too many M&Ms."

He covered the top of the snow with whipped cream and added the candy. "Chocolate chips?"

"Yes, please. Lots of chocolate chips."

When he'd finished topping the snow cream, he filled the spoon and held it out to her. She took a bite. "Yummy." Then he got a bite for himself.

"Isn't that game fun, David?" Sadie said.

He nodded with a smile, taking another bite of snow cream.

Chapter Sixteen

Leah sat with her third cup of coffee steaming in one of Nan's Christmas mugs—it was brown with a red dot and the handle was a reindeer antler. She'd been up half the night, thinking about everything. She'd thought a lot about Nan's last message of regrets and the man named Samuel who, from his letters, seemed to love her so much. She couldn't wait till Roz was here and she could talk everything out in a big swirling mess of sadness, excitement, and confusion.

There was a creak in the floor, and she turned around. "Oh, good morning," she said to June.

June was wearing her housecoat and slippers, but her hair was still as perfectly combed as it had been yesterday, with one side tucked behind her ear. Without her make-up, however, her face revealed the secret that her life hadn't been easy at times. Normally, it was hidden very well.

"You're up early," June said. "You look like you haven't slept."

"I haven't," Leah said, getting up to offer her some juice. She needed a break from all the caffeine.

June accepted and joined her at the counter. She was quiet as she got two glasses down from the cabinet.

Leah wondered if June had any knowledge of Nan and Samuel. She looked tired, but somehow more settled, so she decided to bring up the subject. "Do you know anyone by the name of Samuel Patterson?" she asked.

June poured some juice into the glasses and put the container back into the fridge before she turned around, her eyes squinting in her attempt to recall the name. "I don't think so, why?"

Leah told her about the letters.

"An admirer."

They took their glasses to the table. "It was more than that. He said he loved her."

"He sounds charming." She swirled her juice around in her glass and then took a sip.

"I didn't think she'd had anyone significant in her life since my grandfather Jack died," Leah said. "She'd said how devastated she'd been when she'd lost him. I always assumed she'd just never quite gotten over it."

June's face dropped from curious to understanding; she knew all too well what loss was like. Suddenly, Leah worried that she might have reminded June of the sensitive topic of her friend's death. June's expression confirmed it. "David told me about your friend," she said cautiously. "I'm so sorry."

She nodded, the emotion clearly robbing her of her words.

Leah knew that just saying sorry was what everyone said to someone who was grieving, for lack of anything better to say. There wasn't anything *to* say that could make her feel better. "Since Nan died," she said, "I've felt like a part of me is missing. I'd been going along just fine and it was like getting hit out of nowhere by a speeding van. I didn't see it coming and then my favorite person was gone. I'd never get to hear her voice or feel her comforting hand in mine or listen to her sing to the radio. There are so many little things that I miss every day."

June nodded but looked away. Her hands were tight on the glass. Leah just sat, wondering what it must be like for David to see his mother this way.

"Did Samuel say anything else in the letters?" June asked, her voice still not completely recovered from her emotional moment. She obviously didn't want to go into detail about her friend.

"The most shocking thing he said was, 'Sometimes, we meet people and we know right away how perfect they are for us—Nina, you were that for me.'" Leah tipped her head up to look outside but the view wasn't registering. She had too much on her mind. "I can't believe I never heard about him," she said. "Nan never said anything about a great love affair."

June shook her head. "She never would. She probably didn't want to burden you with a sad story. That was how she was. And she wouldn't have wanted any pity." June's voice was clearer now, focused on the conversation. "What else did he say?"

"He told her that if she ever wasn't okay, she could find him."

"Do you think she left him to come here?"

"I don't know."

June's hands were folded in her lap now, and she had a faraway look on her face. "I remember my mother telling me that Nina had bought Evergreen Hill from us. I was beside myself. Mom wasn't a businesswoman at all. Nina had gotten the business running smoothly, making it more profitable than we ever imagined. She had these amazing plans to take it to the next level, but Mom just wasn't up for it. She didn't want the hassle. My mother had gotten carried away by all that money. She ran up debt that was so large she couldn't afford to pay for the house anymore, and she was tiring of the property and the business. She told me that the house needed Nina as much as

Nina needed that house, and she sold it to her. After we left, I kept in touch for a little while. Nina applied for grants to help her maintain the house, she applied to non-profits, she researched and found all kinds of ways to shave off costs. And she was great at it. Then, when she started to book weddings, hold events for businesses from as far as Washington D.C., people took notice."

Leah knew all of this, but she was glad to see June opening up, sharing some of her own history of the house. As she talked, Leah was brought right back around to thinking about regrets: the regrets she'd feel once Evergreen Hill was no longer part of her life; the regrets Nan spoke of, and Samuel Patterson.

After her conversation, Leah had gone to find David, wondering if they could look at that online list of Samuel Pattersons again.

"Thank you for letting me use your computer so we could look," Leah said, after checking. She got up. "I don't think I'm going to find him."

Leah had re-read every one of Samuel's letters and looked at all the Samuel Pattersons online, bewildered. She was no further forward in her search.

David set his book on the arm of the chair and followed her out of the room. "What are you going to ask him if you find him?"

"Why she let him go."

She kept thinking about how Samuel seemed like a perfect man. He'd said in his letters that he wanted her to move in with him, enroll her children in private schools that he'd pay for, and he'd even mentioned the word marriage. People don't just offer that unless they're in love. Niggling at the back of Leah's mind was the thought that Nan had let go of something she loved dearly. And despite all Samuel's letters, she'd been strong enough to stay away. Why?

"Should we go look in the parlor one more time?" David said. "What if she'd put the address inside something in her desk?"

"I suppose we can check," Leah said, not holding out too much hope. Nan wasn't one for shoving important things into books or drawers. But it was worth a try.

They both looked through the desk again and even some of the drawers on the bottom of one of the old bookcases, but they'd come up empty. At a loss, she looked around the great parlor, taking a moment to really see it. Beneath the period furniture was a hardwood floor in light wood that was so glossy it shone. The walls were done in thick, ornamental cream-colored woodwork that stretched over the large, rounded doorways. At both ends of the room there were windows that filled the whole wall, the light from outside pouring through them. She'd done a lot in this room: danced, thrown parties, listened to Nan read to her from the history books in the bookcase at the front of the room.

"I'm sorry we couldn't find anything," David said.

"It's okay." She tried to downplay her disappointment.

"Mama?" Sadie said, peeking around the oversized doorway. "Oh! May I play the piano?" Her hair was in a crooked ponytail and she was wearing pink, sparkly lip gloss.

"Sure."

Sadie climbed up onto the bench and lifted the lid, sliding it into its pocket. With her little fingers spread as far as they could reach, she began to play. It was a simple song, the notes tinkling into the air and echoing in the large space.

"That's very nice," David said, sitting down beside her.

"Thank you," Sadie said, not looking up. "Nan taught it to me." She missed a note and went back over the keys to replay it.

"What else did you and your nan do?" he asked, visibly curious.

"All sorts of things!" Sadie stopped playing and twisted around on the bench to face him. "She taught me how to dance in here!"

"She did?"

"Yes," Leah chimed in, the memory so vivid it made her chest ache for that day again. "Nan was the lead."

David stood up and held out his hands to Sadie. "Would you show me?"

Sadie jumped off the bench and grabbed his hands, a smile spreading across her face as she slid a little in her socks on the highly glossed floor. "I'll bet you don't know the dance like Nan did!" she said with a giggle.

"I'm not so sure about that." David twirled her outward and then spun her back in, taking her hand again.

Sadie shrieked with excitement. "Do it again!" she said.

David began to move across the floor, twirling Sadie, moving her in and out as effortlessly as the tide in the ocean. He was a natural.

"Where did you learn to dance like that?" Leah asked.

"My grandmother taught me in this very room. She also taught your nan." He twirled Sadie one more time and then let go of her hands. "Sadie, why don't you play us something on the piano and I'll dance with your mom?"

Sadie went back over to the piano and began playing a song. David took Leah's hands. He began to move across the floor, so she followed his lead, his embrace more affectionate than it had been with Sadie. The feelings that Leah had been trying to push away were coming back in full force. He dipped her, surprising her and causing her to laugh.

"What's all this laughing I hear?" June said, coming in.

Sadie stopped playing for a minute to address her. "We're dancing!"

"I can see," she returned happily, but her eyes were questioning, curious, as she looked at David and Leah.

"Keep playing, Sadie," David said, letting go of Leah. He walked over and took his mother's hands, waltzing across the shiny floor. June's lips were pursed, her eyes at the ceiling, but her attempts to be annoyed were failing because she found herself laughing along with them all. David twirled her around and caught her at the back with his arm, dipping her dramatically.

"You like that dip move, don't you?" Leah said with a grin.

"I hated learning this as a kid. Do you remember, Mom?" He pushed her outward and drew her back in, Sadie's little notes rising into the air. "But my grandmother insisted, telling me that it would wow the ladies. And now, here I am, in a room with three!" He turned June around and then back toward him.

Lydia had been correct, Leah thought. He was definitely wowing her.

"This room isn't just good for dancing," Sadie said, pulling off her socks and laying them on the piano bench. She did a front walkover, landing right in front of all of them. "When we move here, I'm going to set up gymnastics mats and practice my handsprings every single day! There's so much space!" She did a cartwheel. "I've been waiting my whole life to have space like this every day! I can't wait!"

Leah felt like she had a thousand pins sticking her skin, the anxiety over telling Sadie filling her up. She looked over at David and his expression said it all: he'd only just realized that Leah hadn't told Sadie anything yet about selling the house. He looked worried, and suddenly, she wondered if she'd waited too long to tell Sadie. Had she only made things worse? She broke eye contact with David, still unsure of when would be the right time to give her daughter the news.

Chapter Seventeen

"I'm ready!" Sadie said, holding her coat and standing at the front door. She had been up at the crack of dawn, since today was the national gymnastics meet in town. They went with Nan every year that they were in town, and this year would be no different, except for the fact that Leah had asked David and June to go. June had decided to stay at Evergreen Hill, but David was coming with them. Leah could see now why David was so against opening up the house to endless strangers. He was just thinking about what his mother needed.

Leah hurried to the door. David had started the old farm truck, having decided that the snow was still too deep for their cars, and knowing that more was supposed to fall later that day.

"Off we go!" he said, his eyebrows raised, his face showing excitement for Sadie's benefit. The old door creaked against the cold as he opened it.

"Be careful, Sadie. It's slippery." Despite her mother's warning, Sadie went bouncing down the stairs and out to the drive, and then set off in a run toward the truck as Leah watched her with trepidation. "She's so excited," she told David.

"I can tell."

They all piled into the old truck and David put it in drive. Sadie bounced along in the backseat happily. "Do you think I could ever be good enough to do a competition like this?" she asked.

"I believe you could. You have great potential," Leah said.

David put the truck in gear and started through the heavy snow that had filled the front drive. Once they got onto the main roads, they were relatively clear, a plow having finally made it down more than once, followed by a salt truck. The school was only minutes into town, and they were driving amidst the throng of other spectators.

"I'll drop you two off at the door," David said, "and then I'll find a place to park." The old truck idled as David pulled up at the curb.

Sadie had the door flung open before he'd even come to a complete stop. She grabbed Leah's arm and tugged. "We'll save you a seat, David! Hurry! Don't miss anything."

He grinned at Sadie's enthusiasm. "I'll go as quickly as I can."

Inside, the energy was electric, considering it was only ten in the morning. But it didn't matter what time of day it was—these events were always buzzing with excitement. The high school building was brand new—an enormous facility with shiny white, tiled floors, vaulted ceilings, and skylights. They passed by the cafeteria; that one room was bigger than Sadie's entire school, with two lines for food, stainless steel drink coolers, and rows upon rows of tables with the bobcat mascot printed in the center. Sadie dragged her into the ticket line; they were about ten people deep.

While Sadie held her hand and bounced beside her, the music kicked up inside the gym—a world-class high school band that marched in the Macy's Thanksgiving Day Parade every year. A thrill zinged through Leah as the drums echoed in her chest. She turned to read the flyers that were pinned to the bulletin board on the wall—

parents' coffee night with the principal, drama club try-outs, swim team meetings. The town was small, but with the wealthy families that lived in it and supported the schools from elementary to high school, the education that one could get here was among the very best—a stark contrast to the overcrowded, old school Sadie attended.

"Hi," David said over the sound of the band as he joined them in line. Sadie, who was still holding Leah's hand, grabbed David's with her other. "I had to park down the street. This is quite an event."

"It's so awesome!" Sadie said, smiling up at him.

When they got to the ticket counter, David insisted on buying their tickets, promising a disapproving Leah that she could get their drinks and snacks. But after they were seated, David excused himself and returned with two large plumes of pink-and-blue cotton candy on sticks.

"For you," he said, handing one to Sadie. Her face lit up as she grabbed it. "And for you." He handed one to Leah.

"Haha!" Sadie laughed as Leah took the stick from him. "You got one for Mama!" She threw her head back and laughed again.

"Well, I didn't want to leave her out. Plus, then you can have all yours and I can steal bites of hers."

"Thank you, David," Sadie said. She held her cotton candy out and hugged him with her free arm.

The gymnasium's glossy floor reflected the overhead lights as the area above the stadium seats became dark. A spotlight shone on the uneven bars and a wisp of a girl in a blue leotard, her hair yanked back into a bun and secured with clips on each side, dipped her hands into the bucket of chalk and clapped them together, causing a small cloud of dust to rise in the air. A hush came over the crowd when the announcer called out her home school. With a hop, the little girl swung herself onto the lower bar, her feet only inches from her hands as she circled it, gaining speed.

Leah caught a glimpse of Sadie. She was on the edge of her seat, her cotton candy barely touched as she hung on every movement that little girl on the bars made. She was in her element, and Leah thought again about the gym where Sadie took lessons. It was all Leah could afford, a small space at the back of an old warehouse. It wasn't well lit, and they had to wear coats when it wasn't their turn because it was so drafty. And the coach was nearing retirement. She didn't know what would come of the gym once the coach decided to finish working. But now, Leah could afford lessons for Sadie by a coach with a track record of success, in a gym with brand new equipment, and Sadie would have a chance to realize her potential. Maybe she could lead with that good news when she told Sadie she wasn't going to get to live at Evergreen Hill. Leah bit her lip. She knew that even news that good wouldn't overshadow the sadness Sadie would have at not living at the plantation.

Sadie didn't move the rest of the time, and two and a half hours later, she was still holding her cotton candy. David had picked on Leah's and they'd finally abandoned theirs by their feet when they'd both had enough. The lights came back on, and the crowd began to filter out. Leah scooped up what was left of their cotton candy to throw it away on the way out.

"That was so cool," Sadie said, with stars in her eyes. "When I get back, David, I'll show you what I can do. I can do a one-handed cartwheel!"

He smiled at her adoringly and Leah couldn't take her eyes off him. Leah had dated a few times in Sadie's life, the last time being a man named Rich. Sadie had fallen in love with him herself, and when things ended, she'd gotten her little heart broken. Leah had had long conversations with Nan about it, and she'd told Nan, "No more men. I don't want to ever do that to Sadie again." But both Sadie and David had that look when they were together and the chemistry was undeniable.

Making matters worse was the way he looked at Leah, and the response her body had, no matter how hard she tried to control it. They were sliding down a slippery slope and she didn't know how to slow it down. In the back of her mind, she knew one thing: Sadie was going to get her heart broken again if she didn't do something. Perhaps she should pull back. She'd meant to, but then David had put those lights in the trees outside... *Come on, Leah,* she thought. *You've got to be stronger than this.*

Chapter Eighteen

"Christmas Eve is in three days anyway," Roz said on the phone when she called to tell Leah she was on her way. Leah had texted her earlier to let her know to come after the gymnastics show. "I've called Louise and we'll come up together. If you're all right with that, Louise and Ethan are packed and ready."

Whenever Roz wanted to change Leah's mind, she always called on Louise, because Louise had that quiet determination about her. She listened so well and when she offered her opinion, it always ended up sounding like the best option. "You won't change my mind about signing the papers," she warned. In fact, Leah had already signed them. They'd come through on email just after they'd gotten home. Leah wanted to sign them quickly while Sadie was watching a movie, so she'd done it without even taking a moment to think it through one last time. She knew her answer.

"Who said anything about that?" Roz's voice came through sugary sweet. "I just thought we'd get there early to help you plan for family Christmas. Who's coming? Are Mom and Dad back from China?"

Leah smiled and shook her head. She loved how Roz called her mother and father Mom and Dad. She even did that to their faces. Louise had attended last year's family Christmas, but Roz had said she couldn't come even though Leah's entire family loved Roz and begged her to join them. Leah had tried to explain how Roz felt about Christmas, and Leah's mom had texted Roz one word: *Scrooge.* At New Year's Eve, Roz had relented. "Okay, I give in, next year I'm coming."

"Yes, everyone's coming—Mom, Dad, Uncle William, and Aunt Claire. Then, of course, you and Louise and the kids."

"I'll be there as soon as I can get us all in the car. Let me just make a quick call to Louise."

We're in town! Roz texted as Leah made it to the bottom of the stairs. She'd figured they'd be here soon so she'd gone up to her room to freshen up just a little, run a brush through her hair. *We're at that little coffee shop with the big front window and the row of little flowerpots inside it. The roads have gotten treacherous. Can you come get us?*

She stood with one foot on the last step while she finished reading.

David still hadn't returned. He'd gone into town with the farm truck to get a new router, as the Wi-Fi wasn't working up to par. Just getting the contract across this afternoon had been spotty. Leah knew her little car would never get down the long drive in all that snow.

She texted back: *David has the truck. Could you get a cup of coffee and hang out there a few minutes? I'm so sorry to make you wait.*

No problem, Roz texted back. *There's a big case of donuts. We'll get the kids all hyped up on sugar and then let them run all over that big house.*

Leah laughed and, just then, saw Sadie running past her into the living room. "Guess what," she said to Sadie, stopping her.

She screeched to a halt to hear what Leah had to say. Leah hadn't wanted to tell her until she was sure that Roz was actually there, so as not to get her too excited.

"Roz and Jo are in town. So are Louise and Ethan. We're going to get them as soon as David comes back with the truck."

Sadie pumped her arms and hopped around just as June came down the steps. "Oh, I can't wait!" Sadie said, her elation clear. "I'm going to get my stuff ready for Jo and Ethan!" she called on her way upstairs, her little feet pounding all the way up.

June watched Sadie as she ran away, her gaze lingering on the now-empty staircase. "What has her so excited?" she asked, finally turning away and entering the sitting room with Leah. They sat down on the settee and June clicked on the silver floor lamp with the beaded shade to allow a little more light into the room. The clouds had rolled in again, making the room dark. "She went up the steps like a flash."

"My friends Roz and Louise are coming to visit with their kids. They're waiting for me at the coffee shop. I'll go get them once David comes back. They're great friends. I think Sadie's missed them."

"Oh, that will be nice," she said. "Why don't you just text David and ask him to pick them up?"

It would make things easier if David did just get them. He was already in town. June gave Leah his cell number, and as she texted, she prayed that Roz wouldn't say anything regarding the house on the way over.

Her phone lit up with a text from David. He'd get them in two minutes. Then Leah texted Roz to let her know they'd all be squeezing into the farm truck. There was only one road between the coffee shop and the plantation, but it was hilly and narrow. She told Roz to belt the kids in the small seats behind the front bench of the truck so they'd all be secure. Then she impressed upon Roz to be on her best behavior with David and not to say a word about the house.

Roz texted back: *Zipping lips... For now.*

Leah got up to straighten a few things and turn on all the Christmas lights before her friends' arrival. June helped her. Leah noticed her quick movements. She wondered if having a bunch of people in the house worried her, if she was jumping around because she was nervous, but it didn't seem like that to her. June had seemed more relaxed and easy lately, and Leah even caught a few smiles. If anyone could make her feel comfortable, it would be Roz and Louise. In their own unique ways, they were the easiest people in the world to get to know. They finished tidying the kitchen and settled in for a cup of hot chocolate.

"I remember when David was Sadie's age and he'd be just like that." She pointed with her chin at Sadie, who had run back downstairs to wait at the window since the text. It was the first time she'd spoken without Leah starting the conversation. "He loved it here, but there were times when he got a bit lonely, and whenever we had friends around, you'd think he'd won the lottery."

"I see them, Mama!" said Sadie, leaning on the large windowsill. "They're coming up the drive now!"

"Would you excuse me for just a second?" Leah said. She went to the window where Sadie was jumping up and down, her fingers still wrapped around the oversized windowsill.

David got out of the truck with a shopping bag and walked around to let everyone out. Roz had on her burgundy coat, the color like spilled wine against the white of outside. Jo climbed out. Her usually messy red curls were pinned back today, and Leah smiled at that. Louise scooted to the edge of the bench, her legs gracefully swinging off the side before she did a little hop onto the snow. She reached in and helped Ethan, offering him a hand.

Before shutting the truck's door, David pulled out another large shopping bag and two small suitcases. He shut the door and led them up the walkway.

Sadie had already left her spot at the window and was sliding across the hardwoods in her socks as she ran to the door. She swung it open and waved wildly at her friends. Leah joined her daughter, the air so cold she could almost smell it.

"Hey, girls!" Roz called, her eyes bouncing from Leah and Sadie to the icy walkway.

Louise waved as she steadied Ethan, his little feet struggling to balance on the ice.

"I like your boots," Leah said to Jo when they reached the door. "Are they new?"

"My nannie got them for me." Nannie was the name she used for Roz's mother, who was a whole lot like Roz. She lived out of state but would visit occasionally and Roz would invite everyone over for a party whenever she did.

"They're pretty." Leah moved out of the way so they could enter.

"They arrived yesterday—perfect timing!" Roz said, her eyes wide with curiosity as she took in the entryway—the antique round table at the front, the delicate chandelier above them, the grainy historical photos and paintings all mounted in original frames against the pale blue walls. "Leah, this is so you!" she said, her head turning in all directions. She peered up at the ceiling. "Oh my gosh! I'll bet this is heaven for you!" Then, she leaned in, her eyes darting around again before focusing on Leah. "David's a tall drink of water…" she whispered under her breath.

Leah gave her a look of warning.

"I flirted with him on the way here."

She shot her another look, this time pressing her eyes open to make her stop.

"Don't worry. I'll let you have him," she teased. Louise nudged her, but both Leah and Louise knew that Roz had a mind of her own, and she'd only quiet down to appease them.

Leah batted away the comment, glad to have her friends there. She wondered what David thought of Roz, but when she looked over at him, he didn't seem affected. He asked The Girls if he could take their coats; he was already holding Jo's. She and Sadie skipped arm in arm down the hallway, Jo pulling a very happy Ethan with her other hand.

Roz shrugged her coat off and thanked David as she handed it to him. He hung it in the hall closet and set her suitcase beside the staircase. Louise followed her lead.

"This is for you!" Roz said, holding out the shopping bag.

Before Leah could look inside, she blurted, "It's a candle. They had a sale, so I bought three—one for each of us." It was just like Roz to give away the surprise. "It isn't your Christmas present, just something nice. Maybe you could use it here!" she said suggestively.

"Thank you," Leah said, unable to hide her grin. Even when Roz was being annoying, Leah just loved her.

"There's also a bottle of wine—the fizzy kind. I figured we could get started on that early."

"Great," Leah said, leading her friends into the kitchen. "David, join us," she said over her shoulder.

She set the bag down at the table as June came in.

"Hello," June said. She held out her hand, her oversized sweater sleeve reaching her knuckles. "You must be Roz. I'm David's mother, June."

"Nice to meet you." Roz squared her shoulders and shook her hand, offering a polite smile. She was certainly putting her best foot forward.

"It's positively freezing. I've gotten the fire going pretty well now, and it's nice and toasty in the sitting room. Come in when you get settled."

"That sounds wonderful," Roz said.

June left them, returning to the sitting room just as David came in and took a seat at the table. "You aren't that scary at all," Roz said, plopping down next to him and bumping him with her shoulder. He looked at her. "I thought you'd be scarier. I'm not sure why." He shook his head just slightly, but Leah noticed a very slight grin on his lips. He seemed to like Roz.

"Would you two like some hot chocolate?"

Louise nodded, lowering herself down into one of the kitchen chairs.

"I have candy canes for stirring in my bag," Roz said.

"We've got some," Leah said with a grin, knowing her friend always stirred her hot chocolate with a peppermint swizzle stick.

Once everyone had their hot chocolates, Leah pulled Roz's candle from the shopping bag and lit it, setting it in the center of the island. It wasn't burning for long before it sent the sweet smell of pumpkin pie sailing across the kitchen. David had stayed for a bit of small talk before excusing himself to get some work done.

Leah sat down at the table. The house was clean and draped in greenery, all Sadie's presents were wrapped—she'd done them early that morning—and the trees were lit in twinkle lights. The house was just as it had always been when Nan had decorated it. She'd taken a few photos of it all for her book.

"I have a great present for you this year," Roz said, her eyebrows bouncing up and down.

"Why am I a little apprehensive?" Every year The Girls exchanged Christmas gifts and Roz managed to outdo everyone with the most ridiculous gifts.

"I toned it down this year. I went the sentimental route."

"You?"

Louise laughed.

"I took a risk. I can't help it. I love ya."

"While we're on the subject of risks," Louise said, looking back and forth between Roz and Leah dramatically, "I asked Bret from the office if he'd like to have dinner."

"Oh, I'm so excited for you!" Leah said, clasping her hands together.

Roz nodded enthusiastically.

"What did he say?"

"He said if I hadn't talked to him by Christmas, he was going to ask *me* out." She offered a shy smile.

"That's awesome," Roz said. "But don't go getting married. Once Leah leaves to live here, I'll be on my own."

Leah wasn't going to get into her decision to sell Evergreen Hill. The afternoon was going too well.

Chapter Nineteen

Sadie, Jo, and Ethan were in the kitchen, doing a puzzle on the floor that Louise had brought for them. They'd insisted on doing it themselves, promising a big surprise for everyone when they'd finished it all. Sadie had tried to hide the box so Leah couldn't see what they were making, but she'd seen it already when Louise brought it—it was of all Santa's reindeer, with a Christmas candy border. The kids had allowed June in to finish making herself another mug of hot chocolate. As Leah had left her in the kitchen with the kids, she'd noticed how their laughter had seemed to brighten her spirits a little bit. One time June had even laughed too, the smile remaining in her eyes as she wiped down the counters.

Leah had just come back downstairs after showing Roz and Louise their rooms so they could get unpacked. Louise had brought her a book she'd finished and was raving about, telling her she'd never guess the ending and she needed to start right away. While The Girls were unpacking, Leah settled in one of the side chairs that were angled around a small antique end table to the left of the settee and started reading it. She was glad that Louise had thought to bring it, because she always read a book at Christmas and this year, with everything going on, she'd forgotten to pack one.

David walked in, smiling at her. Her ankle almost normal now, she'd been able to curl her legs under her and cover them completely with the quilt, although the fire was doing its job, warming the room. "You look very comfortable," he said, sitting down on the settee and opening his laptop. "I still have work to do, but I thought I'd be social and do it down here."

She grinned, glad to have him downstairs.

"I like your friends," he said, amusement bubbling up, and she knew his laughter had to be over Roz. She didn't even want to think about what her friend might have said on the ride here—although Louise had been beside her, thank God.

They'd settled in to a little moment of quiet when the doorbell rang.

David looked up and the two of them made eye contact. It wasn't usual to have visitors when the house sat two miles off the main road. Her family wasn't expected until tomorrow, but maybe someone had arrived early. June came into the doorway holding her mug.

David got up and went to see who it was. Leah tried to make out the conversation he was having, but they were too far away. She could hear another man's voice, and then the door shut. When David walked back into the room, he was with an elderly gentleman. The man had a head of gray hair, receding just above the temples, and an honest-looking face. But David's expression was unreadable. Leah asked him with her eyes to tell her what was going on.

"This," David said slowly, "is Samuel. Samuel Patterson."

Leah had to force herself to say something, to push through the millions of questions that were filling her mind. "Hello, Mr. Patterson," she said, standing up, curiosity whirling around inside her at warp speed. This was the man who'd received Nan's letter, the man her grandmother had been unwilling to explain to anyone, the man who might have brought her so many regrets.

"Please," he said, with a smile and a nod, "call me Samuel."

"Okay, Samuel," she said. "It's nice to meet you."

"Please come in and have a seat," David said.

Samuel walked into the room, unwound his scarf, and wiggled out of his coat sleeves, draping his coat over his arm.

"This is my mother, June," David said, as he took the coat and scarf from Samuel and draped it on the settee. June nodded hello and took a seat in the rocker they'd moved to allow room for the Christmas tree.

Samuel sat down in the antique chair that Nan had always used. It was positioned in the direction of the fire. He put his hands on his knees. "This is Nina's home?" he asked, looking around. He'd said it more to himself than to them. With a look of amazement on his face, he put his weathered fingers over his mouth and shook his head. What was he thinking about? Leah swore she saw tears in his eyes, but he straightened up and cleared his throat.

"I'm assuming you received Nina's letter," David said. He looked just as inquisitive as Leah felt, but she hadn't found her voice yet. Maybe Samuel could provide some answers for her, and, from the look on his face as he struggled to hide his emotions, she was hopeful.

"Yes," he said, clearly climbing out of his thoughts. "I was so surprised to get it. It made me the happiest man in the world."

What did it say? Leah wanted to yell out, but she kept quiet. The letter wasn't for her, and if Samuel wanted to share it, that was up to him.

"She enclosed a letter for someone named Leah and told me to come to the address on the letter."

"I'm Leah Evans," she finally said, realizing she hadn't even introduced herself. "I'm her granddaughter."

Samuel's face lit up with that news, and he looked at her as if he'd only just now seen her—he was searching her face for something. Finally, he said, "You have her cheekbones and her eyes."

He was right. Both she and her mother had gotten those traits from Nan.

"Did you know her well?" David asked, as Leah took in this man she'd never seen before.

He smiled at whatever the memory was he had of her and then, with a dignified sniffle, he said simply, "I did." That smile remained there on his face. "I was glad she asked me to come. I live alone, and I've been struggling with that somewhat. Her letter came just when I needed it."

"Hello," Sadie said, coming into the room

"Where are Ethan and Jo?" Leah asked.

"They're still doing the puzzle. We're almost done! I heard the doorbell and thought it was Gran and Gramps."

Samuel's eyes were moving from Leah to Sadie and it was clear that he'd found the resemblance. "And what's your name?" Samuel asked, a gentle smile on his face as he said it.

"Sadie."

"Sadie?" His face dropped as if she'd said something wrong, something that took him back in time. He recovered and smiled, but as he studied her, she could see a look of awe come over him. Then, he turned to Leah. "She's your daughter?"

"Yes." Suddenly, she wondered about Sadie's name. When she was pregnant, and she'd found out it was a girl, she'd gone straight to Nan. Nan had a pink cake waiting for her when she arrived, and even

though Leah was single, struggling to handle an unplanned pregnan-
cy, Nan had turned it into a celebration.

"What will you name this little princess?" Nan had asked.

"I have no idea," she'd said, honestly. She was still so bewildered
by everything. She hadn't thought anything through yet. "Help me
think of a name," she said.

Now, reflecting on it, Nan had been emotional at that moment,
and Leah had just thought that she was excited about having a great-
grandchild. When she'd told the story later, Leah had always said how
funny it was that the first name Nan had said was The Name.

With tears in her eyes, Nan had looked up at Leah and said, "I
have the perfect name. You should call her Sadie Marie."

Marie was Nan's middle name and Leah's mother's name, and she
loved the idea of Sadie. Leah had thrown her arms around Nan's neck
and they'd cried together, with relief, Leah had thought, that things
were going to be okay. But now she wondered, after seeing Samuel's
face, if Nan had been crying over something else.

Clearly still trying to get himself together, Samuel patted his pocket and said, "Her letter suggested I come this weekend, telling me
that there was someone I should meet. Originally, I'd thought about
ignoring it because it wouldn't bring Nina back, but if she wanted me
to meet you, then I supposed I should. And now I see."

"I'll get us all some wine," David said, standing up. June followed
him into the kitchen, clearly giving Leah some time to talk to this
man that Nan had known so well. Sadie had gone back into the
kitchen to do her puzzle, the conversation obviously not keeping her
attention.

"Is there some connection between you and the name Sadie?" She
had to know.

Immediately, his breathing became slow and steady, as if he were working to make it so. But he didn't say anything.

"It's my daughter's name," pressed Leah. "I'd like to know if there was some sort of family connection."

He shook his head, almost as if he were telling himself that he couldn't say it out loud.

"I've read your letters," she admitted. "Please, tell me."

He looked up. "She kept them?" But he didn't say anything more, as though he couldn't verbalize the enormity of his thoughts. By his reaction, there was a connection, and he was having some kind of inner struggle about telling her. Perhaps she shouldn't have asked.

Finally, he spoke. "That was the name that Nina and I had picked out for our daughter."

Leah stared at him, the words hitting her like a wrecking ball. She realized after a second that she needed to breathe. "You had a daughter? Where is she?"

Samuel clenched his jaw tightly, clearly trying to push back the emotion. "For about three months we had a daughter growing in Nina's belly. Well, she thought it was a daughter. Nina had said she knew by the way she felt, but I never asked her to tell me what she meant. We lost her."

"Oh my God," Leah said, clapping her hand over her mouth. "Why didn't she ever tell me this?"

Still clearly deep in his memories, Samuel's eyes were on the floor, as if searching for something, but she knew he was probably processing as much as she was at that moment. "Your grandmother dealt with a lot in her time. But she was proud, and she never let on that there were any breaks in her perfect life. She was a strong woman."

"I know she worked with you at a college," Leah said.

"Ah," Samuel said, throwing his head back, a melancholy smile on his face. "That was the beginning of everything."

"Would you tell me your story?" she asked boldly. If Nan hadn't been able to share it with her, then perhaps Samuel could.

"Maybe you could come visit me one day and I'll tell me everything. It would be nice to have somebody else in the house. I don't want to take too much of your time. I should probably be heading on."

"Why don't you stay this evening? There's plenty of room here if you need to stay."

"Oh, I wouldn't want to impose. I was just following Nina's letter."

"Well, if she sent you that letter, then I'll bet she wanted you here, and she'd be quite upset with me for not offering."

He smiled at that. "Yes, she probably would," he said with a chuckle. "I don't know…"

"It's snowing again, for goodness' sake." She pointed to the flurries out the window. "Once the sun dips down, it'll all be ice. It's probably already dangerous out there. I won't take no for an answer."

"Well, if it isn't any trouble. I was going to get a hotel room in town."

"Nonsense," she said with a smile.

"She wanted me to give you this." Samuel stood up, put his hand into his pocket and drew out an envelope. Leah immediately recognized the handwriting as Nan's, and her name was on the outside. "She said you can't open it until family Christmas."

Chapter Twenty

"It'll be Samuel and Mom," David said, "Roz and Louise, and I'll be with Leah. Leah's made the punch, but we also have beer. Who's up for a drink?"

"I put together a veggie tray too," Leah said, getting excited. "I'll get it out and bring in the game. I hope it's still in the hall closet."

When Samuel arrived, it felt like Nan was right there, introducing everyone, and this unlikely group of people, from all over the place, had settled in like old friends. It had gotten late, the kids tucked in for sleep, and the snow coming down in the darkness outside. The candles were lit, the fire going, and the Christmas lights shimmering everywhere.

They all piled into the sitting room and Leah, glad to have found the game, brought it in, David helping with the veggie tray. They set it all on the coffee table in front of the settee.

Once they were settled, Roz said, "I think we should let Leah and David go first." She had a flirty look in her eyes, and a smile behind her bottle of beer as she put it to her lips, and Leah knew she was trying to play matchmaker again.

Leah took a giant swig of her own beer and then drew a card.

"Okay, David. Ready?" She turned over the sand timer and read the card to herself: *Flying around the world.*

"I'll hold the card," said Roz. "I want to see what it is."

Leah handed Roz the card and began making airplane arms, tipping back and forth to simulate flying while Roz showed Louise the phrase and then handed it to Samuel.

"Fly," David said, his brows puckering in an adorable way.

Leah nodded. "Does that count?" she asked Samuel.

"Yes. The word is 'flying,' David," Samuel confirmed.

Leah drew a circle in the air with her pointer finger.

"Propeller," David said.

She balled her fingers and used her other hand to orbit her fist.

"Flying…" David said while he thought it through, but he seemed distracted as he looked at her, as if he were thinking about something else.

"Time!" Samuel said, pulling her out of her thoughts. "It was 'Flying around the world.'"

Roz stood up and grabbed a card, and just like that, David turned his attention away, leaving Leah wondering what he'd been thinking.

"Easy!" Roz said, handing it to June to moderate. "Okay, Louise. You've got this." She turned over the timer. With her fingers, she drew an hourglass shape and then gestured drinking.

"Wine."

"Yes!" She held out her hand and pretended it was a plate, picking up little invisible pieces of something and putting them in her mouth.

"Wine… Wine with… Wine and… Cheese? Wine and cheese?"

Roz did a fist pump in the air. "You got it! High five!" She smacked Louise's hand and sat down beside her, grinning from ear to ear.

David pulled the next card and handed it to Samuel, who thought for a moment and then turned over the timer. "Ready, June?"

She smiled and nodded.

They continued on, the game tied three ways, and the longer they played, the more Leah second-guessed her choice. They were all there, together, just like Nan would've wanted. It was wonderful, but Leah felt as lost as ever. She knew in her heart that Nan, always the lover of family, wouldn't have understood how Leah giving David half the house would ever lead to a life of no regrets. Right now, in this place, with these people—*this* was how it should be, and it was about to end. Leah sighed and regrouped. Her family was arriving soon, and she needed to focus on making this the best Christmas she could.

Chapter Twenty-One

David had been up early again. He was dressed in a sweater and jeans, showered, and now in the chair, reading by the fire in the sitting room as if he'd been there all along, but Leah had heard the front door opening and shutting at an early hour, and his nose was still red.

"Good morning," she said, trying to hide her curiosity.

"Good morning. Is anyone else up yet?" He grinned at her as if he were holding in a secret, following her with his eyes as she moved across the room.

"Louise and Roz are up, and the kids. They're all bustling around upstairs." She sat down in the chair beside him. Did she smell sausage?

"I made a quick casserole since we have so many people. It's eggs, sausage, cheese, and pastry. It should be done in just a few minutes."

"That sounds great," she said, eyeing him. Finally, unable to take the suspense any longer, she said, "What were you up to this morning?"

He offered a crooked grin. "I have something planned for us."

She sat up straighter in her chair. "Really? What is it?"

"I'll tell you when everyone gets downstairs."

* * *

They'd had an informal breakfast, each person grabbing a bite to eat whenever it was a good time, and they'd relaxed the whole morning. The kids had played upstairs and the adults had alternated between Christmas TV programs and small talk.

David had told them all they'd be leaving around twelve forty-five, and they'd all been waiting for this surprise of his. Once they'd had a light lunch and were all gathered in the sitting room, standing around, waiting to see what David had planned, he came in, handing out coats.

"Grab your hats, gloves, and boots! We're taking the farm truck across the property to the main road where I've rented a shuttle to pick us up."

"We can't all fit in the farm truck," Leah worried aloud. The large bench seat only held four adults and then there were two smaller seats behind.

"Don't worry," he said. "I've thought of that."

Sadie and Jo were looking at each other, shrugging their shoulders, while Roz offered a glance to Leah, her eyebrows raised, a smile on her face. Louise had her long coat on, her hands in the pockets, her attention on David, and Ethan at her side. Leah turned to June and Samuel for any further explanation but June raised her shoulders as if to say, "I have no idea."

David led the group to the front door and opened it. Leah, who had been walking beside him, was the first to peer out. She couldn't wipe the smile off her face. The back of the farm truck was full of rectangular hay bales to make seats. There was a speaker in the back, next to the cab of the truck, playing Christmas carols. Both sides of the vehicle were draped in fresh greenery and tied with large red bows at either end. He'd even put a wreath on the grill at the front and a small stepladder against the tailgate.

"What is this?" she asked, turning to him, still unable to stop smiling.

"They're having carolers in town. I figured we could all take a walk and watch them, maybe stop in the coffee shop to warm up."

"Somebody's a keeeeeper," she heard Roz say quietly under her breath behind them. Discreetly, Leah batted her away with her hand by her side. She heard Louise giggle.

"The kids can sit up front with me, and I'll drive very slowly down the drive so it won't get too cold," he said to the group. "The shuttle should pick us up right at the main road."

"This sounds lovely," June said, giving David a kiss on the cheek. He smiled at her.

"Okay! Everybody in! Kids, would you like to take turns driving?" David asked. The three children cheered. "I'll take that as a yes," he said with a laugh, shutting the front door after everyone had come out.

They all piled in, but before Leah got up into the back, she pulled out her phone and snapped a photo for the book David had bought her. David set the stepladder behind the front bench and got into the driver's seat. He pulled out very slowly, the tires making shushing sounds in the snow. They bumped along down the tree-lined path to the main road, the Christmas music playing happily, and the group chattering. But Leah was quiet as she watched Sadie take her turn driving the truck through the back window of the cab. While David sat in the driver's seat, Ethan had climbed off his lap and Sadie had climbed into position. David put his hands by his sides, hitting the gas with his foot while Sadie held the wheel with both of her little hands. She kept looking back at him and laughing.

When they arrived at the end of the drive, a small shuttle, white with rental options and a phone number painted in orange on its side, was waiting to pick them up. The driver opened the door and waved as David helped Samuel out of the farm truck, down the step-ladder, and onto the ground. They all filed in to the shuttle and the warmth felt like fire against her face.

Leah sat down in the bucket seat beside David; the others had paired up on their own, and the three kids were all sharing a small bench at the back, giggling. With a quick look in the rearview mirror at everyone, the driver shut the door and pulled onto the road.

"When did you plan this?" she asked. June, who was sitting across the aisle from them, was looking on, grinning at her son.

"Last night, after we all went up to bed, I checked to see if there were any events in town—you know, just something small. I found the carolers' performance. I thought it might be fun so I booked the shuttle online. There's the park in town too—they've filled it with lights and we can walk through it. I'll bet with the cloud cover and all the trees, the lights will still be quite beautiful in daytime."

Leah nodded, the excitement of it all settling in her chest. She glanced over at June, but she was still looking at David, her face gentle, as if something had just occurred to her. She caught Leah's look and offered a warm smile, her gaze darting back and forth between Leah and David.

The driver pulled over in front of the town hall, one of the prettiest buildings on Main Street, and let everyone off. The building was white, with four columns stretching two stories high, and an enormous lantern-style light hanging by large chains to illuminate the platform in front of the double front doors. A group of about twenty people were assembled on the platform. They were wearing black trousers and red sweaters, some of them with Santa hats on. They stood in perfect rows on risers up there, the white, marble steps of the town hall cascading down to the sidewalk in front of them.

The people on the ends of the group began to ring hand bells and passers-by started to take notice, stopping to see what was going on. Leah snapped a picture and slid her phone into her coat pocket. The group started to sing "Carol of the Bells" and their voices echoing off the surroundings and sailing into the street sounded like angels, making Leah's arms prickle with emotion. She rubbed them to diffuse the sensation, but it only got worse when David, standing behind her, put his hands on her arms and rubbed them for her.

She looked over at Sadie, who was transfixed on the group, her breath billowing out in front of her and her cheeks pink as she tipped her head up to watch. Jo and Ethan were doing the same thing right beside her.

She took a minute to look at Roz and Louise; they were alternating between quiet conversations and watching the carolers, and she wondered what they were talking about. June was smiling as she watched, tapping her foot. And Samuel was blowing into his hands and rubbing them together, but he looked content. She didn't know what came over her, but she reached back and found David's hands and held them, their fingers intertwining. It was almost as if she needed to hold on to someone, the perfection of the moment hitting her. She felt the caress of his thumb and she had to remind herself to breathe.

After a few more songs, the kids were starting to get antsy, so David suggested they take a walk to the coffee shop. Ethan hung back and walked with Louise but June had taken Sadie and Jo by the hand and the three of them were walking together, Sadie talking to June, laughing at something June had said.

When they got to the coffee shop, David let everyone in. With all nine of them, they nearly filled the small dining area.

"I think the kids should have their choice—anything they want. On me." He winked at Leah.

Louise tried to offer to pay him, but David refused, telling her this was all his planning, and it was on him. It would be his Christmas gift to the group.

June took charge of the kids, leaning down to peer into the glass cases of pastries with them, pointing to various cakes and cookies.

"They won't be hungry for dinner," Leah said with a grin, standing up beside him to view the coffee menu.

"Ah, that's okay," David told her. "You only live once, right?"

She smiled, nodding, but his comment pulled her back to the drag of her pen as she looped the s on Evans, her signature complete on the sale documents for Evergreen Hill.

The kids had all eaten cookies, and they were ready to go again in mere minutes, it seemed. June was happily chatting with David, and had taken it upon herself to look after the kids most of the time, keeping them together on their walk to the park to see the lights. The adults carried their coffees with them, Roz linking arms with Leah as they made their way down the street.

They walked along the sidewalk until they reached the arching brick entrance for the park. The trees in this park had been here for over a hundred years, their bulky trunks wrapped heavily with white lights that followed the branches all the way to the top.

Sadie tilted her head back, following the branch line up to the sky. "How did they get the lights up that high?"

"Maybe Santa helped," June said, and Ethan's eyes got big. He looked at the tree again, and Leah caught June smiling at him.

"Look at that!" Jo said, pulling Sadie and Ethan into the park.

Roz dropped Leah's arm and went to show Jo a turtle sculpture that had been outlined in lights. The whole clearing was full of white wicker deer and other animals, their entire surfaces glowing. The ground, the benches, the decks around the ponds—it was all just covered in lights. Christmas music played over speakers, and there were little stands set up for onlookers to get hot chocolate and snacks. The town had lined all the historical stopping points in the park with rocking chairs, each one with a red bow, a park attendant wiping the snow from the seats.

"Pretty, isn't it?" David said, coming up behind Leah.

"It's gorgeous." He was smiling, looking around, and she had to pull her eyes away from him. She focused on Samuel, who seemed to be having a great time, laughing with Louise. He'd said he'd been struggling living alone, she remembered. Leah was so glad he was here to share this with them.

Leah and David walked together quietly, just enjoying the scenery. The kids were entertained, and the coffee warmed Leah's hands. She couldn't remember a Christmas as full as this one, and her family hadn't even gotten here yet! She felt for a moment like Nan had had a hand in it.

After they'd seen every inch of the park, David suggested they should probably get back to catch the shuttle. As they walked, Roz inconspicuously pulled Leah with her, falling behind the others.

"Tell me quickly," she whispered to Leah once Louise was also in earshot. "What's going on with you and David?"

"Nothing," Leah said, already feeling the heat in her face. What had made her so defensive was that this time, Roz's face was serious.

"I saw you two when we were watching the carolers. That's not 'nothing.'"

"We have a history together..."

"I know," Roz said. There wasn't a hint of sarcasm in her voice. In fact, it was almost sympathetic. "I just don't want you and Sadie to get your hearts broken. You've been down that road. I know I tease you that David's a great guy, but how's this all going to end? I'm worried. He's bought your house. There's no going back now."

Louise was going to say something but stopped, nodding toward Sadie. She was looking at them, her little lips set in a straight line as she clearly tried to make sense of what Roz had said.

"What's going on, Mama?" she asked.

Leah eyed the group, but no one else seemed to have heard anything, all of them still walking and chatting on their way to the shuttle.

"Let's talk about it when we get back to Nan's, okay?" she said, as gently as she could.

Chapter Twenty-Two

After they'd all gotten settled and had had dinner, Leah pulled Sadie aside. She just couldn't keep her in the dark any longer. She might as well just break the news to her. She took Sadie's hand and walked with her into the kitchen. "Sadie, I need to tell you something." She squatted down in front of her and took in a breath to steady herself. "We aren't going to live here."

David came into the kitchen and Leah saw him stop in the doorway, but she wasn't taking her attention off of Sadie. She didn't want anything breaking her complete focus on her daughter. This was big news.

"What?" she asked innocently, her head turned to the side.

"David's going to live here. After Christmas, we're going back to Richmond."

"Will we come back?" Her eyes began to move around Leah's face, all those big thoughts now going through her head.

Leah shook her head slowly, every movement registering the answer in Sadie's mind, the disappointment and loss flooding her face. "Probably not."

"Ever?"

"I'm sorry, Sadie. It just wasn't meant for us to have it."

Tears brimmed in her eyes. "I miss Nan," she said quietly. "I don't want to leave here. I'll miss this too, and it makes my heart hurt." A tear escaped down her cheek.

"I know," Leah said, the finality of her signature on that document making her feel heavier with every breath. "My heart hurts too."

"But Nan said…" Sadie started to cry, her breath catching with her emotion.

"I know what Nan said, but she changed her mind and decided that David should have this house too. And we can't both have it." She knew David was still there, probably waiting to say something, but she couldn't look at him.

Sadie started to sob, her chest now heaving. She'd really struggled with Nan's death and now this was being taken from her too. Leah's heart was breaking all over again. She tried to say something more, but she had no words. She knew there was nothing she could say to make this any better. Sadie took off down the hallway, squeezing past David. Leah let her go. When Sadie was upset, it was best to give her a little time, even though she felt like her heart was being ripped right out of her chest.

Leah stood, facing David. He opened his mouth to say something, but she gently put up her hand to stop him. Her head was too clouded with grief to hear what he had to say. The sadness in his eyes only made her feel worse. She walked past him and went upstairs to Nan's room for a moment to get herself together. She just couldn't face him right now.

She went into Nan's room and shut the door, feeling so lost. Nan would never have meant for Leah and Sadie to have the house taken from them, right? Clearly, Nan had been affected by David's story, but in this scenario, Sadie's fate was now just like David's had been. Nan would never do that to Sadie.

There was a knock at the door and it opened, Roz walking in. "You okay?" she asked, sitting down on the bed.

Leah rolled over to face her. "I shouldn't have told her before Christmas."

"Don't beat yourself up. It's a tough thing all the way around. There isn't a right way to do it."

"I've broken her heart and there's no way I can make this better."

There was another knock on the door, and David came in, but as he saw Roz, he backed out. "Oh, sorry." His gaze fluttered over to Leah.

"Come in," Roz said, even though Leah didn't really want to see him.

"I can come back." His jaw was set, his eyes showing his concern.

"Nope. I can." Roz stood up and walked out of the door. "I'll be down the hall when you need me," she said from behind him. Then she left and shut the door.

"I can't talk," she said before he could speak. She noticed how exhausted her voice sounded, and she realized then how it was all taking a toll on her. She closed her eyes as he sat down on the bed beside her.

"I feel terrible," he said.

She turned away from him, her heart ready to explode from the sadness. She felt his hand on her back but didn't respond to it. He sat there for a while, and she wanted to say something to him but just couldn't. Finally, he said quietly, "I'm sorry," and got up. She heard the door shut and she was alone again.

After lying there for quite a while, Leah realized that isolating herself wouldn't change anything. She needed to be there for Roz and Louise, and she should help with the kids. With a deep breath, she sat up and rolled her head on her shoulders to relieve the pinch. Then she got out of bed and went to find Roz and Louise.

As she got to the top of the stairs, she heard the kids' voices down the hall, and was glad to hear laughing. Perhaps having her friends here would help Sadie to cope a little better. She hoped they'd take her mind off losing the house.

Louise was in the sitting room, reading, and Leah joined her. She kept getting up to make drinks and stoke the fire because she just couldn't concentrate. After a while Louise came over and curled up next to Leah like they always did when they'd comforted each other over the years. At first Leah was grateful, but as she sat there she realized Louise's act of kindness was only going to make her cry. She decided to peek in on the kids. If Sadie was managing to smile, it would lift her own spirits. She went up to her room to find a warmer sweater and sat for a moment on the bed, wishing things could be different. She was full to the brim with regret. She went to find the kids. They were gathered in Roz's room, so she quietly pushed open the door.

Ethan was on the floor with his Legos, and Jo was making a house for her doll on the bed. She'd used pillows to section off various "rooms" with the baby on one of the pillows at the very end. Leah surveyed the room from the reflection in the windows. It was black as night outside already, so, with the lamplight, they reflected like mirrors. She didn't see Sadie. She peeked in further, looking toward the closet. It was open and she didn't see her so she waited a moment to see if the kids addressed her. When they didn't, she pushed the door open and went into the room.

"Where's Sadie?" she asked.

They both looked at her.

"I don't know," Ethan said.

"She's probably gone downstairs with Roz and your mom," Leah said, smiling at them; she enjoyed having them here. "Come down if you get hungry. We'll have snacks."

"Okay," they both said.

Leah headed down toward the kitchen, hearing June, Samuel, Roz, and Louise's voices as they each gave their opinions about the benefits of real Christmas trees versus artificial. She came in and sat down at the table with them, noticing Sadie's absence.

"Where's Sadie?" she finally asked when the conversation had hit a comfortable pause. "Have you all seen her?"

"I thought she was upstairs," Roz said.

Leah thought about her daughter sitting somewhere in the house crying, and she wanted to find her and comfort her. "Let's see if we can find her," she said, looking directly at Louise, knowing she'd read her expression instantly. Samuel had stood up already, clearly wanting to look for her, worry on his face.

"I'll check the front rooms," Louise said. "Roz, check the parlor."

Leah stood up. "I'll do a sweep of the upstairs. She might be in Nan's sewing room, sewing a quilt. She likes to do that."

"I'll ask David if he's seen her," June said.

"I used to hide in the closet when I was a kid. I'll start checking them all," Samuel offered.

They all got up and went in different directions. Leah took the stairs as quickly as she could and went into the sewing room. "Sadie?" she called. It was dark, so she clicked on the light. "Sadie?" she said again. Nothing. She went in and looked under the sewing table, but there was nothing there. With nowhere else for Sadie to hide, she turned off the light and left the room. She went to Sadie's room and checked in there. No one. She looked under the bed, in the closet like

Samuel had suggested—nothing. She checked all the rooms upstairs, looking in all the spots that a little girl might go to be alone, but she'd come up empty, so she went downstairs to see if Roz had found her.

David joined them as they stood in the sitting room. "Any luck?" she asked. They all shook their heads, looking back and forth between each other.

"I'll go ask the kids if she said she was going anywhere or anything," Roz said. "It's snowing again and dark now. She wouldn't have gone outside, would she?"

Fear building in the pit of her stomach, Leah went to the coat rack and, to her complete panic, saw Sadie's coat and boots were gone. "Oh my God," she said. "Where has she gone?" She looked to Roz for help but she knew that her friend had no answers.

"We'll split up," David said. He was already putting on his boots, the door open before he'd even gotten his coat on. "I'll take the back yard," he said over his shoulder. "You all take the sides and front." David flew out of the door, the wind picking up and pushing it open wider. Leah shut it behind him, worry spiking her veins.

"Louise, can you stay with the kids inside?" Leah asked, her voice manic.

Louise nodded, starting up the stairs.

Leah grabbed Nan's flashlight from the closet and handed it to Roz. "Here," she said, "I know the land inside and out. I'll be fine in the dark. You take this. Check the sides of the house. I'll go out front and down the drive through the trees."

The front door swung open as Leah ran through it. She could hear the angry, icy lapping of the river, and she tried not to let herself completely freak out at the thought that the land literally dropped off into it, and it was dark enough that Sadie might have run in that direction by accident. She rushed out to the front yard where Nan had held all those weddings. "Sadie!" she called, straining her hearing for the faintest sound. "Sadie!" She ran down the path, between the lines of oaks. "Sadie!"

She heard a sound, causing her to stop, but it was just the wind. She listened again as the air froze her face. She hadn't brought a scarf or gloves, and the dark had brought freezing temperatures. Worried she might be losing time, she picked up speed again, slipping as she stepped on a patch of ice, and tweaking her ankle. She squeezed her eyes shut, running through the pain. "Sadie!" she called.

Silence.

Leah kept running all the way to the main road, her limbs losing feeling. Before she searched off of the property, she needed to see if anyone else had found her daughter. Sadie had never ventured as far as the main road, and Leah just couldn't imagine she would on a night like tonight. She'd have been too cold.

What was I thinking? she scolded herself. The plan had always been to move to Evergreen Hill. Leah may have been uncertain at times but Sadie had known that plan since she could talk. They had never considered that it might not happen—until Nan's death. It had always been "When we move to Evergreen Hill," not "if." Leah should have tried harder. She could've taken out a loan, fought the will in court. Maybe if she'd begged the rest of the family they could all have gone in together to buy David out. She had been exhausted, taking the easy way out because she couldn't face the fight. But she hadn't stopped to really think about how this would affect Sadie—only herself.

Leah started the long walk back up the drive, wincing at the pain in her ankle with every step. But there was no pain like the pain she felt right now at the loss of Sadie. She was everything to Leah, and she found herself nearly unable to finish the journey because she was shaking so badly—not from the cold, but from complete heartbreak.

"Sadie!" she called again, this time through her sobs. An icy patch caused her to stumble, falling into the snow. She got back up. "Sadie!" She was winded, frozen to the bone, and absolutely terrified.

"Leah!" she heard Roz's voice in the darkness, a white beam of light nearly blinding her. She shielded her eyes, squinting to keep her head from throbbing worse than it was. "Leah!" Roz said again, breathless as she reached her. "David has her."

Barely unable to stand, Leah threw her arms around Roz and heaved over and over again, the relief like nothing she'd ever felt.

"She was in the servants' quarters out back. She said she saw that everything was being moved out of there, and she wasn't going to let David have that building. She said he'd already taken her house, he couldn't have that too."

"It's damaged. The tree... She could've frozen! Is she all right?" She wiped her eyes with a jittery hand.

"In the dark, she couldn't tell what the damage was. She thought the hole was because he was tearing it down. She said she was going to sleep out there if she had to, but he wasn't destroying anything of her nan's."

They went inside and shut the door. As Leah rushed forward to find Sadie and hold her, Roz stopped her. "Leah." Her tone had never been as serious as it was right then. She turned and looked at Roz. "David cried with relief when he found her," she said quietly. "I've never seen a man hug a child that tightly when he isn't even related to her. He promised her he wouldn't tear down that building."

Leah nodded in understanding. Then she pulled away and rushed toward the voices in the kitchen. When she got there, David was sitting down with Sadie in his lap. He was talking to her, his eyes tired. He nodded at something she said. They both noticed Leah and looked up.

"Sadie." She walked toward her daughter, scooped her off of David's lap, and hugged her like she'd never hugged her before. "You can't do that. You scared me to death." The tears returned.

"I'm sorry, Mama," Sadie said. "I didn't mean to scare you. I was so sad, and I didn't know what to do. You'd always told me to be strong when I have a problem, and solve it myself. I was trying to."

"Oh, honey. You can't solve this by yourself. It isn't something that can be solved—believe me, I've tried." She looked over at David, but his gaze was on the floor, his forearms on his knees, his head lowered. He didn't look up. They were all exhausted. "I think we've had a big night. Let's get a good night's sleep and we can talk about it all in the morning. Want to sleep in my room again?"

"Yes. I'm afraid I'll have bad dreams."

"Okay then. Go upstairs, I'll be up in a minute." Leah waited for Sadie to leave and walked over to David, and he finally looked up at her. "Thank you for finding my baby," she said, the words struggling to leave her throat.

He stood up and put his arms around her. "I'm so sorry," he whispered. And they stayed like that, her head on his chest, until she put her arms around him too. She could feel his heartbeat against her cheek. It was racing. Every single emotion it was possible to feel seemed to be running through her, but bigger than it all was the warmth from David's body, and his strong arms embracing her. She drew her arms up around his neck and kissed his cheek, the feel of his skin on her lips making her dizzy. Then she pulled back and hurried for the door before she went any further.

Chapter Twenty-Three

It was late morning. They'd all turned in early last night, and Leah had risen with the sun, although the snowy sky had hidden it considerably. She'd worried that she would spend the night coming down from her panic, but losing Sadie had been such an ordeal that she crashed and didn't wake at all until the morning. Sadie was still in her pajamas and had been playing with the others upstairs Sadie hadn't mentioned losing the plantation again, but Leah knew it would just be a matter of time and she'd want to talk about it. Louise and Roz were both getting ready for the day, but Leah had been downstairs, taking in every last minute at Evergreen Hill.

The old house was slightly drafty, the radiators working at top speed to heat the morning air but not quite warming it completely. Snow had fallen again overnight and the fields were covered in white. David seemed to be giving Leah the silence she was craving. After their initial "good morning," he'd looked over at her quite a few times, but hadn't spoken. He was working between his computer and fiddling with the new Wi-Fi connection, finally standing up and telling her he was running out to get a few things and that he'd pick up some groceries.

June was having a second cup of coffee in the kitchen. Samuel was reading a newspaper from earlier in the week quietly in the sitting room, and Leah thought it might be a good time to chat with him. She went upstairs and got the stack of letters.

"She kept *all* of them," Samuel said in a whisper as Leah handed them to him, the ribbon from the bow that tied them together draping over his hand as he held them. In an instant, his eyes were brimming with tears. He set the bundle in his lap and folded the newspaper back up, placing it on the end table beside him. "I missed her so much when she left that I wrote her letters begging her to come back, but she didn't respond."

"She never wrote you back?" That wasn't like her at all. Leah sat down on the floor beside his chair, her back to the fire, and hugged her knees casually as she waited for his explanation.

"I couldn't find her. She'd moved. But the mail must have been forwarded to her new address for a while because I kept sending them to the old address, relentlessly, until one day they started coming back to me. I told her I loved her. When she didn't respond, I'd occasionally send her a note asking about her, wondering where she was, if she was okay. I should've given up. Anyone with any dignity would've. But I was so worried about her, and I cared about her so much, that I just couldn't."

Her sweet, always happy Nan had had a secret. "She never said anything, Samuel."

"No, she wouldn't have. That's why she wouldn't see me either. She pushed all that emotion right out of her life. That was how she dealt with it." He held up the letters. "May I keep these?"

"Of course." Leah noticed his hands were shaking.

"I got a ton of food," David said, interrupting them before darting into the kitchen to unpack the brown paper grocery bags he'd been bringing in. Leah was thankful he'd run out before the snow got too deep. It was coming down again. She left the conversation with Samuel apologetically, and went to help David put the groceries away, Samuel getting up and following her into the kitchen.

David was chipper now, happy, and Leah couldn't help but wonder if it was because once the drama with Sadie was over, he'd realized that he'd won. He'd gotten Evergreen Hill, and there was nothing Leah could do about it. But she thought about the hug they'd shared after he'd found Sadie, and she didn't really believe that could be the source of his happiness. Since when did she care about what made David happy? She pushed it out of her mind. This was about enjoying her friends and having one, final Christmas near Nan.

"On the way in, I slid a few times even in the truck. It's still early so the ice is heavy, but I worry the weather's getting worse."

Leah reached into one of the bags and grabbed a ketchup bottle and a can of crushed tomatoes, setting them on the counter.

David leaned in toward her. "How's Sadie?" he asked, so close she could feel his warmth. He was looking down at her, his face now full of concern.

She reached into the bag again, pulling out two cans of vegetables, unable to look back at him because his concern for Sadie made her want to put her hands on his face and kiss him. "She's still low," she said. She didn't want to go into it right there in the kitchen. She didn't want to tell him how the whole ordeal had taken the wind right out of her sails.

"I saw on the forecast that we're supposed to get another five inches. That's a record, they said. We never get snow this early," June said as she helped David put away the refrigerator items, seemingly unaware of Leah and David's exchange.

"I shouldn't have been so impulsive in coming," Samuel said. He was sitting at the kitchen table, holding one of Sadie's crayons. She'd just brought her coloring books out and asked if he'd like to color with her, running off again to see if her friends wanted to join her. "I didn't expect to impose like this."

"It's really no problem at all," Leah said, hoping David and June felt the same. She was so glad he'd decided to come. Just having him there made her feel closer to Nan. "I'm happy you're here."

Samuel smiled, looking a little relieved.

"It's perfectly fine," David agreed. "In fact, why don't we celebrate? We can make a big meal, put on some music?"

"Yes!" Roz piped up. She and Louise had come down, leaving the kids to play upstairs, probably just dying to hear what was going on. Leah hadn't had a chance to tell them anything— the house was always so busy. Roz sat down at the table. Louise, ever the quiet observer, sat beside Roz, taking everything in, Leah could tell. She couldn't wait to have some time with her friends alone.

"I'd enjoy that," Samuel said. "Although I wouldn't want to be any trouble."

"You're not," David promised. "I'll get some music on. Let me see what Nina has in the old stereo." He finished putting away the vegetables and left the kitchen.

After a few minutes, "Dream a Little Dream" by Louis Armstrong poured through the speakers, and, without warning, the memory of Nan dancing to it flooded her mind. Emotions hit Leah fast and hard; her beautiful fantasy of all those family moments she'd wanted to create at Evergreen Hill was gone, instead belonging to June and David, and she felt the panic about her choice to sell.

"You okay?" David asked. She only realized then that tears had surfaced. She blinked them away and saw that Louise was paying close attention—she recognized her look of concern.

"This song just takes me back." She sat down in the kitchen chair next to Sadie, trying to play it down.

June came over and patted Leah's leg. "Your grandmother loved old classics. They've become so much a part of me now that I'd forgotten it was she who had introduced me to them. This was one of my favorites." June was smiling, happy, that sadness in her eyes slightly lessened. Like low tide, it had receded just out of view.

Leah nodded, thinking back to the music box she and David had bought. When she was finally able to squelch the tears, she noticed Samuel. He had his hand on his face as if the music had just hit him, but he was grinning, his eyes glassy. Leah moved into his view, hoping he'd share whatever the thought was that had put such a sparkle in his eye.

"I introduced Nina to this song," he said.

"Really?" Until that moment, Leah had always thought this song was just Nan's. She'd never even considered that it might have been someone else's song before that.

"We'd worked late one night. I had been working on a presentation to the faculty, and she'd helped me rehearse and tweak my lines until it was perfect. We'd worked so long that I couldn't think straight anymore, so I went over to my old record player and put on this record."

He leaned forward to address Leah specifically. "My office was full of all sorts of historical artifacts, but she'd always gravitated to that record player. I can still see her: she fiddled with the buttons, ran her fingers along the surface of the machine, focused as if it were telling her stories. I don't know what came over me, but that one time, I took her hand, pulled her close, and danced with her."

Leah wished Nan were here to tell the other side of that story. What had she felt for Samuel? What had it been like to dance with him? It seemed so romantic.

"David danced with Mama," Sadie said quietly as she walked back into the kitchen, pulling them out of their story. "And me."

David locked eyes with Leah, his stare and the slight grin on his lips making her feel as though all her thoughts about him were being exposed. She looked away and focused on Samuel.

Samuel turned toward David, his eyes telling him something, but his lips still. He smiled a knowing smile and then looked back at Sadie. "Dancing is fun, isn't it?" he asked her.

Sadie nodded, when normally she'd have jumped up and done a twirl. "I love to dance," she said.

"When faced with dancing or not, always dance," he said, but he'd looked back at David when he said it. With Sadie safe and sound, Leah wanted to take those words to heart. She didn't want to waste a single minute being upset or worried. Instead, she wanted to create a few more memories of this place while she could.

Sadie had pulled Samuel into the sitting room, asking to color on the coffee table so she could stay warm by the fire. Everyone else was settling in there as well, and June was just finishing tidying up the kitchen before going in. She was whistling quietly, and Leah hung back to be with her.

"I enjoy seeing you smile," she said to June.

"I've smiled a lot lately," she said. "I got up early this morning. For the first time in a long time, I wanted to start the day."

"Oh?" Leah said, glad to hear that. She'd noticed June coming out of herself more and more, spending time with the group rather than being alone.

"When Christine died, my whole world was changed, and I didn't know quite who I was anymore. Life didn't mean much to me because I felt like I could work my fingers off and the life I made could still be stolen at any moment, so what was the point?" She began fixing Leah a mug of coffee without asking. "But being around you all is helping." She poured just the right amount of cream into the coffee and stirred.

"How is it helping?"

She handed Leah her coffee and said, "Because with both Nina and Christine, I realized that the focus shouldn't be whether my life is important or unimportant. It's how all of our lives intertwine, and by isolating myself, I'm not allowing pieces of me to be shared and left when I'm gone. I've really enjoyed being around you all."

"I'm so glad to hear that."

"I'm excited to see Marie," she said, her eyes big and a smile on her face that took Leah back to when she was a little girl. "Your mother and I haven't seen each other in years. While we were very different people, we talked a lot when you kids were little."

"I know. My mom remembers those talks too."

"When's she coming in?"

"Tomorrow morning."

"It's supposed to snow again. I hope her flight isn't delayed."

"I know. I'm a little worried about that." She was more than a little worried. This was her very last Christmas at Evergreen Hill and she wanted everything to be perfect. Sadie's memories of this place had to be strong if they would carry on throughout her life. She was so young.

"While it's under difficult circumstances, I'm glad we could all come together one last time. Do you need any help preparing food or anything for tomorrow?"

"Actually, that would be amazing, thank you."

Samuel had agreed to take all the kids sledding for just a bit before the afternoon daylight faded into evening while The Girls prepared for tomorrow's dinner. Sadie had said she didn't want to go and when David had dropped down on his haunches to convince her, she'd turned away, and David looked like he'd been punched in the gut. He got up and Leah went over. "You'll have fun," she said, drawing Sadie close.

Sadie shook her head.

"Ethan and Jo will miss you if you don't go." She ruffled Sadie's hair. "I bet they won't dare go down that hill without someone brave to show them."

Sadie nodded. "Okay." She trailed out after Samuel, and Leah sighed with relief.

The kitchen was brimming with flour, sugar, pie pans, spices, vegetables, fruits—the women all working on separate dishes. June had offered to go out in the farm truck and get a few more things they'd need that David hadn't thought of. She wanted to be sure, with the snowstorm looming, that they'd have enough wine and breakfast items.

The candles were lit, the fire roaring, and the smell of roasted sweet potatoes, pumpkin pie, and Christmas sugar cookies filled the air. Leah clicked on the lights, illuminating the back woods. She couldn't wait to show them to her family. They'd be so happy to see it.

"It smells so good in here that I can't get my work done," David said, entering the kitchen. Leah had hardly seen him all day. His eyes were on Roz and Louise, rather than her, and she wondered how she should handle being around him now.

"We've been busy," Roz said with a sugary smile.

David nodded and then his eyes met Leah's. When they did, he offered a careful smile and then turned back to Roz and Louise.

"What are we having tomorrow?" he asked.

As Louise was explaining her recipe for stuffing, Samuel and the kids came barreling through the door, Sadie running in front. "Mama!" she said, a smile on her face. It was the first time she'd seen Sadie smile since she'd heard the news.

"What is it?" Leah set down the kitchen towel she was holding and went over to her daughter.

"We were sledding," Sadie said, nearly breathless, her little friends looking on. "And we heard crying. We went to the creek by the road, and there was a kitten! It's stuck! We need to save it!"

Samuel put a hand on Sadie's shoulder and added, "It's stuck on a rock and the water is icy and rushing so fast because of the melting snow so it's scared. We think it might have climbed out on a limb and fallen. I tried to get it, but I was too worried my old back would give out and I'd slip."

"Oh no!" Leah said, thinking of a poor little kitten out in the cold.

Sadie rushed over to David. "David, will you save it?"

David smiled at her, his fondness for Sadie clear on his face, and Leah wondered if he too was glad to see her smile. He went straight over and put on his boots and coat, darting out the door. He'd saved Sadie the other night, and now he was saving her kitten. Leah grabbed the towel and started wiping the counters again, trying not to acknowledge her undeniable affection for him.

A few minutes went by, and they came back in, Sadie holding a mewing little ball of brown-and-white fur in her coat. "You're soaking wet," she said to David, as he came in behind her.

"I'm fine," he said, winded but smiling, although he looked miserably cold. "We'll need to check the little guy for frostbite."

Not stopping to take care of his wet clothing, David went upstairs and got an armful of towels. Leah and Sadie took the kitten in by the fire. It seemed exhausted from its ordeal. It was wet and dirty, but its paws seemed okay. She pressed on the pads of its feet but the cat didn't wince or anything. She checked its ears and its tail—all seemed to be fine.

As she sat in front of the fire, David wrapped the kitten in warm, dry towels.

"Is it okay?" Sadie asked as everyone gathered around.

"It's a little girl. And she seems to be," Leah said, shrugging off her coat and cuddling her like a baby. "You caught her just in time."

Sadie squatted down beside her mother and put her hand on the cat's head, stroking it gently. "Maybe she fell out of Santa's sleigh," Sadie said with a big smile.

"What makes you think she fell out of Santa's sleigh?" Leah asked.

"Because she was on my list and when she was crying and we all went to her, she looked just at me." Then, worry spread across her face. "What if he was on his way to Richmond and he didn't know to stop here?"

"Sadie, he isn't even flying yet. He'll know where to come. I promise."

"Even if he doesn't come, I know she was meant for me. See?"

Leah looked at the kitten and saw that she had tilted her head back to view Sadie. Leah smiled, glad for the distraction for Sadie and feeling again like Nan might have had a hand in all this.

* * *

"When David texted me to get kitten supplies at the pet store, I thought he'd gone a little crazy," June said, carefully buckling a petite red collar around the kitten's neck. They'd told her the story when she'd come home. She set her down and the cat ran to her bowl of food for the second time. "But judging by the shape she's in, she hadn't wandered far. She'd have frostbite if she had."

"But there aren't any houses around. And there were no other cats. Where has she come from?"

"I don't know. You don't think someone would drop her off in this weather, do you?" June asked, concern flooding her face.

"No one dropped her off," Sadie said, as she and the other two children crowded around the cat, petting her as she ate. "She was meant for me."

June leaned over them to get another look. "What are you going to call her, Sadie?"

"Lucky," she said, as if she'd always had a name in mind. But then she explained. "Lucky, because I'm so lucky to have her and she's so lucky we found her."

"I love that," Leah said.

Chapter Twenty-Four

Sadie had scooped Lucky into her arms and taken her with the kids upstairs. David was up behind them, changing into dry clothes, and the others were all in need of a break, so June had opened an early bottle of wine since they'd spent the whole afternoon cooking, and they'd settled in the sitting room.

"I feel like Nina put that cat here," June said, taking a sip of her wine and looking at the glass for a long time.

"I thought the same," Leah agreed as she sat down next to Roz, Louise across from them in a chair. "Thank you for watching Sadie and the kids today, Samuel. I know it was a lot of work."

"Oh, it's fine." He was visibly tired as he sat in the chair by the fire, a glass of red wine in his hand. "I never had kids of my own. I feel like I missed out, and I'm happy to spend time with them." He looked over at the fire as if deciding something. Then, he said to Leah, "Would you like to hear about my little Sadie now?"

"Are you sure?" She worried that he might feel uncomfortable, having everyone else in the room.

Samuel insisted it was just fine.

"Then yes."

David came down in a clean outfit and sat on the other side of Leah on the settee, just in time for the story.

"Nina had complained of lower back pain all day—I still remember it," Samuel said, looking at the fire for a moment before he continued. "I promised I'd come over and give her a back rub that night. She'd refused to move in with me, for the sake of the children, and she hadn't told them she was expecting our child. She was waiting to find a good time." He swallowed, the sadness evident on his face as he tried to continue the story. "She'd said she was fine, and she went home. That night, she called me. She was having terrible cramps, and she said something just didn't feel right. A neighbor sat with the kids while I took her to the hospital. We lost Sadie that night. The kids never knew a thing. Nina hid her pain and her sadness from them. But I've always missed our little girl."

"Wow," Leah said, at a loss for words. No wonder Nan had been so understanding when she'd told her she was pregnant. And now, knowing what she knew, she was so thankful she'd used the name Sadie for her own little girl. After that story, it had new meaning for her.

"Being with Sadie today doesn't make the pain go away completely, but it makes me feel like I've found a missing piece of the puzzle."

She took a moment to look around and every eye was on him. Louise's elbow was resting on the arm of the chair and she had leaned her head on her fist as she listened; Roz had taken the sofa pillow and put it in her lap, her legs curled underneath her, her complete attention on Samuel; June was in the rocker, her legs crossed, her wine untouched. Leah turned to look at David and was surprised when she realized he was looking at her. She smiled and turned back to Samuel.

"Did you ever try to marry Nan?" she asked, feeling protective of her grandmother. Nan should've had Samuel to go through life with her. He could've helped her in her last days.

"When I found out she was pregnant, I orchestrated the perfect sentiment, the most heartfelt way to tell her how much I loved her. I proposed to her that night, and she said no."

"Why?" Leah was baffled by this news.

"She didn't want to get married just because of the baby, and I couldn't convince her that my proposal had nothing to do with that. We should've done things the other way around, but in the end, we didn't, and that was just how it was."

"I like having you here," Leah said out of the blue. "I feel closer to Nan than I have since we lost her. I feel like you were the only one who really knew her."

He was leaning back in the chair, his glass swinging from his fingers. "She was the love of my life. I like being here too. It makes me feel… whole again. For so many years I've been missing something, and I feel closer to her here as well."

"How are you still fond of her when she refused to marry you and she ran away and never answered your letters?"

There was a moment when Samuel was silent, as if he were trying to find the right words. The candles flickered on the mantle, their flames vibrant despite the daylight coming in through the large windows. Finally, he spoke. "Because I separated her fear from who she really was. It was her fear that drove her away from being happy. It wouldn't do me any good to allow that fear to ruin what we had. I never held her running away against her. There was a part of her, after your grandfather died, that was so fragile I felt as though I needed to hold her hand to keep her together. In the end, when she lost the baby, that fragile part of her shattered and she shut me out completely. That's my take on it anyway."

"So what happened? Did she just leave you?"

"A week after she lost the baby, she sent me a letter telling me that she couldn't take any more loss. She wasn't ready to be vulnerable, she said. To her, love was vulnerability, but to me, you see, love is strength. Loving Nina was what gave me the energy to see life again. But I'd never get the chance to convince her of my view or change her mind. When I went to her house, she was gone. It was empty. I remember the sinking feeling as I peered into the dark windows, every single shred of her having vanished."

"You must have felt terrible." The whole room was looking on, and as Leah listened, she felt the strength in having that quiet support of her loved ones around her.

"Yes, I didn't know what to do. That was when I started writing the letters. It wasn't just a quick romance. It was years in the making. Nina worked for me the whole time and I was a perfect gentleman. Our mutual loneliness was how it began. We'd eat lunch together, have dinner when the kids were at parties or sleepovers. She stopped by the house when they were at school... Then, one day—I still remember it—the change in her eyes when she looked at me. That friendliness, that excitement, and happiness when she saw me deepened and I saw love in her eyes. It scared me a little. I'd never felt like that, and all of a sudden, I knew I wanted to see that look for the rest of my life.

"She'd told me once that she'd gotten quite good at being on her own and she just didn't have the courage to allow anyone else into her world. But that night, when she looked at me the way she did, I could tell that her resolve had faltered. I kissed her right then. It was the most glorious moment. I knew then that I loved her."

"That's a beautiful story," Leah said, wondering how Nan had had the strength to run away from that kind of love. Was that what Nan had been trying to tell her about regrets? Don't run away from what makes you whole? And right there, with everyone around her, she felt whole.

After Samuel's story, David had gone up to the sewing room to work. Leah felt the need to make sure he was okay, not believing his story about working since it was so late in the day, so she went up there. She closed the door behind her, and he looked up.

"I just wanted to check on you," she said, walking over to him. "You look like you have a lot on your mind."

He stood up, facing her. He wasn't smiling; he looked concerned, his gaze swallowing her up.

It could've been the fact that she had a house full of people she enjoyed, the Christmas decorations, the smell of the food, and her parents in flight to Evergreen Hill, but all she wanted right now was to forget about the fact that she'd signed the house over to David, and just enjoy being with him. His compassion today made her realize how much she liked having him around.

Suddenly unable to say anything, her emotions were welling up. She blinked, successfully keeping them from spilling over, thank goodness.

"Sadie's crying over the house broke my heart." He looked at her for a long time before speaking as she scrambled to get herself together. "And so did yours," he finally said.

He put his arms around her in a comforting way, but as she wrapped hers around him, he pulled her closer. When she'd gotten herself together, she looked up into his eyes, trying to find the reason for his affectionate embrace. He reached up and moved her hair off her shoulder, putting it behind her.

"I've been thinking a lot about the house," he said, looking down at her with concern in his eyes. "Losing Sadie scared me to death. That night, all night, all I thought about was what it would feel like when you left—how empty that would be for me now. I don't want to lose you and Sadie."

"What are you saying?"

"What if you and Sadie stay here with me?"

Was he asking to share the house? "I couldn't... afford it." She hated to even admit that, but he was being so honest, she felt like she could be too.

"With a million dollars in your pocket?"

"You mean you'd want me to live here, while you owned it, and what—me pay rent?"

"Or you could keep your half. I'll take care of things until you can get a job here."

While it was a very generous offer, she did have her pride, and she wasn't going to take handouts. That wasn't who she was. "I'm sorry," she said, shaking her head at the same time. "I can't do that." She pulled away from him. "I've signed the papers, David. I did what you wanted. There isn't any other way."

Ultimately, it was still David's house, and she couldn't live there and watch him make changes to it, make the sole decisions for it, while he spent his hard-earned money to keep her and Sadie afloat. That wasn't how things should be.

"That's not what I want anymore," he said, his voice almost pleading.

"David, I'm flattered, but things wouldn't end the way we'd want them to in that scenario."

"How do you know unless you try?"

"I just know." She started toward the door. "I'm going to check on Sadie," she said.

But he caught her arm. "Wait," he said urgently. "If I let you go, I'll regret it."

They both stared at each other, the word "regret" hanging between them.

"Stay a little while after Christmas. We'll figure it out."

"I signed the papers," she said again for emphasis.

He locked eyes with her, his stare direct and focused. "But I never sent them."

"Why?" Her voice came out in almost a whisper. She was so confused. She'd signed those papers well before Sadie had gone missing, before David's revelation that he didn't want to lose her.

"Because I can't take the house from you. I felt awful." He took a step into her personal space and placed his hands on her arms gently. "I don't know where to go from here. I just know that I want you with me."

Then he put his hand on her face, drawing her near. As if asking permission with his look, he moved his lips closer to hers. She closed her eyes in response. Then, there was an explosion in her body as she felt his warm lips on hers, and it was as if they were meant to be together. Like pieces of a puzzle, their lips moved perfectly together, his breath mixing with hers. She reached up and grabbed the back of his neck, running her nails along his hairline as he grabbed at her waist. They kissed so passionately that she forgot where she was or why she'd come into that room anyway. All she could think about was that one moment.

When they'd finally slowed to a more regular level, he pulled back and looked at her, a grin on his face. Neither of them said a word.

Then lightly he bent down and touched his lips to hers one more time.

"Ah–hem," Roz said, when Leah went back to her room to freshen up. She wanted to make sure she didn't look like she'd just made out with David. Roz was sitting on her bed. "Would you like to tell me why you just came out of that room with a weirdly happy look on your face?"

"I was just thanking David for saving Lucky." She tried not to give herself away, straightening her face to a more regular look.

Roz squinted her eyes. "And *how* were you thanking him, exactly?"

"Roz!" Her voice came out in an exasperated gasp.

"Don't play Mrs. Manners with me. I can see it all over your face."

"It was just a kiss," she admitted.

Roz's mouth hung open and she lifted off the bed like a rocket, landing right in front of Leah, grabbing her shoulders and shaking them. "You kissed the enemy?"

Leah tipped her head back and laughed.

"Look at you. Laughing like you've been hit by some sort of love arrow. Get a grip, woman."

"I'm totally fine," she said, still laughing as she pulled away.

All of a sudden, Roz clapped her hand over her mouth and gawked at her friend. "Did you seduce him to get Evergreen Hill back?" she teased. "You are brilliant!"

Leah rolled her eyes. "*He* kissed *me*. And he asked me to stay after Christmas."

Roz's eyes got big with that news. "Whatever you're doing. Keep doing it!"

Chapter Twenty-Five

The Christmas tree was lit and the turkey was baking when Leah's family pulled up to the house in a rented SUV. They got out, carrying loads of shopping bags in their arms. "Sadie!" Leah called. "Gran and Gramps, Uncle William, and Aunt Claire are here!"

Sadie, Jo, and Ethan all came running, Sadie holding Lucky in her arms with an enormous smile spread across her face. Leah was delighted at the sight of her daughter so flushed and happy.

"Hi, Gran! Hi, Gramps!" she called, stepping precariously onto the icy porch.

"Sadie, come back in. You're in your socks, your toes will freeze," Leah warned.

Leah's mother struggled to climb through the snow in her red designer heels, despite the path that David had shoveled earlier that morning, while her aunt and uncle were pulling their bags from the vehicle. As the cold temperatures had dipped even further, the walk had gotten icy. Leah's father was holding her arm, steadying her.

June hurried in from the kitchen and met them at the door, followed by David.

"Oh my gosh! June?" Leah's mother said as she planted her feet on the solid hardwoods just inside the door. She set down the carrier bags and gave her a warm hug. "It's been so long."

"You look amazing!" June said, shaking her head.

"Thank you!" Leah's mother looked over at David, recognition finally hitting. She put her hand to her chest. "Davey?"

He grinned, nodding. "I go by David now," he said with a chuckle. He shook hands with William and nodded at Claire as they arrived at the door with more bags.

Leah's mom gave David a hug, and she said, "You'll always be Davey to me."

"Hi, pumpkin," Leah's dad said to Sadie, giving her a big bear hug and sweeping her up into the air.

"Oh, you're cold, Gramps!" Sadie said with a wiggle.

He set her down and greeted Leah, "Hi, sweetheart. How are you doing?" His face was consoling, and she realized that it was the first time he'd seen her since the funeral. So much had happened since then —she'd had so many emotions—but she wasn't sad. She felt Nan with them.

"I'm okay. I can't wait to introduce you to Samuel," she said. "You'll never believe his stories."

"Everyone's in the sitting room," June said. "I'll get us all a drink. What will you have, Marie?"

"I'd love a glass of white, but whatever's open," she said, before turning to Leah to give her a hug.

Leah took their coats, and they all settled in the sitting room. Every chair was full. Sadie and Jo were on the floor, while Ethan played with the cat, using one of the new mouse toys June had bought. David patted the spot beside him on the settee, and Leah sat down. When she did, he put his arm around her. She didn't even flinch.

After a little bit of conversation, and once they were all relaxed, everyone having taken their bags upstairs, Leah passed out drinks and took the lead. Nan usually did, so she thought it would be fitting for her to do that part. She stood up. "For the new folks, family Christmas starts with an opening toast to celebrate another year together, where we all say one thing we're thankful for and then we have a big group toast. Does everyone have drink?"

There was collective nodding and June stood up. "May I go first?"

"Of course," Leah said. David had his arm on the back of the settee, and she sat back down, leaning against his side. He moved his hand to her shoulder and scratched it lightly to show his affection.

"I'm thankful for this room of friendly faces. How comforting to know that we are not alone."

"I'll be next! I'm thankful for Lucky," Sadie said, and she gave Lucky a big cuddle, the kitten purring in her arms.

As everyone went around saying what they were thankful for, Leah thought about all the blessings she'd had: Sadie, Nan, her family, meeting Samuel, and… David. The times she and David had shared together flashed in her mind like a slideshow: the moment she'd first seen him, the M&M hitting his face, the way he'd looked at her when she'd thanked him for stringing the lights outside… She smiled.

"Your turn, Leah," Roz said. "Tell us what you're grinning about."

She stood up. "I'm thankful for so many things that it's hard to say just one. But I suppose I'd say that I'm thankful for Nan. Every Christmas, she brought us together, and here she is, still doing it. I'm so thankful you all are here."

She turned to David, who was the last to go, and then sat down beside him. He stood up, but his eyes remained on her. "I'm thankful for a lot too. But I'm mostly thankful for seeing Leah again after all these years. And for meeting Sadie."

There was a silence in the room, his comment clearly taking everyone by surprise. It seemed as if they were all waiting for an explanation.

"Until now, I've been completely on my own. I've put all my energy into work and starting my business. That was what got me excited. But now something else can get me excited too. I wake up in the morning and I can't wait to see Leah. Her smile lights up my day." He held up his glass. "So, a toast," he said, "to family, and the people we meet along the way."

Everyone stood up and raised their glasses as they exchanged curious glances.

"Wait," Leah said, putting her arm around David. "Nan has something she'd like to say." She pulled the letter out of her pocket and held it up. "She said I couldn't open it until family Christmas, so I figured I'd read it now." Leah's fingers tingled with anticipation as she pulled the familiar lacy paper from its envelope and unfolded it.

She cleared her throat as she read, "'Dear family,'" she began, the tears rising in her eyes. She took a deep breath and continued. "'If you are reading this, then I can rest happily because I know that all the people I love have met each other. I may not be with you this Christmas, but if not, it is my sincere hope that you are all together. In different ways, each of you has been part of my life, and now I'd like you to be part of each other's. Leah, meet David. He's the kindest person I know. David, meet Leah, she'll do anything for the people she loves. To the rest of you: support one another and spend time together, because at the end, that's all you'll have to take with you—the love. Love each other and everything else will fall into place. Merry Christmas, Nina. P.S. Now go have fun!'"

They all laughed, their eyes glassy as they looked at each other.

Leah was quite emotional, although she was able to keep her composure. As she went to slide the letter back into the envelope, she noticed something else inside. She pulled it out. David took her hand, looking down at her for support. To her complete surprise, it was a photo of her! She had on a navy blue double-breasted coat with white tights and silver-buckled, black patent leather shoes. Her curly blonde hair was pulled back in a clip. She was probably only about five years old. But that wasn't the most unexpected part.

"What is it?" her mother asked.

Leah looked up briefly but went back to the photo. She was holding hands with a boy, and she knew right away who it was. He was looking down at her, a smile on his face as he walked beside her. Exactly like he was now.

"This was at Christmas," she said, completely stunned that she remembered such a thing. She'd been so young. "We had a nativity hunt after church. Nan had hidden bible verses about Christmas all over the yard. For every one we found, we got a tiny gingerbread heart cookie. David read all the verses to me." She turned the photo around for them to see. "That's me. And David…"

"Dinner's ready in the dining room," Leah said. The Girls had been busy setting the table and getting all the dishes ready for serving while the others mingled in the sitting room. With the help of her friends, Leah had cooked every recipe of Nan's that she could remember— stuffing, green beans and ham, buttermilk biscuits, sweet potatoes with candied walnuts, butternut squash, and the turkey.

The dining room was spectacular, with an ornamental tray ceiling and an enormous glass chandelier dripping from its center. The floors were dark wood with a cream-colored rug taking up most of the space. Leah and Roz had draped the Georgian dining table with a white linen tablecloth and set a small candelabrum, surrounded by Christmas greenery, in the center, its spruce-colored candles dripping wax while they burned. The white plates shone in the yellow lamplight as everyone awaited the food that Leah and her friends had prepared.

Sadie came in with Jo and Ethan, and Leah told them to pick their seats. She poured them all some sweet tea over ice in short tumbler glasses that matched the larger ones that were going to be used by the adults. As everyone else came in, they seated themselves.

"You've outdone yourself, Leah," Samuel said, scooting in his chair. He placed his napkin in his lap.

Leah finished setting the last of the food in the center of the table and took a seat herself. "Thank you," she said.

"I think Nina would be quite delighted seeing this—all of us at her table, food cooked with her recipes, sharing this night together. It is such a blessing." He raised his glass of tea. "Another toast! To Christmas with family," he said.

"To Christmas!" They all clinked their glasses. The kids raised their tumblers of sweet tea.

The others began to dish their food, passing bowls and plates around the table. As the clinking of spoons and tinkling of dishes filled the air, Leah knew without a doubt that this was where she belonged. The only thing that hadn't occurred to her until now was that everyone else belonged there too.

After dinner, Leah insisted that everyone relax and enjoy themselves while she cleaned up dinner. Nan had always done the same. Louise was playing cards with the kids, and Roz and the others were in the sitting room, watching football. June had popped back in and was clearing dishes with her.

"Please don't feel like you have to help, June. I'll get it all. I enjoy hosting," Leah said, piling the plates at one end of the table.

"I actually wanted some time alone with you. To talk."

"Oh?" She set the last plate down and turned toward her, giving June her undivided attention.

"I shouldn't have quit my job," she said. "At the time, I was grieving so much that no one could've told me differently. I was exhausted mentally. I wanted to come to Evergreen Hill to get away from everyone. But now that I've been here with you all, it's given me some perspective." She took a deep breath. "I've been talking to David. He doesn't want to take the house from you and Sadie. He can't bear it. And I've been thinking—I couldn't handle my job when I was low because I was never truly invested in it. Losing Christine made me feel I had nothing to live for. But Evergreen Hill, this is a place I love. Working here—that would give me a reason to wake up in the mornings."

Leah's heart was pounding. Was June about to suggest what Leah suspected?

"I'm still not entirely myself, but I'm getting there. Give me a few months, with something to look forward to, and…" She looked Leah directly in the eye. "How would you feel about running this place together?"

Leah couldn't breathe.

"David, may I see you for just a minute?" Leah asked above Roz's cheering for the East Carolina University football team as they ran twenty yards toward the end zone. Roz gave Samuel a high five.

David stood up.

"Let's go to the parlor," she said. He joined her and, together, they walked down the hallway.

The room was dark, the historical memorabilia still pushed against all the walls. She clicked on the chandelier, spilling light onto the shiny floor. She turned toward the empty piano seat, thinking about David and Sadie sitting there last time.

With her back to David, still too worried to get her hopes up, afraid that it was some sort of dream or giant misunderstanding and she'd come crashing down, she said quietly, hearing the hope in her words, "I talked to your mom." She struggled to say more.

Then, out of nowhere, she felt his strong arms around her, his face at her neck. His breath gave her goosebumps down her arm. "What did she say?" he whispered into her ear, clearly knowing the answer. She turned around.

"She said she wants to run the business. With me." She looked up at his warm eyes, the satisfied smile on his lips, and the complete adoration for her that was written on his face, and she knew that this was right. She could never regret this. "But I thought you didn't want anyone running a business in your home."

"I changed my mind," he said, his hands moving to her waist, his fingers unstill as he caressed her sides. She felt that nervous energy too—as if she were about to explode. "I realized it when I admitted to myself that you and Sadie were the last thing I thought about every night before I went to sleep. What makes you happy, makes me the happiest man in the world."

He grabbed her sides, her sweater in his fists, as if he'd been trying to control the impulse this whole time and had finally lost the battle. His lips were on hers, urgently, his hands holding on to her tightly, making her woozy. She wrapped her arms around him and kissed him back. When they'd finally slowed and then stopped, he pulled back and looked at her. "Evergreen Hill is not home unless you're here. Will you stay?"

She couldn't hide the smile on her face as she said, "Yes. Of course I will." She threw her arms around his neck and kissed him again. "We have to tell Sadie."

They went up the old staircase together, like they had so many years ago, but this time holding hands. Sadie was in her bedroom with Jo and Ethan. The room was a complete disaster—coloring books on the floor, her dollhouse items spread out, quilts in piles with baby dolls on them. "You all look like you've been having fun!" she said with a laugh. "Sadie, may I see you just a second? David and I want to tell you something."

Sadie scooped up Lucky from the bed and followed them into Nan's room, where it was quiet. She stood against the foot of the bed, stroking the kitten.

"I think that kitten is going to need quite a bit of care, and we're going to have to give it the very best we've got."

Sadie nodded, Lucky purring in her arms. The cat pressed the top of her head against Sadie's chest, showing its affection, and making Leah smile.

"It's going to need a lot of trees to climb."

Sadie nodded again.

"David and I thought the best place to find trees is here, and maybe the three of us might need to live at Evergreen Hill. Together."

"What?" Sadie's mouth hung open in surprise as she stroked the cat, remnants of her pink nail polish showing as her fingers moved through the fur.

Leah smiled. "And I'll take care of Lucky while you're at those big gymnastics lessons you want to do so badly." Leah's smile widened. "Sadie," she said, finally allowing herself to be as giddy as Sadie looked, "you and I are moving to Evergreen Hill. We're going to live here with David and June."

David squatted down beside her. "What do you think about that? Want to live here with me?"

Sadie threw her arm out, wrapping it around David's neck and leaning against Leah while awkwardly holding the kitten. She yanked David toward them so hard with her embrace that for a moment Leah worried about the kitten. "Careful with Lucky," she giggled. When she pulled back just a little to give Lucky some breathing room, she noticed tears in Sadie's eyes and she bent down to be eye level with her.

"Mama, I'm so happy," she said, looking back and forth between Leah and David. Then, she whispered, "I put Evergreen Hill on my Christmas list. When nothing was working, I thought maybe Nan in Heaven could help Santa give it to me."

Leah smiled, her own tears brimming. "Maybe she did."

Chapter Twenty-Six

Leah was the first to notice it. It led from the bed to the closed door of her bedroom and trailed underneath it. Sadie had been sharing her bed since the rooms were all full, and Leah knew that it hadn't been there when they'd all gone upstairs early, to give Santa enough time to come. Sadie had just gotten up and hopped down, her Christmas nightgown billowing out around her as she jumped.

"What's on the floor?" she said, her eyes bright despite having just opened them. Her blonde hair was still in braids from yesterday, and the loose strands had fuzzed up while she'd been sleeping. She bent down and ran her finger through the silver sparkles.

"It's glitter," Leah said, curious as to where it had come from. Last night, once Sadie was asleep, she had brought in her Santa gifts from the trunk of her car and displayed them near the fireplace like she always had. Next to the gifts for Jo and Ethan, she'd put out an art set she'd gotten on sale—a little case with markers and stencils. She knew Sadie would love it. She'd opened it up and set some of the pieces out to make it look bigger. Then, she'd put out a new hairbrush and some fancy clips that Sadie had asked for. She'd filled her stocking with candy and set it down on the floor by her gifts. Then, she'd gone to bed. She hadn't done anything with glitter…

Sadie was already opening the door and she'd barely gotten her bathrobe around her. She shuffled herself into her slippers and tried to catch up, the glitter still going, along the hardwoods of the hallway and cascading down the staircase. Sadie was going down so fast that Leah couldn't keep up. She rounded the corner at the bottom of the steps as Leah tried to get down the staircase as quickly as she could without waking everyone.

"Oh!" Sadie nearly screamed, her elation so unexpected that Leah knew the glitter wasn't the only thing in that room. She got to the bottom of the stairs and entered the sitting room, clapping her hand over her mouth.

The art set had been moved, the pieces returned to the box, but it was left open and displayed beside a thick blue gymnastics tumbling mat. Sadie hopped on, doing a cartwheel in her nightgown. To the side of the mat, there was a basket full of cat toys, food, bedding, and a climbing tree for Lucky.

Sadie turned to her mother, the reality of it all settling in. "Did you buy all this?" she asked.

Too stunned to speak, she answered truthfully and shook her head. That was when she saw it for the first time in Sadie's eyes—magic.

There was a creak in the floorboards and Leah turned to find David. He was leaning against the doorframe, smiling. She didn't have to ask, to understand that smile. As he locked eyes with her, she knew he'd been responsible for this. She walked past him, nodding for him to join her just out of earshot of Sadie.

"You didn't have to do this," she whispered.

"I know," he was still smiling, so clearly happy. "It's like Samuel. I don't have a daughter of my own. And I adore Sadie. She deserves to have an amazing Christmas. You didn't ask me to do this—no one did. I did it myself. Because I wanted to."

"Thank you." She didn't have a clue how to repay him, but she wanted him to know that she was thankful.

He leaned down and touched his lips to hers. "You're welcome," he said against her lips. "Let's go back in and see Sadie." He took her hand and they walked in together.

Sadie dug through her stocking. It was fuller than it had been last night. She pulled out candy canes, chocolates, a small stationery set, glitter pens, hair ribbons, rolled-up coloring books, all sorts of things. The stocking covered her entire arm as she plunged her hand in one more time to get the last few treats at the very bottom. She wiggled around, her legs shimmering with glitter from sitting on the floor, and Leah couldn't imagine a better Christmas.

When everyone was up and had eaten a quick cinnamon roll while the real breakfast casserole was in the oven cooking, they gathered in the sitting room to open gifts. Sadie was doing a handstand on her new mat while Ethan built with his deluxe Lego set and Jo combed the hair of her brand new, life-size baby doll. Leah reached under the tree and pulled out Roz's gift, laughing out loud at the packaging. Stretched along the bottom of each of Roz's gift bags for her and Louise was a pair of lacy Christmas undies with two green bows side by side where the bikini top should be. Samuel raised his eyebrows and David laughed out loud. Leah turned it around toward the tree to shield the children.

"I couldn't resist," Roz said, holding her coffee with two hands and sitting cross-legged on the sofa. "Let's do yours first, though! Save mine for later."

"Okay," Leah said, shaking her head in amusement and switching gears. She pulled out the one she'd wrapped for Louise. "This one is for you." She handed Louise the gift she'd wrapped in silver paper, decorated with a dark red ribbon and fresh greenery tucked beneath the bow.

"This is beautiful," Louise said, pulling delicately at the bow to untie it. She slipped her finger under the flap of paper and unfolded it. She opened the box to reveal the navy-and-tan hand-knitted scarf that Leah had found at a craft show. As soon as she'd seen it, she knew it would go beautifully with Louise's complexion.

"Oh, I love it!" she said, pulling it out and wrapping it around her neck.

Marie and June both leaned in closer to view it, chattering together about how pretty it was.

"It's just gorgeous." Louise got up from the settee and kissed Leah on the cheek. "Thank you."

"You're welcome," Leah said, pleased with herself. "Okay, Roz." She passed Roz her gift.

Roz took it from her kindly, yanked the ribbon down the box and tore the paper, wadding it all into a little ball and setting it on the table. She opened the box and gasped, staring at it a moment before speaking. "What. Is. This?"

Leah started to laugh uncontrollably as Roz turned the picture frame around for Louise to view it. The others in the room looked on with confusion, David even turning his head to the side, his brows furrowing. Louise threw her head back in laughter.

"You gave me a picture of Delivery-guy Stan?"

"It's for your desk," Leah said, barely able to get the words out. "It's his employee photo!" She doubled over.

"Ha. Ha," Roz said, trying not to laugh herself for the sake of drama.

Once Leah could stop laughing, she told her that the gift was really the frame. It was stained glass, using recycled glass from antique soda bottles. It would match Roz's living room perfectly. By the look on Roz's face, she was truly touched.

"Okay, my turn," Roz said, getting up and scooting the obnoxious gift bag toward Leah.

Leah pulled the unmentionables off the bottom and stuffed them into the bag. Then, she rooted around for the gift. When her fingers hit something hard, she pulled it out, and peered down at a beautifully hand-carved cedar box. As the carving came into focus, her mouth nearly dropped open. It was Evergreen Hill. "Oh my gosh, Roz. How did you get this?" She turned it around so her parents could see. Then she held it in view of the others.

"I found a photo of Evergreen Hill online from one of the old ads that your nan had put up. I gave it to the artist and asked if he could carve it. I figured that, as you go through your nan's things, you could put keepsakes in it."

Leah stood up and threw her arms around Roz. "This is amazing." She blinked away her tears, unable to say anything else.

"Don't go getting all sappy on me," Roz said, but her embrace told a different story. She pulled away, and Leah let her, knowing how she was about showing emotion. "Go ahead, Louise, open yours." Roz handed the other gift bag to Louise.

Louise took her undergarment off the bag and hid it as well. Then she reached inside to retrieve her present from Roz. It was a snow globe with a little boy in the center that looked just like Louise's son. He was holding a blanket, with the name Ethan. "You are so thoughtful, Roz," Louise said, giving her hug.

Both ladies unwrapped their presents from Louise. They'd been meticulously wrapped in brown paper and tied with a dark green bow. Louise beamed as Leah and Roz held up tote bags made in their own individual fabric patterns. "I figured that you can fill them with your books and things when we take trips," she said.

"I love it, Louise," Leah said, giving her a hug. "Thank you."

They took a break to grab breakfast and help Ethan set up one of his racecar tracks. "I got presents for Sadie and Ethan too," Roz said, lighting the new candle she'd bought for Leah and setting it on the coffee table. The sulfur smell of the match took Leah back to all the nights she'd had with The Girls. They'd been through so much together—broken relationships, laughter, and long nights just being there for each other. She'd never seen Roz so sentimental and she wondered if her friend was going to miss their time together as much as she would.

"That's thoughtful of you!" Leah said.

"When I saw Sadie's, I couldn't pass by it. It screamed 'Sadie.' I think we should get the kids in a minute and let them open them." Roz followed her back into the kitchen and ran the match under the water at the sink, then tossed it into the trash. "They're from both Jo and me. Jo wrapped them."

"Thank God for that," she teased, remembering the Christmas undies. She made eye contact with Louise and they both laughed.

"Everyone needs new underwear." Roz was looking back and forth between them, pretending to be put out by their laughter.

"Yes," June said, sneaking in on their teasing. "And socks."

"I was just being practical," Roz agreed with mock-seriousness.

"Thank you," Leah said, chewing on a grin.

She set the empty dishes in the sink but her mother shooed her away, telling her to relax and enjoy herself. Even her father and her uncle were helping to clear the dishes to free her from the duty. Could they tell how much this Christmas meant to her? With a happy heart, she snapped a photo.

"What was that for?" her dad said with a playful grin.

"I just needed to document that you and Uncle William were doing dishes," she teased.

"Oh, they're good men," June said. "And good men do dishes." She lumped an armful of plates toward David with a wink.

"I'll get the kids ready for more presents," Louise said, standing up and leaving them in the kitchen.

When everyone was back in the sitting room, Roz pulled two haphazardly wrapped presents from the shopping bag by her feet. Jo had written Sadie's and Ethan's names in large uppercase letters across the front of them and added a premade bow to each one. She set them on the table. Christmas music was playing in the background—"Rockin' Around the Christmas Tree".

The kids came barreling down the stairs before Louise, having taken some of their toys to Sadie's room. They sounded like a herd of reindeer as their feet pounded on the hardwoods. Sadie was the first to enter, sliding to a stop in her fuzzy red socks. Ethan came in shortly after, and Jo pulled up the rear with Louise.

"Ethan first!" Jo said, recognizing her own wrapping, her excitement making Ethan smile. She grabbed the present from Roz as the family gathered around.

The three kids sat down on the floor and Ethan ripped open the paper. He gasped, recognizing the box before he'd even turned it over to the front. "It's a Lego landscape kit!" he said with a huge grin as he looked up at everyone. "Thank you, Roz! Thank you, Jo!"

"You're welcome! Now you should have everything you need to make that Lego city," Roz said. "You all can take them upstairs and play with them today." She reached over and handed Sadie the rectangular present.

With a thrill in her eyes, Sadie tore it open and held the large frame in her tiny hands, a look of astonishment on her face. "I love it, Roz," she said, not taking her eyes from it.

Leah leaned around to view what it was. In the style of Norman Rockwell, it was all white with a simple painting of a blonde-haired girl wearing a blue leotard, her thin body stretched into a dismount pose, a tiny shadow by her feet.

"I can put it on the wall in my room upstairs!" she said, her words tumbling out in her elation. "The blue and white will look so pretty in that room because they match my pillow and comforter! I want to hang it up right now!"

Leah remembered the day Sadie and Nan had gone out shopping for the bed linens for that room. Nan had let Sadie pick, telling her that one day it would be her room. And now it was.

By the time the tree skirt was empty of gifts, the whole floor was full of balled paper, boxes, and piles of goodies by each person's feet. David had even thought to buy some gifts for Samuel when he'd gotten Sadie's surprises. Leah smiled when she realized he'd signed Samuel's card from the both of them. Leah hadn't been sure what to get David, but she knew she'd wanted to get him something nice. She'd found a

Pete Rose baseball card online, using her phone. The most inexpensive one she could find was still more than she'd ever spent on a gift, but she knew he'd love it, so she put it on her charge card. She'd gotten both her mother and June a pair of earrings, and her father a new sweater. She hadn't forgotten Samuel either. He'd been the hardest to buy for. But she'd settled on a leather journal so he could write his stories down.

Everyone was looking through their gifts, sharing small talk, when David handed Leah a tiny box. It was wrapped in holly paper with red berries and a matching red bow. "You didn't think I'd forgotten your gift, did you?"

Until that moment, it hadn't occurred to her. She was having such a perfect Christmas that she didn't need anything else. What he'd done already was enough. She took the box as he sat next to her on the settee, and pulled the end of the ribbon to untie the bow. Then, she slipped her finger under the paper where it was taped shut, and opened one end. She slid the box out. It was a flat, square box, and she was baffled as to what could be in it. It was as light in her hands as if it were empty.

Her parents, Samuel, and June looked on as she lifted the lid. It *was* empty—except for a business card. She took it out and read the name. "The Mason-Schuster Company," she said. "Historical Restoration." She looked at David.

"They're the company that will be here on Thursday to begin the restoration of the servants' quarters out back. It's the company that your grandmother always used. I'm having them restore it to exactly as it was during the Truman era. I never told you this, but your nan had shared the blueprint with me, and she'd told me she'd always wanted to do it, but in retirement it would require more funds than she was willing to provide. She also mentioned that it was one of your favorite places."

"You're keeping the building?" she said, excitement swelling in her chest. She wrapped her arms around his neck, making him chuckle.

"Yes," he said in her ear. "*We're* keeping the building." He looked over at June. "I've got the restoration crew on a tight schedule. I'd like to get it done by the time the weather breaks."

Leah waited for further explanation.

June leaned into view. "I want to get the business up and running sooner rather than later. I have our first wedding scheduled for February in the ballroom. It's a small affair but it would help us get our feet wet. Think we could be ready for that? Could you be all moved in by then?"

Leah put her hand to her chest. "Absolutely."

"Well, I hope she'd be here by then," David said. "I picked up Sadie's entry forms for school. And I grabbed the forms from the gymnastics gym too so she can get started using that mat Santa brought her."

Unable to stop the tears, Leah smiled.

He took her face into his hands and kissed her in front of everyone. After, she looked around, ready to explain, but it was as if they already knew.

That night, with the presents all set aside, Leah's mother slipped on the fuzzy Christmas socks that June had gotten everyone as a present and sat next to June on the floor. The house was drafty in the evening, as it always was, and they'd all lined up in front of the fire. "Put yours on," she told Leah.

"Everyone should put them on," June said. David and Samuel playfully rolled their eyes, but they all did, and sat next to each other—Sadie in the middle, with Lucky on her lap—and warmed their feet by the fire. Leah had always wanted a big family, rows of fuzzy-socked feet in front of the fireplace, an enormous tree with so many presents she couldn't fit them all beneath it, and a snowy house filled with friends and the golden glow of lamplight. Well, she got just what she'd always wanted. And more. She knew what Nan meant now about regrets, and she suspected that Nan hadn't been warning her; she was paving the way for her, so she wouldn't have any regrets in life, and Nan had done a little matchmaking while she was at it.

Chapter Twenty-Seven

Leah had slept like a baby. As she sat in the kitchen the next morning, stroking Lucky, who'd balled herself up in Leah's lap, she was completely at ease.

Roz and Louise had gone with David to get their car from town and then packed it that morning. They'd headed back home to their respective houses. Once he'd dropped them off, David had stayed out quite a while with work errands, he'd said. Her family had spent a lot of the day with Samuel, hearing about his life both with and without Nan. And Leah had been able to finally kick back and read that book she'd been given by Louise. It had been a relaxing day.

"Sadie," David called, startling Leah, coming into the house and looking from room to room. "Sadie!" he called again.

"What is it?" Leah asked, just as Sadie started down the stairs.

"Get your coat on! Where are your boots?" David seemed almost frantic with excitement. "You too, Leah! Hurry! I have a surprise!"

Leah and Sadie dressed for the snow as quickly as they possibly could, David's enthusiasm causing them both to rush, Sadie nearly falling over trying to put her boots on. Samuel, June, and the rest of the family were at the windows, curiosity getting the better of them.

David took Sadie by one hand and Leah by the other and led them outside, down the steps, and onto the long front lawn. The entire property was completely white, except for the few tire treads left by the farm truck, the trees leading the way out, covered in fluffy snow. David stood with them right at the front of the drive as Leah waited for what he had to show her.

Then, faintly, she heard bells. Jingling bells. She strained to make out the source of the sound but couldn't see anything.

Then, Sadie gasped, her eyes round, her mouth open, her hand squeezing Leah's. Coming up the drive between the lines of evergreens was an enormous red-and-gold sleigh, pulled by eight reindeer, each one wearing a thick collar of golden bells around its neck. Sitting in the seat of the sleigh was Santa Claus, his red velvet hat bouncing as the sleigh slid along the snow-covered path.

"Ho ho ho!" Santa cried, raising his white-gloved hand in greeting. "Miss Sadie! Is that you?"

To Leah's surprise, Sadie started crying. "Yes!" she gasped again. "Yes! It's me! I didn't think you knew me!"

"I know every child in the universe, little lady."

Sadie squinted. "You're a day late."

Santa Claus burst into a hearty "Ho ho ho!" and Leah and David bent over laughing.

"Ah. I've already been here!" he said. "Didn't you get my gifts?" Santa said, his cheeks storybook rosy. "That chimney gives me trouble every year. Those old ones are a tight squeeze."

Sadie looked over at Leah in amazement.

"How did you do it?" Leah whispered to David.

"It only took a few phone calls and a trip into town," he said, looking down at her with a smile. He leaned in and kissed her nose.

Santa said he was just passing through, and he couldn't stay long, but he asked if she'd like to climb up in his sleigh. With undeniable excitement on her face, Sadie got up into it and sat down on his lap.

"Did you get everything on your wish list?" he asked.

Sadie nodded. "And I got something even better that I didn't even think to write down." She looked over at David and Leah, who were arm in arm.

Santa pointed at Sadie then tapped his temple, like he'd read Sadie's mind. Sadie laughed.

"You were a very good girl this year," he said. "You think you can top it next year?"

Sadie nodded furiously.

Santa's bright cheeks lifted with his grin. "Well that's good to know. Now, I have a lot of other little boys and girls to check up on."

"Okay," she said, climbing out of the sleigh and hopping down onto the snow. "I'm glad you came to see me," she said.

"And I'm glad I could make you happy, Miss Sadie. Merry Christmas!" With that, he shouted, "On Dasher and Dancer! Prancer and Vixen! Comet, Cupid, Donner, and Blitzen!" The reindeer all turned slowly, two by two, until the sleigh was facing away from them, then, the jingle bells sounding once more, Santa Claus headed back down the long drive between the trees.

"Merry Christmas!" he called out just before he disappeared. And that, it was.

Epilogue

It was a warm summer's night. Leah lit the white lanterns in the weeping willow tree, the James River lapping happily beside her, the evening sun making its surface look like diamonds. The Virginia heat had relented somewhat, but just in case, she had peppered the yard with enormous white buckets of ice containing iced tea, water bottles, and lemonade.

June unrolled the white satin runner that stretched from the front steps of the house all the way to the yard. They'd lined the entire path with gardenia bushes in white pots, their sweet perfume filling the air. The lush green grass was shaded from the sun by white tents that stretched across the property, their edges dripping with white lights, paddle fans and chandeliers wired in to the ceilings underneath. Beneath the tents were large, round tables covered in linens, more gardenia blooms in their centers. Leah set out the place cards in heavy stationery that she'd had printed, catching a glimpse of Lucky, who was pawing at something in the lush grass under the tree. In the past couple of years, she'd planned more weddings than she could count, but this one was special.

Before long, it was time to get the kids into their wedding clothes. She hoped that David had Sadie's eight-month-old brother, Mason, dressed in the cool cotton onesie she'd bought just for the wedding. She looked down at her own wedding ring, the diamonds set in Nan's wedding band, and remembered her day like this one, on this property, when she'd said "I do" to the man of her dreams under the night's sky. She had a picture of the two of them sharing a kiss, her long white gown blowing slightly in the wind, her blonde hair pinned up into a diamond clip, his hands on her face like he always did when he kissed her. They were standing in the center of that path, Evergreen Hill behind them.

Leah stopped and looked around at what she'd done today. She'd worked her fingers to the bone to make it perfect for Louise and Bret. Today was their day, and she couldn't wait to celebrate it.

"Somebody's fussing for his mama," Roz said, walking toward her in her pale pink bridesmaid's dress and a pair of flip-flops. She had a cloth diaper over her shoulder to protect her dress, and Mason in her arms. "David's making sure Sadie's getting dressed in her flower girl dress now."

"Fantastic," she said, taking little Mason into her arms.

Leah and David had named him Samuel Mason Forester, after Samuel, who was like a grandparent to the kids. They'd changed plans completely, and decided to have the servants' quarters converted back to a residence, the relics moved to a room off the parlor, and he lived at Evergreen Hill with them.

"I think it's time to get ready!" Leah said. "Better go get those heels on before Louise sees you," she teased. "The guests will be showing up shortly. I'll wait out here to seat them."

The business had taken off, and, while June had mentioned she might want to retire, she loved it so much that she kept working on the next project as it came. Leah didn't mind at all. She loved having June with her, and she'd continue on as partners as long as June wanted to work.

She walked with Mason into the cool shade of the oak trees, where the branches were so large from age that they made a natural canopy over the rows of white chairs she'd set up earlier. She took a seat and bounced Mason on her lap. He smiled, looking so much like David that it made her heart want to burst.

She turned around as she heard the crunch of feet on gravel. It was the most glorious sight: her family and friends, all walking toward her, Sadie's pink flower girl's dress with the satin belt billowing out with the breeze, her hair curled in ringlets. David looked amazing in his tuxedo as he locked eyes with her. He was helping Samuel down the walk. Roz took Sadie by the hand as she talked to June, laughing at something. Then, behind them, Leah got a glimpse of Louise, her veil cascading around her face and contrasting against the brick of the house as she peeked out the door to make sure everyone was ready.

"Bret's coming around from the servants' quarters," Roz said. She'd taken control of everything inside today, wanting it all to be perfect for her best friend.

Leah remembered how Nan had said she'd like everyone she'd brought together that first Christmas without her to be part of each other's lives. In true Nan form, she'd done her job better than anyone else could. Leah smiled to herself as she cooed with Mason, remembering that final letter from Nan. *Support one another and spend time together, because at the end, that's all you'll have to take with you—the love. Love each other and everything else will fall into place.*

Acknowledgments

I am so thankful to have my husband, Justin, along with me on this journey. His constant encouragement has carried me through.

I am very blessed to have such a talented and supportive publishing team.

Thank you to my editor, Natalie Butlin, an amazing, creative talent, who works wonders for me every day.

A very special thank you to Oliver Rhodes, who first put me on this rollercoaster ride of publishing. He continues to keep me on track, and I am so grateful.

To the many friends and family who allow me to pick their brains with relentless texting to tap into their various areas of expertise, I thank you.

Letter from Jenny

Thank you so much for reading *All I Want for Christmas*. I really hope you found it to be a heart-warming winter escape!

If you'd like me to drop you an email when my next book is out, you can sign up here:

www.itsjennyhale.com/email/jenny-hale-sign-up

I won't share your email with anyone else, and I'll only email you when a new book is released.

If you did enjoy *All I Want for Christmas*, I'd love it if you'd write a review. Getting feedback from readers is amazing, and it also helps to persuade other readers to pick up one of my books for the first time.

Until next time!
Jenny

P.S. If you enjoyed this story, and would like a little more winter fun, do check out my other Christmas novels – *Coming Home for Christmas, A Christmas to Remember,* and *Christmas Wishes and Mistletoe Kisses.*

8263960R00156

Printed in Germany
by Amazon Distribution
GmbH, Leipzig